It Just So Happened

The Life and Times of Allan Brown.

By

Allan Brown

Copyright © 2026

All rights reserved.

This book contains autobiographical accounts of childhood abuse, trauma, and emotional and physical violence that some readers may find distressing. Readers are encouraged to read with care and to prioritise their wellbeing. If you or someone you know is experiencing emotional distress, confidential support is available in Australia through Lifeline on **13 11 14**. In an emergency, please contact local emergency services.

Dedication

I want to dedicate this book to my wife, Wendy, who has stood by me through every struggle and been my greatest source of encouragement each and every day.

Prologue

Proverbs 4:23 (NIV)

Above all else, guard your heart, for everything you do flows from it.

It Just So Happened

I didn't set out to write this book. I started by simply journalling a few stories from my past.

Like many of the chapters that shaped my life, it just so happened.

It just so happened that I grew up in fractured places, homes that didn't quite hold, systems that tried their best but often missed the heart. It just so happened that faith found me in the margins, not loudly announced, but quietly persistent. Purpose arrived long before I felt ready for it, often dressed as interruption rather than invitation. And it just so happened that, over time, people began sitting across from me, asking questions that echoed many of my own.

For the past fourteen years, much of my professional life has been lived in those conversations.

Coaching, at its best, isn't about fixing people. It's about creating a space where truth can breathe, where insight surfaces, and where the next brave step becomes possible. I've had the privilege of doing that work with business leaders and elite sports people; with couples and coaches, pastors and practitioners; athletes under pressure, and teams navigating high performance and deep uncertainty, across boardrooms and kitchen tables, church halls and correctional facilities; marriages on the brink and leaders staring down transition.

Along the way, I've trained and qualified, becoming a Gallup Strengths Coach, a Working Genius Coach, a Professional Supervisor, a Gottman and Prepare/Enrich marriage facilitator, and a mentor to leaders navigating complexity, faith, and failure. These frameworks have given language to what I had come to believe through experience and prayer: that people already carry strengths, wisdom, and hope, sometimes buried beneath survival, sometimes forgotten under success.

Yet this book isn't a summary of my coaching credentials.

It's the story behind them.

Before I coached others, I learned to listen in silence. Before I asked courageous questions, I lived inside unanswered ones. Before I spoke of resilience, I watched it form slowly and imperfectly, through disappointment, risk, failure, surrender, and grace. My life didn't unfold in straight lines, more like holy interruptions, unexpected doors, and quiet moments where something whispered, *Pay attention. This matters.*

This book traces those moments.

Some are tender. Some are confronting. Some still surprise me when I reread them. All of them shaped the coach, the husband, the father, and the man I continue to become, under the steady, often unseen guidance of a God who seemed far more patient with me than I was with myself.

Today, my work lives through **TheAllanKey.com**, a place devoted to unlocking insight, clarity, and transformation, for individuals, couples, athletes, teams, and leaders who sense a calling forward, even if they can't yet name it. But this book isn't an invitation to my work.

It's an invitation to yours.

As you turn these pages, my hope isn't that you admire the story, but that you recognise something of your own. That brave honesty. That unresolved chapter. That quiet turning point that didn't look significant at the time… until it was.

Because so much of what shapes us doesn't arrive announced.

It comes gently. Faithfully.

It just so happened.

Endorsements

Nigel Benn, Former World Champion Boxer

It Just So Happened is a powerful story of redemption and hope. This isn't just another autobiography; it's a testimony of what faith can do when life feels broken beyond repair. Allan's journey shows that no matter how far you've fallen, God's grace can lift you up and set you on a new path.

What struck me most about this book is its honesty. It doesn't hide the pain or the mistakes, it faces them head-on and shows how faith and perseverance can turn even the darkest chapters into something meaningful.

For anyone who's ever wondered if change is possible, this book is living proof that it is.

As someone who's walked my own hard roads, I know how much courage it takes to share a story like this. It's not just inspiring, it's real. And that's why it will connect with people from every walk of life.

If you're searching for hope, if you need a reminder that second chances are real, this book will speak to you. It's about grace, resilience, and the power of believing that your story isn't over.

Read *It Just So Happened*. It might just be the spark you need to start your own comeback.

— Nigel Benn, Former World Champion Boxer

Chandika Hathurusinghe, International Cricket Strategist & Coach

"When I met Allan Brown, I didn't expect to be drawn into one of the most compelling life stories I've ever heard. From the silence of care homes to the chaos of Central America, Allan's journey is marked by grit, grace, and a relentless pursuit of meaning. His coaching style is unlike any I've encountered; deeply relational, spiritually grounded, and strategically sharp. I invited him to coach with the Bangladesh national team because I saw in him not just a coach, but a mentor who could shape culture. This book is more than a memoir; it's a legacy of hope, leadership, and transformation."

— Chandika Hathurusinghe, International Cricket Strategist & Coach

Nicole Partridge, Writer and Literary Agent

"From the moment we met at my creative writing class, I sensed that Allan Brown was carrying a book within him. A natural storyteller, he renders his life with vivid precision and quiet courage. Tracing a journey from brokenness and searching to leadership and service, his story bears gentle yet unmistakable witness to the faithfulness of God. Warm, witty, and deeply human, Allan's writing invites the reader not only to know his story, but to see something of their own reflected within it."

— Nicole Partridge, Writer and Literary Agent

Table of Contents

Dedication iv

Prologue v

Endorsements vii

Chapter 1 1

Chapter 2 5

Chapter 3 10

Chapter 4 12

Chapter 5 15

Chapter 6 17

Chapter 7 21

Chapter 8 23

Chapter 9 26

Chapter 10 28

Chapter 11 31

Chapter 12 34

Chapter 13 37

Chapter 14 41

Chapter 15 45

Chapter 16 48

Chapter 17 53

Chapter 18 56

Chapter 19 59

Chapter 20 62

Chapter 21 65

Chapter 22 67

Chapter 23 69

Chapter 24 73

Chapter 25 76

Chapter 26 79

Chapter 27 82

Chapter 28 85

Chapter 29 89

Chapter 30 93

Chapter 31 96

Chapter 32 100

Chapter 33 103

Chapter 34 107

Chapter 35 110

Chapter 36 114

Chapter 37 118

Chapter 38 122

Chapter 39 126

Chapter 40 129

Chapter 41 132

Chapter 42 136

Chapter 43 139

Chapter 44 143

Chapter 45 146

Chapter 46 148

Chapter 47 152

Chapter 48 156

Chapter 49 160

Chapter 50 163

Chapter 51 166

Chapter 52 170

Chapter 53 173

Chapter 54 175

Chapter 55 178

Chapter 56 182

Chapter 57 186

Chapter 58 198

Chapter 59 200

Chapter 60 209

Chapter 61 215

Chapter 62 218

Chapter 63 222

Chapter 64 227

Chapter 65 233

Chapter 66 239

Chapter 67 244

Chapter 68 249

Chapter 69 254

Chapter 70 259

Epilogue 265

Chapter 1

What happens inside a young person when they decide to run away from home? I remember my own first night on the run at around twelve. It felt alien, being up so late, but I'd been well prepared, with my clothes neatly placed under the mattress and a bag packed, ready to go. Trying to stay quiet, every noise amplified in my head as I filled my school bag with such a foreign cargo and crept towards the front door.

There was no way I could close it; the noise would wake the whole tenement. So I snibbed it open, feeling a flicker of guilt, pulled it to behind me, and slipped down the five floors of the blackened-sandstone stairwell towards the final obstacle, the clattering, half-hinged downstairs entrance door.

What was I feeling? What was I thinking? I was a little scared, but mostly relieved. Relieved to escape the stifling discipline and painful beatings that had plagued my life and closed in my future. Relieved to have an open road almost before me, to embrace an adventure, and to hope that somehow this road to nowhere might lead to something more.

Slowly, like paint drying, I eased the stairwell door open, straining to take its weight and soften the creaks. Then I was out in the street, the sulphur-yellow streetlights casting a strange, quiet glow, shadows of hidden danger lingering at the fringes. The memories of endless tears faded a little; a sense of purpose and hope gripped my young heart as I stepped out, tight against those shadowy edges, heading towards freedom.

I remember it as if it were yesterday, squinting at the oncoming car headlights reflected in the rain-washed, chilly Edinburgh streets. The sour smell of brewed hops drifted nearby in fleeting wafts. Heading to Portobello on foot, bag slung over my shoulder, I kept up a decent pace to fight the cold. Yet it felt as though the whole world had opened to me, that nothing was impossible, and opportunity would come knocking if I could just stick it out. I think I was sensing the call of the open road, taking risks, travelling light. Something new was forming in my green-stick-fractured character: a rising hope that change could be mine, waiting somewhere just ahead.

Memories of Enid Blyton's *Famous Five* blended with *Horatio Hornblower*, *The Jungle Book*, and the echoes of Zane Grey urging me on from *Riders of the Purple Sage*. Oblivious to risk, I walked for hours. I did have a plan, if I could reach the outskirts of the city, I could put my thumb out, and I had faith someone would help me make some distance.

My mind was fixed, and distance felt like the natural, straightforward goal. The real task was covering that initial stretch before daylight broke. Was I missing my warm bed, thinking of breakfast, or picturing my family waking up? To my embarrassment, none of that crossed my mind. I was an adventurer, willing to travel as far as needed and endure whatever hardships came rather than return to an emotional prison, where sterile enamelled gates waited with silent anger, dour, violent, and vindictive.

As I walked along the mostly empty streets, I kept clear of the busier main roads and did my best to avoid any lone pedestrians. Self-conscious and aware of my own strangeness, I slipped briefly into the far-off shadows at the edge of the pavement, away from the random sweep of prowling car lights. As I walked, my mind drifted back to a past event. There were no soft-focus effects or harp music, only the sound of my own breathing and the irregular pulse of distant, sporadic traffic.

I was about four years old, sitting on the sink's draining board, feet in the basin as my dad washed me. He asked me a strange question: "Is it sore?" I'm fairly certain I didn't understand what he meant, but my eyes followed his gaze down to my own legs and buttocks. As I stretched to look, I remember feeling a kind of amazement at the many shades mottled across my lower back and down to the backs of my knees, greens, blues, purples and even pinks. The colours carried a worrying depth, yet strangely, there was no real pain.

"No," I answered simply, although uncertainty echoed in my voice.

"Hmm," he replied, pausing before saying, "I think I'll use something harder in future then, maybe a shoe or a cane."

Said with such a straight face and calm manner that, at my young age (and even now), a wave of uncertainty passed through me, settling in with a shudder. I remember so clearly that I simply didn't know what to say.

All-night garage lights glinted in the distance, a sign of normal life, open and welcoming. A car sped past with its indicator already on, leaning toward the kerb as though it wasn't sure it would make the turn. Normal life. How do I explain the disappointment that lived in my chest? The longing? The wonder at friends whose mums and dads laughed, had messy homes and open doors. I wanted to steal a bit of their family joy and hide it under my jersey, holding it close in memory if I couldn't have it in reality.

Soon I reached the petrol station, watching cars, and lives, go about their carefree business. Doubt settled into my mind and heart. Where was I going? I hung back at the edge of the forecourt, watching, thinking, waiting, uncertain. I sensed, more than understood, that I was at a defining moment. Leaving the house had been easier than moving on now. Some sort of reluctance was rising; something final waited beyond the pumps, somewhere across the far pavement. A decision would be made there.

Hesitation reached out as if to shake my hand. It wasn't quite a stalemate, more of an impasse. A conversation churned in my head, but the words were thick and slow, making no sense. A hint of anxiety crept in; it wouldn't take much to push me into panic.

For the first time, I felt the weight of my bag. I'm not sure how long I stood there, shuffling back and forth. Hesitation had invited indecision in, and they were settling comfortably.

A van pulled up at the nearest pump and a man stepped out to fill the tank. He looked up and smiled at me. I stared back with a faint smile, not wanting to be rude, but unfamiliar with the whole situation. When he finished with the pump and locked the petrol cap, he looked my way again and beckoned me over.

"Hi son, cumoan over here," I heard.

Head down, eyes fixed on my feet, I walked towards him.

"Whear ur ye goin'?" he asked.

In that split second, I decided I was going back. I gave him the name of a street near my home. I think I already knew he would offer me a lift before the words even left his mouth. He went inside to pay and made me come with him.

I still wonder if he saw through the half-formed story I told him, even I can't remember what it was, and simply wanted to help me get home.

Amazingly, though I had walked for hours, it took only a short time before we reached the street. He asked for the exact house number, but I dodged the question and jumped out with a quiet, "Thank-ye, mister."

I headed down the street, nervous. Maybe my parents had woken in the night, seen the open door, and the whole game was already up. Rushing without running, I pressed on towards the stairwell. With a little less concern for noise now, people were up and about anyway, I climbed to the door. Still open. House still in darkness.

Silently, I worked the snib back into place once I'd closed the door, then slipped into my room and, like a mime artist, put everything back exactly where it belonged before climbing into bed. I knew I had about ten minutes before the 5.30 alarm would ring and I'd be ordered to get up.

It felt like a defeat in some ways, but my heart was singing. Something new had opened up inside me, a possibility. I'd discovered a potential escape route, and although I hadn't used it fully, it now existed in my mind. I had no idea, of course, that future journeys would last much longer and take me hundreds of miles. But I sensed there were adventures ahead, experiences that would reshape my world..

Chapter 2

At times, the morning newspaper round I had as a young boy made me feel like an explorer. Up at 5.30 am and quickly out the door, the cold morning air greeted me sharply the moment it opened. Down the street I went, stiff trees overhanging a long wall on one side, reflected in the tenement windows like a hundred one-way mirrors on the other. Into the shop I'd go, just long enough to grab the heavy bag of morning papers before lugging it out again and along the high-walled streets that marked the start of my round.

Stealing wasn't really part of my everyday thinking, apart from one rather bizarre incident when I took a jar of Marmite from a local store, thinking it was some sort of chocolate. The shock I got that night was unforgettable. Needless to say, my dad found the jar with a fingerful missing, the police were called, and after they left I had the unenviable task of taking it back and owning up at the checkout on my own. But after my first escape as a half-overnight runaway, as I considered possible routes of escape, stealing began to take on a hint of promise. Gradually, I was forming a new plan in my mind, one that involved stealing a bicycle and cycling away from home. I suppose I had a bit of a fantasy about what it would be like to run away on a bike (if that's not an oxymoron).

My paper round became the perfect place to scout who kept bicycles in their sheds or behind their houses. Creeping around in the early morning's frosty half-light brought a tension and excitement to an otherwise routine and tiring job. One morning I found a tired old ten-speed bike left unlocked in the garden of a big house, a house I didn't even deliver papers to. I took it stealthily and hid it in the basement of an unused building. For the next few weeks, I took it out early each morning before my round, practising my cycling skills in preparation for the big day. One morning I rode the bike for my entire paper round, then cycled the five miles to school as well.

Gradually, the attempt was taking shape in my head. At that time, I was sometimes shut in my small bedroom for the whole weekend, and often the same in the evenings. This sense of entrapment steeled my resolve to try again. Lasting memories of hurts, real and perceived, fuelled my desire for escape, and captivity sharpened my appetite for freedom. But events would take a surprising turn before the next daring plan could be launched.

It was at school that the real opportunity presented itself. The bike I had stolen was on its last legs, but it had introduced me to a new group, the ten-speed racer club. School wasn't a great experience even then. For some reason, I'd been sent to a secondary school five miles away that none of my friends attended, so I knew no one. I got to know Mr No-one very well, as most of the kids already knew each other from the junior school.

Even with all that, school still felt like a kind of escape. The long bus journey, the overly warm classrooms, the breaks, and the teachers who could be easily distracted, all of it formed a sort of grey, Orwellian victory-gin sedative for what I faced at home. I think I dreaded going home. Pushing against it was like leaning into a thin wall of warm, clinging clay; I fought with all my emotions to delay the moment.

I remembered lying awake in the dark nights, waiting for the inevitable door to be flung open, the sharp light, and then the beating, forced to stand and take it, hands by my sides. I knew I was bad, always doing things wrong, but still trying with everything I had to stretch for a moment of praise or even acceptance.

I wondered how God could play such a cruel joke, to have me born only to deliver this fate to me. Some days I longed for a kind of un-birth, a release. In the small hours, I'd question whether the whole world was acting in some elaborate conspiracy, just so I could be caught in every mistake and every wrong move. Fear plagued me, and I became overly needy for friendship and acceptance.

The bike shed was, however, a friendly place, and boys often loaned out their bikes to anyone who had money for the local shops, about a five-minute ride at lunchtime. So I cultivated a friendship and borrowed a bike a few times, always bringing it back, locking it securely, and earning the owner's trust. I had a fifty-five-mile bike ride in mind, one that would get me far enough away to hitch-hike into a peaceful oblivion. If I didn't turn up at school, my parents were notified straight away, so I needed to get through registration and then disappear at the end of lunch. That would give me at least a four-hour head start. I'd made a habit of borrowing a bike and returning late from lunch, but the owners always found their bikes locked and safe at the end of the day, so they'd learned to trust me.

On a warm summer's morning, I decided this was the day. I packed my schoolbag with different items and felt excited and free already. At lunchtime I borrowed a bike, but this time I rode straight past the shops and kept going until I reached the nearest public toilets, where I changed into less school-like clothes and set off. Was there any guilt about stealing the bike? Yes. I felt the weight of shame and the fear of being caught, and that fear powered my legs through the first dozen of many miles.

My memory of the exact route is hazy now, but I was heading south. From the north of Edinburgh, straight through the city and out the other side by the A7, down to Galashiels, Selkirk, and then Hawick. It was a sunny, warm day, the road was fairly quiet, and I was making good time. Stopping occasionally to gather my thoughts and tuck in my shirt, I was actually loving the day.

It made me think of the happy moments from my childhood.

My cousin lived in the country on an estate, and visiting him felt like a true boys' own adventure. Fast country lanes and a ten-speed racer to ride, fields and hedgerows to explore, wild imaginative escapades, and simple pleasures savoured. Large chestnut trees became ammunition for slingshot battles; small streams became jungles leading to King Solomon's Mines; morning rides turned into Tour de France stages. Freedom, acceptance, and home baking, a recipe for happiness. My thoughts turned easily as the miles slipped behind me.

I remembered camping holidays too, morning dew on canvas tents, the first heat of the day, the patter of midnight rain. Carrying jerry cans of water, running on the beach, playing a wind-driven version of beach badminton. Strange memories, but remembering the good never quite banished the bad.

In truth, I had no real idea what I was doing. Though I'd travelled further than on my first attempt, nothing about this escape suggested success. Eventually, cycling downhill in the dark as I passed through Hawick, I was pulled over by the police for having no lights, rookie mistake. The game was up, and I was taken to the station. I gave up my details embarrassingly quickly and was left in a cell to wait for my parents. Even then, I was already recovering, processing what had happened, and considering what I'd learned from the two attempts so far. The next one, I was convinced, would be more successful.

My next escape was the most successful in terms of distance, and it became the last of my "one-day" breakouts. Again, it was a middle-of-the-night effort: quiet, tiptoeing, every sound amplified, but with more determination than ever. Looking back now, I wonder what went through my parents' minds each time they found me gone in the morning. As a parent myself, the thought is terrifying. But back then, my only concern was getting far away.

By now the exit routine was familiar. I slipped out to the street, bag slung over my shoulder, woolly hat pulled low, and the early-morning wind hitting my face. A light, cold mist tugged at any skin left exposed. All I could hear was my own breathing and the soft tread of my shoes on the damp pavement. My plan was still simple: make distance.

Just being away was so much better, no matter what hardships lay ahead.

I walked through the dark hours when even the city seemed asleep, apart from the occasional lonely cab, gliding past with a dull swish on the wet tarmac, like a sleeper turning in the night, oblivious to the repeating drama of my life. Millisecond memories flickered: muffled screams, my head buried in bed blankets wet with fresh tears, pleading for the beating to stop, pain on top of pain. These peripheral memories shuffled forward with a muffled insistence. Subconsciously, I lengthened my stride, perhaps trying to leave them behind.

I had a first-base destination in mind, a launch pad for escape. No more stalled attempts or back-road renegade risks. This time, I was heading for the city outskirts and motorway slip roads, a gateway, in my mind, to anywhere other than here.

Chapter 3

Standing at the slip road onto the motorways would become a normal part of my day over the coming weeks and months. Somehow, again, I found myself making my way towards the Scottish Borders, thinking ahead to where I might sleep. I caught a couple of short lifts courtesy of my novice thumb and eventually found myself walking along a quiet main road in the last of the daylight, a time sometimes called the gloaming.

Seeing a barn off to my left in a field, I jumped the fence and, under cover of a convenient hedge, half-scuttled and stumbled over the furrows to the barn, where I made myself as comfortable as I could on a couple of bales of hay. I was lonely, but too tired to be scared, and quickly fell into a broken, fitful sleep that carried me through to a very early, cold morning, when even the air seemed dull and grey. I had passed a checkpoint that had previously seemed impossible, and now I had stayed out for a whole night. An entirely new day lay ahead, with an open road and as-yet untold adventures.

Crossing back over the field, I was quickly picked up by a passing truck and soon out of Scotland. Straw stuck out from several places on my jumper; it must have been obvious that I'd been sleeping rough.

I needed a cover story. I decided to tell anyone who asked that I'd been offered a job in London but had no money to get there, so was hitching my way down. I was already nearly six feet tall and, although just turned thirteen, could easily pass for sixteen. The lorry dropped me at the edge of a town, and I began walking, looking for a suitable place to hitch my next lift, somewhere a car could easily pull over and where traffic wasn't moving too fast.

I had a long walk ahead, taking me through the town and out the other side. Hungry and thirsty, I had little idea of what I was doing, and my plans barely extended beyond the immediate. The day went on, and I eventually found myself at a roundabout leading onto a motorway. I stood and hitched for several hours with no luck. Eventually, traffic thinned, my legs and back ached, and darkness fell. I had no idea what to do, having never been in this situation before. With only my small bag of clothes, I headed back into town to a large car park I had passed earlier. I could probably find somewhere to hide and rest.

There were several big lorries, and I stood behind one, unsure what to do next. Another older man was there too, apparently relieving himself under a lorry before walking off in another direction. About ten minutes later, a police car pulled straight up to me, as if they knew I was there. I was taken to the local station and initially blamed for the mess under the lorry. Eventually, once they discovered who I was, their attitude changed. I was given a sandwich and a drink, which I demolished, before being put in a cell for a short time.

Later, I was woken in the middle of the night and taken to a foster care home, where the woman was so kind that I simply cried. I immediately wanted to stay there forever. The next day, I was transported back to the police station, where my dad and mum waited, quiet, like oncoming thunder. Back to Edinburgh I went. I remember the feeling of being cared for at the foster home, and my eyes were watery most of the way back. Nothing was said, and once home I was sent straight to my room and told to sleep.

I was far too tired to think about any further attempt that night. I lay under the covers, shivering, waiting for the footsteps in the hall, the light being switched on, and the shouting and hitting to start. The fear kept me awake longer than I thought possible, but eventually, I must have fallen asleep.

Chapter 4

My next journey started with all the usual stealth and apprehension, with a long early morning walk to the roads out of the city followed by a hitched lift to the furthest point possible. After a full night and day of hitching and travel, I found myself somewhere in the north of England, walking slowly on a country road, tired, head down with no real thinking going on other than the need to put one foot in front of another. This would be my longest time away from home and would last over two weeks.

I did not really mind the silence or the empty road; in some ways, I was able to take ease from the sense of being alone. I found a new place in my mind during most long walks, a place where I could explore who I was and who I wanted to be. Walking up a long hill with the dark grey grassy corridor on both sides of the tar-black road, a half-moon gave enough light to see glimpses of the distance and much of the close-up. An occasional cloud changed the landscape and mood, whilst a wind that had grown chilly continually surprised me with its sudden embracing push and pull. Once again the safe loneliness of the explorer settled on me. I found comfort in my all-night walking pace, even though I did not know where I was going.

I was a little unsure of what to do. Did I want to walk to the nearest town and get my bearings, or would I jump in the first car that stopped and go wherever it took me? As it happened, I kept walking for many hours before a weariness came over me and my eyes had a mind of their own, casting around for a safe place to rest or even doze, but for the longest time nothing of that nature was in view and the wind grew colder as the night grew darker. Not a car on the road.

Eventually tiredness spoke up and I simply lay down at the side of the road, curled up as much as I could to get some protection from the prodding and probing wind. Body tired, but my mind would not co-operate and sleep was not to be; even rest seemed elusive as shivering started in spasmodic bursts. I tried to guess the time and thought it was probably around 3am. A long time to go before light came, and the open nature of the country seemed a barrier to any real rest. What do you do when you are so tired that you can't go on, but there is nowhere to rest, when lying down is more exhausting than standing up and the relentless wind seems intent on finding you wherever you try to hide?

You get up and go on, at least that is my experience. So, on I went, and in honesty this was a difficult period where if a way out had presented itself I may have been tempted. In the stories I had read of great adventures there seemed little mention of drudgery, of long walks along bare empty roads through the night. More often than not the hero had to venture into a dangerous forest and take on fantastic foes, or stow away on midnight ships leaving on the tide, hearing the shouting and bustle from their hiding place, heart beating with excitement for all that lay ahead. At this early point in my journey all that seemed fanciful and far away.

It was dark and late and I had been on this road for what seemed to me like days. I was somewhere in Yorkshire, a bit lost really. The only thing I knew to do was to keep moving. So I walked along the side of this back road, up long slow hills to windy summits and then down again to rusty cattle-grid gateways. On and on.

Earlier in the day a family had kindly bought me some soup and bread at a roadside café when they had given me a lift, but I was starting to feel hungry again.

I could see a glimmer of light in the distance, and it might be a car, but I could not work out if it was coming from behind me or towards me as the hills all around were confusing. I was not sure about people who were out at this time of night, so I would tend to be cautious at night and then look for a lift in the mornings as it got a bit lighter. But there was nowhere to hide really, so I just kept walking.

The car came slowly up the hill behind me, and I could see its lights flickering around my feet, and then my legs and upwards, until suddenly, when the car was only a short distance away, it slowed and there was a spinning blue tinge to the light. Oh-oh, it was the police. Not good.

There was one policeman in a Morris Minor police car. He had me get in the car and then drove to the nearest tiny village, where it turned out he lived, as he stopped at his house and not a police station. He questioned me at length, and to my shame I lied. I was not ready to be caught, even with the hardships. Previously I would have given up my name and details right away.

I gave the name and address of a friend in Scotland. It was risky. This person would not be reported missing, but if they sent someone to his house to check then the game was up for sure.

The policeman went into his house to use the phone and check out my story. While he was there, I saw his wife come to the back-lit doorway and peer out towards me in the car. The year was 1972, and I guess I was a bit of an oddity in rural Yorkshire at that time of night. I waited. Nervous. A thirteen-year-old masquerading as a sixteen-year-old, lying to the police at 4am in the middle of nowhere. Stomach cramps and an overwhelming need for the toilet were my immediate companions.

The policeman came back to the car, crossing the road slowly with a package in his hands. He said, "yoo are all good man to go on – all checked oot", so I was good to go on. He handed me a package his wife had made of some ham and cheese sandwiches.

I took the sandwiches thankfully and waved an over-the-road thank you to his wife who was back at the doorway.

It was the great escape, and I was on my way. To be honest, as soon as I was out of sight I wolfed down the sandwiches and I sat down at the side of the road and cried. Not much later the sun came up, with the promise of a new day.

Chapter 5

I walked on for several hours that morning, a toughness creeping into my legs and my soul. I had gone further than any previous attempt in many different ways. A pattern was developing that seemed to shape this season: walking and hitchhiking at night, and finding places to sleep during the day. That became my main, though not only, pattern over the next week or two.

I remember being dropped off at Salford on the outskirts of Manchester one night. It was late, the streets were dark, and everyone seemed in a rush, caught up in their own world affairs. This was a new experience for me, walking through city streets late at night. Usually I was in rural areas on quiet roads.

I was hungry; I had probably not eaten all day, if not longer. I walked on, sometimes along stretches of busy uncluttered roadways with cars and trucks forcing their way along, rushing, squeezing every inch they could, noisy and disruptive to a young boy's thoughts. Other times I walked through areas with small shops, one or two lit up with movement and life inside, corner shops open all hours. At one point I saw a bench near traffic lights and I sat and rested as the traffic rushed past in its start-stop rhythm. I did not rest long as it felt like a place to be noticed, and that was not what I wanted at all.

My tired legs lifted me up, and with my bag slung over my shoulder, arm across my chest, and head bent forward, I adopted my long-haul walking position. I set off to walk through Manchester that night. There was no other option but to go on.

I could tell I was getting closer to the city centre. The traffic grew more intense, roads and pavements widened, and shops increased in size and variety, grouping into sprawling clusters.

A grown man fell into step beside me, asking how I was and where I was going. We talked a little and walked along the pavement together; there were many other people around, so I did not feel concerned. We were in an area of nightlife now, with food shops, cafes, and takeaways sporadically open.

At one café door the man stopped and turned to me, saying he was going in to get something to eat. He asked if I was hungry and I said I was.

He turned away from me and walked inside, the jingling door closing behind him as he joined a few others at the counter, all gazing up at the roughly written menu. I stood in the street waiting, watching him stand with his back to me, hands in his pockets, lost in his world. I looked on, afraid and hungry. Afraid of being so close to food and not eating. Hunger pressed at me in those moments. I had been managing it well until the proximity of possibility mocked me and felt almost too much to carry.

I probably stood for forty-five seconds staring at the man's back as he waited to order. A sadness settled on me. I think I was a little surprised that there had been no offer to share. Turning my school-shoe-clad feet slowly, hope fading with each movement, I turned away from the glow of the café. My resolve washed out at that moment, but there was no option. I had to keep walking.

I needed to find a way to secure food each day.

Chapter 6

I continued my pattern of hitchhiking through the late evening and night, then sleeping, or at least resting if the weather was warm, during the day. I became the resident expert in how long you could get away with sleeping on a park bench or in a railway or bus station. Sometimes I slept briefly during the night when the opportunity presented itself.

The stories I told people who stopped to give me lifts were designed to gain sympathy, hopefully with a side of fries or a few coins. At the time I believed my storytelling ability grew with each lift I received. To be honest, looking back now as an adult reflecting on the stories I told as a thirteen-year-old boy, I think most people probably saw through them but were kind to me anyway.

I filled my days dreaming of a better future, travelling, walking, sleeping in parks, railway stations, and once, when someone gave me a five-pound note, an all-night bus until the driver woke me and told me to get off.

I was thirteen now and surviving. There were tough times. Loneliness, hunger, tiredness, fear, and danger were my road companions at different moments. I was abused on three separate occasions by predatory men. I will not go into details other than to say I understand they were broken men. I have truly forgiven them and prayed for them, and thanks to the power of true forgiveness they did not leave a mark on my life.

I saw kindness in so many people: the family who drove me to a service station and bought me food, the drunken couple driving home from a wedding who gave me a sofa for the night, the RAF serviceman who got me a bed and a meal in his barracks, and so many more. Not forgetting the policeman's wife in Yorkshire and the best tasting ham and cheese sandwich ever.

The thing about hitchhiking when running away is that you do not really control your destination. You go wherever the person offering the lift is going, just to be warm and to sit down. Sometimes the hardest thing on cold days was to stay awake once inside the car or truck and keep talking to the driver and any other passengers.

One evening I ended up in Birmingham, dropped off on the north side. I had no desire to head further north and sensed immediately that this was going to be a tough night.

Usually, no matter where I was at night, there were options to rest. There might be a barn, a thick hedge, or an empty midnight bus shelter. I knew straightaway this was a different night, one where I would have to keep moving. I had most of Birmingham to walk through, and I expected it would be a long journey.

I traversed Birmingham that night, seeing the different shades of the city ebb and flow as I crossed unmarked boundaries of culture and race. In some places men spilled out of half-boarded-up pubs, shouting, pushing, often fighting, sometimes laughing. In other streets, sterile shops were closed up. No shutters here though, well lit, well policed, and well kept. Busy dual carriageways forced their path through the urban setting, and finding my way through this maze was at times painstaking and slow.

As the black sky lifted its shades and a hint of morning appeared beyond the false dawn, after a seven or eight hour walk I recognised the road signs to London. I was through the maze, and an on-ramp to hope would be nearby.

Slightly bowed from the all-night test, I stood still by a pale-lit on-ramp and blended in, hoping for a lift. When it came, I was carried down the southern motorways to the town of High Wycombe, close to London.

It was a warmish morning, and a grey tiredness settled over me, my thoughts, and even my steps. I saw the gateway to a local park, inviting me to rest, opening up a place to recover from the trials behind me.

Unperturbed by what others might think, I lay down on the grass. I had a deep six-hour sleep in the warm spring sun that day.

Waking early afternoon and noticing a few people staring at me, I stood and brushed the grass off my clothes. I walked to the park toilets, and since no one else was inside, I took the chance for a fast stand-up bath, splashing water liberally, knowing the sun would dry me.

As I left the park, I realised I had money in my pocket. Enough to eat. Hunger hastened my stride. Walking through the area near the park, my radar for shops switched on fully. I found a Wimpy Bar and wolfed down one of their set meals in record time, paid, and was on my way.

The feeling of being rested and fed made me almost euphoric. Hope rose strong in me. I was loving this adventure, with no thoughts of tomorrow. The moment had become my new permanent address.

On the outer edge of High Wycombe I stumbled upon another on-ramp for what was either a motorway or a main dual carriageway. I stood for a few hours in busy nonstop traffic with my thumb out, when to my dismay a motorcycle policeman pulled up beside me. He made me empty my small bag of clothes onto the roadside verge. I found out later they were looking for an IRA suspect. I was ashamed as cars slowed to stare at my small pile of stained earthly belongings.

The policeman stood with me and radioed for a police car to come, and when they arrived he remounted his police-issue Norton Commando and, with a smooth movement and style, purred off to his next assignment. I do remember that he was quite gentle and kind towards me.

The police took me in their car (a Jaguar) to the station. They did 100 mph down the motorway and had me lean forward to see the speedo. I don't think rear seatbelts were a thing then. They were laughing with me about the story I could tell when I got home.

I had no resistance left for this situation, it was just too hard in the moment, so through snot and tears, and as they handed me tissues, I told them everything. They were so easy with me. Once we were at the station I had to tell them everything again. I was put in a cell, and on a thin blue rubber mattress, uncovered, I fell asleep.

Very late that night, when I was still half asleep, they moved me from the bare cell I was in to somewhere else a long car journey away. When

I awoke I was in a very small room with a proper bed, sheets and a pillow. The door was locked, and it seemed at least like a nicer cell.

During what I imagined to be the daytime, someone brought me food. They did not speak to me and left me in the room. I imagine that either there was a toilet in the cell or I was let out to use one, I can't actually remember. The night went by and no one came. The next day was the same. I was feeling claustrophobic, scared, frustrated, and overwhelmed at times as the fearful swirling thoughts of the future whispered to me. I think I imagined a silent car with my parents hurtling down the motorway to collect me.

I later found out they were keeping me safe and arranging for a social worker to come and talk with me. Certainly, from where I had been earlier the previous day, I was much safer and well guarded, even if at the time I did not fully understand that.

Chapter 7

At the end of the second day, an older woman came to the room and let me out to sit in another bigger room that had a sofa and a table in it. The view from the solitary window was over a large, well-kept garden. It turned out that I was being cared for at a girls' borstal on the outskirts of Birmingham. I was isolated for my own safety, they told me. There was a radio playing somewhere, and I remember the comforting sound of a well-known T-Rex song.

I was strangely happy and content in myself that day. I was safe, warm, fed, and no one would move me on that night. My newly acquired world-view counted only what I could eat and where I could sleep as essential understandings for happiness.

That night I slept well, and early the next morning they let me out again into the bigger room for the day and provided a couple of books. Happiness reigned; I so loved reading.

Memories of Saturday mornings when I was allowed to go to the local library came back to me, bringing such peace. Even though I could not articulate it then, reading was my escape, my happy place, my adventure land. I would walk, jog and run through the city back lanes, knowing every wall, every tiny garden, every crossing on the way. I'd be stood at the library doors at one minute to nine, recovering my breath and waiting with excitement.

In my little school bag I would usually have three books (that was the maximum allowed out) to hand back, and already in my fertile mind I had a shopping list of books I hoped would be available.

I loved Zane Grey, C. S. Forester, Agatha Christie, Roald Dahl and so many more. I read *The Sword in the Stone* trilogy at least three times, *The Man in the Iron Mask*, *The Black Tulip*, *The Three Musketeers*, *Robinson Crusoe*, *Swiss Family Robinson*, *Treasure Island*, *A Christmas Carol*, *The War of the Worlds*, and I devoured the Famous Five and the Secret Seven.

Once I had found my carefully selected prizes for the week ahead, I had them stamped (two weeks was the maximum time then, I believe) and I'd be off, running back towards home, up the familiar stairs into my room, book out and reading before I was on my bed. I'd finish one book that same Saturday and start another. I was usually ready to go back to the library by the Wednesday and had to patiently wait for Saturday to come around again, and hope against hope that my treasure run would be permitted.

That afternoon a youthful long-bearded man came and chatted with me. He was the social worker assigned to get me back to Scotland. He talked about putting me on a train the next day and asked if I'd stay on it. I was honest and told him I'd be out the train doors and away again before it left the station if I could. Even with the hardships, I was happier on the road than I had ever been at home for as long as I could remember.

He left, and nothing much seemed to be agreed other than that he would come back the next day. I read, listened to the radio playing the new top twenty, and went to bed in my little locked room.

The next morning he was back early, and I was taken to his car. No reading and radio today. At the local airport I was put on a plane to Edinburgh. One hostess told me that when we landed I was to remain seated. I had never flown before, so I was a bit excited as well as apprehensive. I think I had developed my ability to live in the moment so much that I did not think too far ahead about what might come next.

The plane landed, everyone disembarked but me, and I waited. Then through the front door of the plane I saw two uniformed police officers enter and walk towards me. They had me stand and accompany them from the plane, down the steps, and at the bottom they went either side of me and took an arm. I was frogmarched across the tarmac apron in full view of the raised viewing gallery, and I was aware of swivelling heads and rubber necks.

I did not know what was happening, but I began to suspect that I was not going home. In that moment I was a thirteen-year-old Ronnie Biggs, or so I thought.

Chapter 8

He was quite a cheery sort of man and gave off an air of confidence that made me feel like everything was going to be okay. The minute the police handed me over to him I felt like at least there was a plan. He had brown corduroy patches sewn onto the elbows of his worn grey jacket and a suitably tired-looking car. He was to be my social worker for the next few years and would see the best and worst of me at times.

As we drove out of the airport that morning I had no idea of the adventure that lay before me. I was entering a whole new world of children's panels (courts), assessment centres, government agencies, and well-meaning people.

He explained that he was taking me to what was called an assessment centre, where I would be placed for the next six weeks and looked after while the social work department tried to work out what to do with me. As I kept running away from home, I could no longer simply be put back with my parents.

While there was anxiety about this unknown place we were heading to, I felt settled in the knowledge that I was not going home. Home held no attraction for me; I did not feel safe or wanted there. The constant discipline and sense of never being good enough was breaking me. I knew that no matter what, I could not go back, even if going forward was scary.

We drove in through the gates of a modern-looking building, set out in blocks in places and surrounded by a soccer pitch and what looked like vegetable gardens. There was a high perimeter fence around the whole establishment.

The moment we walked into the main building I picked up on the atmosphere. There were locked doors, staff with large bunches of keys on their belts, and no children to be seen anywhere.

My clothes were taken from me and I was examined, and my social worker simply evaporated and wasn't seen again for at least three weeks. I was given a green-blue T-shirt that was three sizes too big, one pair of black shorts, and a set of plastic sandals. I was led through a couple of locked doors into the main building.

It was still morning, so I was offered some toast and watched over by a staff member as I hungrily ate every last crumb. Next, they took me upstairs along a long corridor and stopped at one of the small rooms. Each room had a number. This was to be my room — two single beds, both perfect squares, nothing else. I was sharing.

The man with me explained that all the boys did chores in the mornings, and I would now join them. Before I knew it, I was on my hands and knees scrubbing all the boys' toilets. That was my first job in my new home-to-be. Some of the other boys were there, and when the guard (and yes, that's really what they were seen as) wandered off for a while, they asked me questions. It became obvious very quickly that I was the youngest. Most of the boys were fifteen or sixteen or older. Many came from very difficult backgrounds, and some had been in institutions pretty much their whole lives.

There was a lot of bullying and fighting, and that was very new to me. Being the youngest and the newest, the first few weeks were hard as I was picked on by the worst of the boys. The showers were by far the worst place for bullying. The staff didn't come into the shower rooms, so old scores and imagined slights were settled there all the time. Most days I was scared to go in, although most days nothing actually happened to me. Still, there was an air of underlying violence, and the smallest incident, even a wrong look, could spark a furious fight.

There was a solitary confinement cell in each block, where anyone caught fighting was put for a few days and nights.

Anyone who tried to escape and was caught had to wear knee-length bright blue scratchy woollen shorts for a few weeks. Boys climbed over the large perimeter fence while working in the garden. Others smashed their bedroom window at night, threw their mattress out, jumped down onto it, and ran into the shadows. They all returned eventually, straight into solitary confinement and then the horrible scratchy shorts. One boy I knew lived in the nearby woods for two weeks before being caught. I wanted to be like him.

We had basic school during the day after morning chores, then outside for sports or garden work in the afternoons, then chores again before dinner. The last hour before bed was in the common room, where there was a table tennis table. Most of the day was routine: we lined up for meals, stood for roll call, lined up to be allocated chores. So that hour in the common room was precious.

At night a red light stayed on, and a guard constantly checked through the spyhole in the door. We heard his keys clanking as he went up and down the halls. We were locked in and had to buzz for the toilet or if we were sick. Sometimes none of us slept, because all we could hear was the boy in solitary shouting or crying.

My mum came to visit one day. We sat together in the large canteen with the kitchen staff working in the background. We spoke like strangers, asking generic questions. No hugs, no connection. I wanted her to leave. Eventually she did. Her parting remarks were, "Ah knew ye were nae good, and ah told yeh ye'd end up here, but you widnae listen," and, having got the last word, she was gone.

For those who don't know me well, you won't know that I love my mum, and that we began to be reconciled seventeen years later, but that's a story for another chapter.

A few weeks into my stay I was taken to see a psychologist and a doctor, and then told my social worker would visit. One night within the next two weeks I'd have to go before the "Children's Panel", a kind of junior court that would decide my future.

Most boys leaving the assessment centre went to what was called an "approved school". There were several of these schools in Scotland. They were apparently much like the place I was already in but bigger, with longer stays, years rather than weeks. It was not an exciting prospect.

Chapter 9

The day came for me to go to the Children's Panel. A heavy sense of apprehension settled on me. My dad and mum would be there. My social worker would take me but wouldn't be in the room for the hearing. A lot was at stake, and I didn't feel prepared emotionally or mentally.

I had been badly hurt at the assessment centre one night. All I remembered was waking up on the floor of a dark hallway with staff standing over me shouting. I was taken to the first aid room on a stretcher. Someone held my hand and told me it was going to be ok, while other voices talked about an ambulance.

My forehead was split open and I needed fifteen stitches. I was in hospital for a few days, and when I came back I stayed in bed for more than a week. My eyes were puffed up and bruises covered my face.

Once I was well again, I was partnered with one of the maintenance men at the assessment centre to help him each day. We hung out in the boiler room playing cards while he shared his sandwiches. Those were good days, and I remember them fondly.

All this delayed the date of my hearing. But now the day was here, and I was, butterfly stomach and all, on my way. Sitting unaccompanied in the back seat of the car, my thoughts ran riot.

I remembered the days at home, long days locked in my room. I would read and read. I thought about the time my mum gave me 1000 lines to write during the school holidays, something like "I must be a better behaved boy at home, and not tell any more lies to my parents." One thousand times. It took me all day for days and days. My hand was sore. The writing had to be neat or it didn't count. Pages were regularly rejected and had to be rewritten. I don't know what the final total was. The stack of completed pages was put under a mop pail to absorb any spills while washing the common stairs.

My memory flicked to the time I was caught taking a handful of sultanas from the jar in the cupboard. Every meal for the next ten days was a plate of sultanas. I had to stand in the corner on my own as my dad, mum and sister ate at the table. I was in the little scullery area, back to the family, with my saucer of sultanas. Even today they make me gag. I would have been around seven years old.

And the sudden, confusing violence, hit to the floor, kicked off the floor, and implements used regularly for beatings.

I couldn't think about going back home, but I was also really worried about being sent to an approved school, with the likely bullying and abuse that would go on there.

I only have a vague memory of the hearing: serious but kind voices asking questions in a room dominated by dark wood, low lighting. My dad and mum looking so out of place, fragile even. The anger in their voices when they spoke.

Then it was over. No decision made. The panel would consider options.

The car journey back to the centre was quiet and quick. My mind was consumed by the fear I might be sent home. My social worker said he would visit me the next day. My role now was to wait. I think I was so tired I slept well that night in spite of the turmoil and anxiety. The next day or two would decide my future, I was sure.

That night I dreamed about being able to fly, and yet I didn't fly away from the assessment centre. Instead I stayed, enjoying the oohs and ahhs of staff and inmates as I flew around the different spaces.

Chapter 10

The next morning I awoke with a conglomerate of sensations: hope, dread, excitement and fear all bubbling at the top, with deeper, more primitive emotions stirring below the surface. The call came after breakfast and chores, by which time I was starting to worry that maybe nothing would be said. I was instructed by the chores oversight that I was to go to the main office, and a staff member came to collect me.

Waiting in a comfortable chair outside one of the offices, away from the main population, would normally have been a moment of pleasure and escape, but today it was patience that was on trial inside my young frame. Fidgety, nervous and feeling a little nauseous, I waited.

The door opened and I was ushered inside. My social worker was there waiting for me. I sat where I was invited to and stilled my heart as best I could. After the words "going home" were spoken, I did not hear much else. Soon after, I was in a car on the way to meet my parents again at some neutral venue.

My social worker was driving. He told me that the panel, the police and himself had spoken with my parents and had asked for some changes to be made to give me a bit more freedom. He said my parents were willing to do that. Inside my head, the only thought that had any room, any traction and any volume was that none of these people really knew my parents or understood what it was like to live there.

Back home it was sterile. The atmosphere was cordial but impersonal. My dad told me I was allowed to go out now in the evenings, and that he and my mum did not care to know where I went, but they were only doing this because they had been told they had to. It was a weird moment really. I think the curfew was that I had to be home by 8 pm or 9 pm at the latest.

I had never had this sort of freedom ever. For the next few weeks I went out nearly every night, walking miles, roaming all over the city, exploring the back streets and shortcuts, parks and river walks, shopping centres and unused lanes. Just to be out of the house for me was amazing. I took books to the park and read them some nights. I met up with some of the rowdier bunch from school occasionally and managed to get into trouble a few times.

It might be easy for you, the reader, to imagine my whole life at home was unbearable, but in truth there were seasons of normality. We would go on family holidays, camping mostly, and have fun in those days. My dad would take me for long walks up the hills around the city on the weekends. I would walk alongside him, fuzzy headed for the first mile or so at silly o'clock in the morning. We would occasionally all go out and have dinner in a café together or fish and chips in the car.

My mum had been seriously ill for a number of years when I was younger, and I think a lot of the stuff that happened then was part of what was going on. Mum was in and out of hospital for months at a time. Looking back on those years now, my dad was stuck between the proverbial rock and hard place. I would probably have been around seven or eight years old and my sister nine or ten. If my dad stopped working to look after us, he would lose his job and with that our house. If he kept working, then he had to leave us at 6 am and not get home most nights until around 8 pm. He kept working.

So we were on our own, under instructions never to answer the door. My sister and I had some moments of conflict in those months, as any normal brother and sister left on their own may. My memory now of those times is of being on our own except Sundays when we had our best clothes prepared and we all went to the hospital to visit my mum.

One night, when my mum was back home from another long hospital stay, my dad woke me up in what seemed to me the middle of the night but was probably only 11 pm. He pulled me through to the main living room where he and my mum had their bed. My mum was holding on to the headboard, groaning really scarily loudly in pain and twisting under the sheets. My dad told me that this was my fault, that my bad behaviour had caused this.

An ambulance came and took her to hospital. My mum had undiagnosed Crohn's disease and later had yards of her bowels removed.

If I may address you directly, dear reader, please do not slip into any sort of judgement on my parents. Rather, allow the story to unfold and see the way they were shaped and how the story ends.

After a few weeks of me being out most nights roaming the streets until 8 pm, there was a massive shouting match at home. My dad screamed at me as to why I never told them where I was going. In my head, I was recounting him telling me they did not want to know. No way was I saying that. Blows were landed and rules were changed. The next day, on the way to school, I was gone, bag over my shoulder as the now well-known route south was commenced.

Chapter 11

Somehow I found myself in Leeds. To be honest, it was never in my mind as a destination, and even as I arrived my internal compass was already trying to work out how best to get around or through this city. My memories now are of a dark place, grimy, a tired grey city, like a family that had seen one too many tragedies and had stopped even trying. Eventually, I found myself walking along what seemed like a bypass. It was late, after midnight, and the traffic was sparse. A truck, a taxi and then a moped passed by, airbrushing my hitchhiker's thumb out of their world views. I imagined them getting home, putting the kettle on, maybe making some cheese on toast, wilfully enjoying the delayed gratification of their warm bed. I did not begrudge them their comforts.

I walked on. My body, toughened now to the hardships of my chosen path, could do hunger, and could do sleepless, and I could survive for days on no company. All I needed was the occasional moment of hope that a lift in a car or truck would provide.

At my young age, I had yet to experience a violent predator, and Leeds filled that gap for me. A violent, angry man with a rabid Alsatian dog in his car ripped at my clothes from the back of the car, tearing a large gash in my only warm jersey and covering it with dog saliva. I'm not sure if this encounter coloured my experience of Leeds or whether my already poor impression of Leeds was confirmed by this individual. I forgive him today, this scared man, preying on young boys to fulfil his flesh-driven desires. How empty a life, void of connection and meaning, must be. My heart was left unscathed, even if my memories were tainted by this abuse.

Then I was on the road again, breathing deep the cold night air, confused a little I think, but determined not to dwell on the greyness of my surroundings or allow it to intrude, but to push on, shaking the dust from my feet.

When finally a car with a man and woman stopped to give me a lift onto the motorway, away from Leeds, I determined never to return. And to the best of my knowledge, I never have.

For some strange reason, a series of lifts (and I would just go wherever they were going) deposited me in Oxford, a sort of antithesis of Leeds, at least in my first impressions. If my memory is right, there was an easy route towards London from Oxford and I started to traverse this route, back and forwards, snatching short bursts of sleep wherever I could. I experienced male abuse a further twice on these journeys, always late at night, a middle-aged male predator, and once I feared for my life. There is no need for me to dwell on these stories or give any room to details here. Suffice to say they were confusing experiences for a 13-year-old vulnerable boy. I resolved even then that those men would leave no mark on my inner person, only touching my physical body.

I think that on balance I met so many remarkable, caring people that I was able to stay strong in my twofold purpose, which was to learn to survive and not be caught. People who gave me a bed for the night, or bought me food, or even gave me a little money, kept alight the candle of hope in my heart. Yes, I lied. I told stories of a job offer one way and then of a job offer unfulfilled the other way. Back and forwards I went, day after day, the original Oxford/London shuttle.

One night I accepted a lift off the beaten track and found myself walking on a B-road around 1 am. No traffic passed for at least an hour. I had learned to be happy on these solo walks. The sense of the unknown, even the hunger and physical pain, promoted my sense of being alive now. What originally had crushed me was now my daily bread.

… Memories of being alone at home drifted through my thoughts. My dad leaving the house at 5 am and returning at 7 pm stayed with me that night. My mum was in hospital for what felt like months. My older sister and I fought and argued and I became completely out of control. I remember hanging out of the bathroom window on my fingertips, four flights up, trying to scare her into leaving me alone. Perhaps that was when rebellion first took root in me.

My older sister was very different from me. As she grew up, she played the cello, was learning Russian, and sat at the top of her class, a straight "A's" student. I, on the other hand, had not found my rhythm, and only with what felt like superhuman effort managed to claw my way to the middle of the bottom class. Usually a disappointment for my parents, I dreaded parent nights and the interrogation and punishments that followed. I would be locked in my tiny box-room bedroom night after night, with surprise checks to make sure I was doing my work.

Car headlights swept across the treetops in the distance. The car was approaching from behind me. Should I hide or ride? I stayed where I was, hungry and exhausted, and somehow hope weakened my resilience. The car stopped and a young man offered me a lift; he was heading back to an RAF base after a night out. As I told my prefabricated story, he suggested I go back to camp with him and get a bed for the night and breakfast in the morning. I was wary, having been abused several times by lone men. But in the warm car, my hunger and tiredness echoed loudly. I went.

He kept his word: a clean warm bed and a massive breakfast in the NAFFI the next morning. He told me he had told a few lies to get me in, and that he would help me leave after breakfast. He dropped me at a dual carriageway slip road, handing me two one-pound notes, an absolute fortune to me. It was a warm morning, promising heat later in the day. I was full, rested, and safe. This felt like the peak of my hopes: an open road before me and endless time ahead. What could possibly go wrong?

Chapter 12

It had become normal for me, as a thirteen-year-old, to find myself in the back of a police car or in a police cell. Part of me was frustrated, and part of me was oddly relieved each time I was caught. So here I was again, on my way back to Scotland. This time the first stop was the assessment centre. I knew my way around now and slipped back into the routine as easily as the old clothes they gave me.

Weeks passed. A psychologist spoke with me a few times, as did my social worker, and in one surreal meeting my mum was there with another person.

I worked in the veggie gardens after morning classes, played table tennis in the evenings, ate everything I was given, and slept well each night. Mostly I managed to avoid the bullies as best I could, and apart from a few kicks and an occasional wild punch, I escaped most of it this time.

I'm guessing now, but I think I was at the assessment centre for around six weeks before word came that my Children's Panel date was set.

It was a winter evening, dark nights creeping in like slow traffic. Car windows steamed up, blurred reds and yellows from street and car lights making shaky mosaics as we drove to the city centre building that housed the well-meaning people who would decide my future. I could see my breath as we stepped out of the car. I had a split-second thought of running, just as a firm hand gently closed on my shoulder.

We were back in the high-ceilinged, dimly lit room with the large, heavy-set, dark polished table in the centre. On the other side sat four or five well-dressed men and women I didn't know, and the Children's Reporter, whom I now recognised. My social worker was there, as well as my mum and dad. My dad wore his work clothes, and he and my mum sat slightly huddled together, looking strangely out of place in the formal room, like two oil paintings awkwardly overlapping.

They spoke, or at least my dad did. He was measured, but angry. Angry at the people in the room, I think, as much as at me. I remember the tone of the voices: the calm, almost clinical tones of the professionals, the sharper, strained sounds from my dad, and the occasional Morse-code-like whisper of support from my mum.

My dad spent his life providing, my mum spent hers tidying, and they seemed confused as to how those solid efforts had led them to this moment. There was anger in their voices, accusations in their words, and punishment was the currency they sought.

The meeting ended. I was in the car heading back to the centre with no decision yet announced.

… I loved going to the local park as a young boy. There was nothing like the early sun on your back, the rich smell of freshly cut grass, and the sight of a soccer game already underway but still short a few players. Piles of jackets marked the goals, and some unspoken agreement filled in the missing white lines. After 20 or 30 goals, no one bothered keeping score. Some games went on for half a day, or at least until the kid who owned the ball had to go home. Hunger usually ambushed me late in the day.

Back at the centre the next day, my social worker arrived and took me to see a possible new home. So the Children's Panel must have reached a decision after I left.

It was a huge old Victorian building with four floors, including the attic, and a giant kitchen and pantry. We drove for what seemed like hours, it felt like we had left the city behind when we finally pulled up at a small gate. The boys' bedrooms were up a narrow, squeaky, winding stairwell covered in industrial carpet, leading towards the attic. These sloped-ceiling rooms would originally have been servants' quarters. On the way up we passed a common room with a table tennis table, a record player, and a TV. It looked like heaven to me. I asked when I could live there and was told that today was the day.

The other children (usually around twelve) were all out at school or work. A brief shadow of recognition passed over me, I would be going back to school.

Sitting by myself that first day in the common room, I felt strangely safe, as though something in me knew things would settle now.

… I remembered a few years earlier when a relative from New Zealand had come to visit with my mum during the school holidays, Easter, I think. I'm not sure what I had done wrong, but my mum gave me 1000 lines to write out. I genuinely can't remember what they were meant to say. One thousand times, as a ten or eleven-year-old. I spent the whole holidays locked in my bedroom, writing and crying. I hoped there would be no more moments like that.

The other children returned and we chatted a bit over dinner in the massive kitchen. A cook prepared the meals for the children and staff. I met my roommates, four of us in the biggest attic room, two boys each in the smaller attic rooms, and four girls on the common room landing, two in each room. One of the full-time staff also slept on the girls' landing in a third bedroom. He was older, wore leather sandals with bare feet, spoke softly, carried a Bible, and seemed quite angry much of the time. I was the youngest in the house. Some boys were 16 or 17, and one was already working full time.

That first night the pecking order was established, and I landed at the bottom. I also couldn't comb my hair for the next day or two.

There was so much to learn about this new life: the rules, the unspoken rules, the boundaries, and what was expected of me each day.

Chapter 13

The house itself was a marvel. Surrounded by head-high stone walls, it had a small, stony front garden and a large grassed back garden overlooking, in the distance, the playing fields of a girls' school. A gunship-grey metal fire escape clung to the side of the house passing several windows on it's way up. Inside, ceilings were high, wood was dark and polished. A large ground floor bay-windowed dining room to the left was consumed by the deep mahogany coloured dining table and chairs. I think once we somehow got the table out and used this room for a Christmas party. Otherwise it was untouched, week after week. The "office" was also on the ground floor, first door on the right, before a large elegant hardly used toilet. The office was where we were assigned when we stuffed up generally, otherwise it was staff only. The large kitchen, complete with farmhouse table, pantry and cooking range, a place of joy mostly, also was on the ground floor, entrance adjacent to the impressive staircase that dominated the foyer. All in all, it reminded me a bit of the black and white house Sherlock Holmes lived in. At the back of the kitchen was a never-to-be-passed-door leading through to a built on staff house where the head staff and his wife and children lived.

Moving upwards, there was a sort of halfway level. At the top of the first set of stairs was a landing, and then to the left, up two steps, was a small foyer (with a payphone) leading to a large laundry and ironing room, and a girls' toilet. On the other side of the halfway landing was a TV room, reached by climbing a few more steps. From there we went up through a wooden and reinforced-glass fire door at the top of the stairs, bridging the main landing. Here sat the ornate, high-ceilinged common room and three large bedrooms.

Through a door in the wall, a spiralling, creaky stairwell led up to the attic rooms. That was most of the house, although games of hide-and-seek would reveal a few more secrets over the next year or two.

During the first few days, there were many meetings with staff. My social worker came every day, and the basics like clothes and toiletries were sorted out. I spent hours in the common room on my own, enjoying the sense of safety and thinking about my life so far.

…When I was very young, we lived in a street designated as a "play street", so no cars were allowed in unless the people lived there. To be honest, no one on our street even owned a car. The only car we ever saw was a little bubble car that opened from the front, and it came late at night when a boyfriend visited his girlfriend in the next tenement. If it arrived while we were still playing, we would gather around it in amazement as the young man climbed out, steering wheel and all.

Every tenement was just a single room with a bedroom alcove off the main living area. There was no hot running water, and some buildings had outside shared toilets. We had one central grassed area at the back, really meant for drying washing for the hundreds of families who lived there.

All the children played together in the street, and we had brilliant fun with very simple things. As no one had a proper ball except for the odd tennis ball, we often played soccer with used cotton reels. Hard on our shoes. (Nobody had trainers back then.)

One summer afternoon, one of the boys, maybe we were all around seven, came out to play and offered to buy everyone an ice lolly. This was unheard of. Most families had so little money that tripe or mince and tatties were the usual meals. He headed down the street and around the corner, out of sight, which was also unheard of because we all lived under the unspoken rule that if your parents couldn't see you from the window, you were in big trouble.

I remember him returning about fifteen minutes later, both hands full of ice lollies, proper multi-coloured, rocket-shaped ones, the stuff of dreams.

He was about twenty yards away when his mum appeared in their stairwell. I could tell immediately something was wrong. She shouted, "Did you take money out of my purse?" Oh-oh. We all froze on the spot. She grabbed him by the ear and dragged him, and the ice lollies, into the dark stairwell. We were silent. Everyone knew that taking money from your mum's purse was right up there with the major crimes of childhood.

We knew when his dad came home because we heard the wailing as he was punished. (Back then spanking was normal, and wooden spoons, shoes, and canes were often used.)

Even then, I remember thinking that some advice was really worth listening to. Although I could almost taste the ice lolly…

The staff in the home consisted of a large Canadian man who was in charge, the sandals guy, and a student who came and went at odd hours. They were decent enough and usually helped us.

We received pocket money each week. If we didn't do our chores, skipped school, or came home late, we were fined. Usually a fine was a week's pocket money, sometimes two. Money meant power.

The nearest shops were a forty-minute round trip away. If you didn't want to walk yourself, you could often bribe someone else to go. The boys who worked, there were two of them originally, never had to go for anything. As the youngest, I usually had to go, at first under threat with no reward, but eventually I learned to stand my ground.

The girls were mostly polite to me and easy to chat with. They were all working, some part-time while still at school, others having already left at fifteen. Again, I was the youngest by a few years. Two of the girls were dating a couple of the boys in the home. They often sat together, and the boys got rather edgy if you talked to their girlfriends when they were out of the room.

I was learning the rules: don't win at table tennis against the bullies, don't talk to girls when their boyfriends aren't there, and don't expect your dinner to still be on your plate if you were late. There were a lot of fights in the boys' rooms. Sometimes I was called out, and sometimes I was left alone. It all seemed a bit random.

I wanted to fit in, to become one of the boys, so that when a new boy arrived I would no longer be the sole target of attention. The boys in the home came from tough backgrounds: families in prison, no family at all, or families with such serious problems that the kids weren't safe at home. In the years ahead, I would visit some of those homes and be shocked by what I saw. But for now, all I wanted was to fit in.

Chapter 14

Going back to school was not a great experience. If I hadn't really fitted in before, I certainly didn't fit in now. I was the bike thief, just a few rungs down from the book thief. On top of that, I was now the kid who ran away from home, or the kid living in a children's home. There were so many labels to choose from I could have opened a department store.

In class I struggled to concentrate or even take an interest. Previously I had kept trying, but now I disengaged completely. I became the class clown, covering up my failings with deflecting humour, silly stunts, and constant small rebellions.

I can't remember how many times I received six of the belt. I even had the dubious honour of getting six of the belt from the headmaster, something I think was rarer than steak tartare. My heart was hardening towards authority and towards anyone who seemed to care. I couldn't have expressed it back then, but there was a bit of self-destruction in me every day.

There was no money at the children's home for clothes, so we received a voucher from social work and were sent out on our own to buy what we needed. What do you think I bought, school uniform, or clothes that helped me fit in with my new peers? That's right, the peers option.

So I turned up at school with no uniform at all, not even a single item of the right colour. I was sent to sit in the first-aid room, where a long line of people came to peer in the window at this strange specimen. There was a "zoo" feeling about my life that morning. "Do not feed this person, they are dangerous!"

I was sent home. The children's home didn't really care much at that point. It took over a month for the clothing issue to be sorted, and a pair of grey trousers and a white shirt were eventually found. I know older people often talk about how hard they had it, and younger ones roll their eyes. But I actually went to school that winter with no soles on my shoes. It was tough, embarrassing, and very character-building.

I remember one day when I actually went to school, being on the bus home and desperately needing to go to the toilet. I jumped off at the first stop I could and ran, cheeks clenched, for the gate to our home. Twenty yards from the finish line, I knew it wasn't going to happen, so down came the breeks in the street. I was actually at the hedge of the front garden, and one more step and the mess would have been in my pants. In record time, the small brown anaconda made its escape, and pants up, I left it there without a backward glance.

As a young boy I could be stubborn. One day, while exploring the building, I found a trapdoor that led to the large triangular eaves. There was enough room to crawl in and sit, so the following school day that's exactly what I did. I sat in the dark, reflecting in the confined space for probably six hours rather than go to school.

… The first time I really ran away from home, I would have been around seven or eight. I was at primary school and somehow knew about a ruined house with a large garden, around a twenty-minute walk from school. Back then the school gates were open, no one was watching, and children often went home for lunch.

At lunchtime, I set off as if going to the shops but kept walking to the abandoned house. I don't think I was truly "running away," more like exploring. The area had large, thick walls, broken down in many places, the rubble of a ruined house, and small patches of thick, overgrown bushes and trees.

I spent the afternoon climbing trees and imagining adventures. It was a sunny, warm, and still day. I played on my own for hours.

At one point, I left the ruin and ran around the outside on the pavement. Turning a corner, I saw my dad, mum, and the headmaster all getting out of a car. Their backs were to me, and they didn't see me.

I froze for a millisecond, then turned and dashed back to the garden, hiding in the bushes. My mum appeared first in the ruined house's garden, easily spotting my bright school clothes. She came over to the bushes and called me out, which I slowly did.

I was hustled away in the car back home. I don't remember much after that. I don't think I was punished too severely; it was just youthful adventure, without thinking things through. Reading *Tom Sawyer*, *The Famous Five*, and *The Secret Seven* had somehow sparked the desire for my own adventure story. I hadn't really considered how I'd survive overnight.

Around 4 pm, I sneaked downstairs, trying to get past the kitchen door where staff often sat. I congratulated myself on my stealth and cleverness as I managed it. I went to the front door, opened it quietly, and shut it behind me with enough force to make it clear I'd just come home from school.

The staff on duty called me into the big communal kitchen and asked about my day. I said it had been good. He suggested I check the mirror next door, which I did. My face was covered in black dust, my hair had cobwebs, and my throat was marked with camouflage-like streaks. He knew I had been there all day, as the school had called when I didn't show up, and he had let me sit in that space for six hours.

I shudder now thinking about how I treated my secondary school teachers. In Chemistry class, I once set a coil of magnesium on fire and put it in the desk drawer. It burned through the drawer, set off the fire alarm, and emptied the school. Another time, after being unfairly accused, I spat on the blackboard when the teacher stepped out. I also spilled a full bottle of "stink bomb" fluid in English class, again emptying the department.

I skipped classes, arrived late, left early, and was repeatedly disrespectful. Detention was handed out time and time again, but I often just went home in defiance. I can't imagine how many teachers had meetings about me or how much stress I caused. I am sorry now, all these years later. At the time, I think I was reacting to rejection with an extra dose of immaturity.

During this period I contracted glandular fever and was bedridden for several weeks. I was so disconnected from school and schoolwork that there seemed to be no way back. I had just turned 14 years old. Eventually, I was expelled.

The next day, I was having a long lie-in when the staff came upstairs and said the school was willing to give me one more chance if I accepted their conditions. From my reclined position, I declined.

The home I lived in got a new head staff member, a man from Fort William called Iain. Iain would impact my life in ways I had yet to understand.

Chapter 15

Families are weird sometimes. I remember being at home, probably around six or seven years old, during the Christmas holidays. My auntie from London visited unexpectedly one day and stayed for a while. She brought her boyfriend with her. My mum sat and chatted, and I think my dad was there as well, as it was probably Christmas Eve. They stayed for a while, and as they were leaving, they somehow invited themselves to come over for Christmas dinner with us the next day.

My mum was really annoyed with her sister, turning up unannounced with her "latest" boyfriend and expecting mum and dad to suddenly provide two extra Christmas dinners. We did not have many visitors that I can remember growing up; my mum kept the house immaculate, but I'm not sure who it was for.

The next day we were instructed to stay very quiet and keep all the curtains closed. If we went past the front door, we were to be on our hands and knees so we would not be seen through the letterbox. (Wow, work that out.)

Needless to say, my auntie and her boyfriend never came to our door that day. Maybe they sensed something the day before that we kids were oblivious to. I think we probably missed out that day, although as a family, Wendy and I have had "neighbours" and people away from home join us for Christmas dinner.

In her later years, my mum transformed, keeping an open house for neighbours and friends and displaying the uncanny ability to make friends wherever she went.

I was settling into life as part of a family with twelve children and no real parents. I experienced love as the freedom to make mistakes, own up to them, and receive reasonable discipline. We were nearly always up to some sort of mischief, the seven boys, that is. Like the time at Halloween when all of us climbed down the fire escape, dropped the last section into the back garden, and ran through the neighbours' gardens at 2 a.m., covered in pillowcases and sheets, making strange noises and pretending to be ghosts. That stunt was raised at our weekly home meeting:

"Ahemm, boys," Iain started, "wud any of yoos know anything aboot an invashun of ghosts intae oor street this week?"

Stifled snickers were the only answer.

"Next item, please…"

Sometimes our antics were not so harmless, we might talk about those another day.

One summer school holiday weekend, a few of us decided to have a picnic. We snuck into the kitchen, which adjoined the staff accommodation, so we had to be super quiet.

We had to find a way past the padlock on the pantry door, which we did (and then locked it again). We found food suitable for a picnic: three pillowcases partly full of apples, crisps, and some cooking chocolate. Then we went up into the attic, out the side-attic window, and scrambled onto the roof. Looking back now, I shudder at how easily we could have slipped and died.

We all sat on the roof having our picnic, and I must say, cooking chocolate was not quite what I had imagined. Eventually, an apple core was thrown from the roof, alerting the staff to our whereabouts. A few minutes later, a head appeared at the side of the roof, Iain. We were commanded to attend a meeting in the office and to bring our pillowcases of loot.

We all clambered back down, loot in hand, and sheepishly went to the office. We lost our privileges, pocket money, our bedtime was changed, and we were all grounded. In hindsight, it was handled tenderly, and I think we heard the staff laughing after we left the office.

I loved going out in the evenings after school, and as long as I was home by 7 p.m., nothing was said. I could ask to stay out later, but only for a strong reason. One early evening in the city centre, a shop window sign caught my eye: "Dishwasher required, apply within." I went in, applied, and was offered the role that weekend. Mostly it was Saturdays only, but occasionally evenings were needed. I was fourteen, nearly fifteen, which meant finishing work around 9 p.m. and then walking home for an hour. I had to ask the staff for permission, I did so nervously. They said yes! Fourteen years old and I had a job of sorts.

This was the start of a whole new adventure, that had some fairly predictable and some less foreseeable outcomes.

Chapter 16

Iain saw something in me I think, and he wanted to help bring that out. So he somehow managed to convince the Social Work department to pay for a two week Outward Bound course for me in the Lake District. He drove me to the main station one day with my bag full of weird fashionable clothes (I was starting to be influenced by David Bowie, and Marc Bolan in the 70's). I was to be collected at the other end.

Six am. on the first morning, we all run down to the rough wooden pier at the lake and jump in off the end, swim/wade back to the shore, and then run round a short assault course before being let back into the dorms (6 sets of bunks to a room with a locker each). My heart was bursting, and my skin felt strangely well.

The next two weeks were filled with adventure. I was, by far, the youngest person there, as all the other men had been sent by their employers, there were police, architects, engineers, mountain guides, and doctors that I remember.

It was a dustbin lid on the side of a steep slope. We were all kitted out in wetsuits, battery packs, head torches, and gloves. And in we went through the dustbin lid hole in the side of the mountain. It was a cave system, and we were about to have our first experience of "pot-holing". The first passages were around five-foot-high and about chest deep in slow flowing water, so we all mastered a sort of backwards crab-walk. Trying to keep our heads above the water line. A couple of times we had to duck under and swim a few strokes to the next system, where our heads could again bob up and down, keenly sourcing all the oxygen available, eyes wide open. The instructor had us turn all out torches off, so we could experience total darkness. It was definitely "total".

We passed a roped off area where we were told a guy had gone down the sump, where the water flowed down to the lower caves (with an air bottle on), but had never come back. So "sump-diver" was crossed out on a whole lot of career lists that day!

Then we stopped as a group at another small hole in the cave wall. We were asked rhetorically if anyone was claustrophobic (I had no idea what the word meant at 14, but was about to find out a little). And in we went one after another, crawling on our bellies, water running down our chins, roof touching our backs in places. The guy in front of me got stuck, his battery pack caught on the lip of a rock, and he had to jiggle it round before he could move again. I started to whistle with nerves. I found out later is was a hundred yard crawl - called the philosopher's crawl.

Once I was free from the crawl and in the next cavern I had a fit of the giggles, and an overwhelming feeling of wellness flooded me.

The caves now were huge, ceilings out of sight, and as we abseiled down through secretive waterfalls, I found it so exciting to be part of this adventure. A love for mountains and adventure was being stimulated in my young heart.

When we exited the caves, we were fed, re-equipped, broken up into smaller groups of four or five with an instructor each, and headed off in various directions to spend the night camping before being picked up and driven back to the centre the next day.

There was a slow, soaking rain as we set out, and we walked in single file at a steady pace, heading up the hill for a couple of hours, legs and back aching for a rest that never came. The rain gave way to a watery sun that promised more heat than it delivered, but even that false promise was gratefully received.

Then we reached a small, sheltered plateau by a stream and were told to set up our tents and prepare for the night before dark fell. We were warned that under no circumstances should we take our stoves inside the tents. Totally made sense to me. However, the other two men seemed to know better, and once set up, their stove was nowhere to be seen outside. I crouched on my haunches, boiling water to add to our dried rations, when I heard a scream. Suddenly, the neighbour's tent was half-engulfed in flames. One man jumped out the front, and the instructor leapt into the tent, emerging a second or two later with the screaming individual from the back. The tent was now a charred nylon sheet flapping in the breeze.

I remember being surprised that these men would not listen to the instructor. They had a rough night if I recall correctly, having to set up a few capes and a groundsheet as a makeshift cover.

There were so many memorable moments from that short two weeks. I learned to go out on the hills by myself, sleep under a bivouac, fend for myself, read a map and compass, all while it incessantly poured with rain, and make my way to a rendezvous point to be collected, living on dried rations and porridge cake.

I learned how to be part of a team, facing testing challenges and learning how to get along with a group of men who were fitter, stronger, wiser, and better equipped for life than I was. I loved the camaraderie of shared adventure, rock climbing, canoeing, hill walking, solitude, and survival. That two weeks opened the door to new adventures later in life.

Then I was back, back in the children's home, back at my new job, and back trying to find a way to endure school. Although I had been expelled, there seemed to be a path back for me.

Having great friends and spending time with them is surely one of life's great pleasures. At fourteen, I made friends with the family of a boy I worked beside. Over time, I sort of became adopted into his family, sleeping over and spending more time at their house than anywhere else. We both worked at the same place, where my dishwashing skills were becoming legendary. Long before the concept of BFF, we were inseparable for several years, even starting a band together. Oh, the memories.

On weekends when not at work, we would often spend the entire day together. I remember one summer Saturday morning: the sun was out, we were up fairly early, and at my friend's house there was a group of around five of us. They lived on the outskirts of the city in a new development of council housing, which in Australia is sometimes called commission housing. There were dreadful things that happened and, in the poverty and mess of life, much drug and alcohol abuse.

This day, however, stands out in my memory as one when we truly enjoyed our time together.

We all put on our oldest clothes and trainers and walked to the edge of the new housing area, where it changed into countryside and farmland. We found a small river and all jumped in off a low-hanging old bridge, up to our knees and waists in fresh, cool water.

The sun shone through the riverbank trees. Everything looked so clean and fresh; we were transported from a concrete jungle to adventures on the Congo. We walked upstream together, five abreast, enjoying the closeness of shared Saturday adventures. The river gleamed in the filtered sunshine, bringing waves of joy with its whorls of cool water.

We came to a space on the bank where we could climb out. There was a massive tree overhanging the river. I cannot remember how we did it, but we somehow found an old rope and set up a Tarzan swing over the river.

We played there for hours until the sun was past its peak and the shadows were changing shape and length. I think for all of us there was a tinge of sadness at the end of such a glorious day. We set off back to the bridge, dripping as we crossed building sites and partly made-up streets, before returning to the family home.

We made hot chips on bread and rolls smeared with cold butter and laden with tomato ketchup, the hot chips melting the butter as we wolfed them down. With our favourite music blaring, we sat upstairs in the bedrooms, laughing and talking until the last one of us fell asleep.

As a very young boy, I remember collecting "Batman cards" from packs of bubble gum. Each pack had two cards, I think. If you had doubles, you would try to swap with someone who had a card you needed. Once you had all the cards and turned them over (each card had an image from the TV programme, with characters such as The Penguin, The Joker, and The Riddler on the front), the back revealed a part of the full image from the Bat-Signal in the sky. Only when you had all the parts could you see the complete picture.

Back in the children's home, the other boys would come up with ideas for what we should do. Usually, it meant climbing down the fire escape and dropping to the ground around one or two in the morning. Once we went over the fields at the back of the home, looking for another group of boys causing trouble, just because someone said we should, though no one can remember who. The end result was a close encounter with a baseball bat and me running for my life, jumping off a railway bridge as I was being chased by a group of angry older boys. The bridge was over a disused railway line with no tracks. I landed hard, still running, and collided with a heavy bush on the embankment, impaling myself on a thick branch at my side. I limp-jogged several miles back to the safety of the children's home. I would not be doing that again.

I still remember, when I was younger and living at home, climbing over the railings that separated the common areas. My knee slipped, and I impaled myself on a railing. I have no idea how I had the strength to pull myself free and climb down. I lay on the grass in the sunlight as every ounce of strength seemed to slip out of my body. I was carried to a car, then to hospital, before waking up with stitches and a story. By chance, a doctor had been visiting with my mum at the exact time I got impaled on the railings.

Life was starting to fall into shape. Work brought money, which brought opportunity and choice. Some of my early choices would lead to challenges and setbacks.

Chapter 17

Being a dishwasher was a good place to start my career.

The dishes were stacked at the service lift hatch. I would load them in and send them down to the dishwashing area, where I racked them, ran them through the machine, stacked them at the other end, and reloaded them into the service elevator. I would then send them up while running up the back stairs to arrive before the dishes. All the various dishes were returned to their proper locations by me, before starting the process all over again. Sounds simple, right?

Except in practice, things were usually quite different.

The lift would not work, so I had to carry everything up and down the stairs manually. The dishwasher would break down, meaning everything had to be washed and dried by hand. Then the waiting staff would be so short-handed they could not sort the dishes or clear the plates, so each time I returned upstairs with clean dishes, there was a mountain of uncleared crockery and cutlery jammed into a small space in no order. And it just kept coming while I tried to sort it all out. I was fourteen. In 1973, the pay was fifty pence an hour. Two years earlier, that would have been called ten shillings.

At the end of my shift, I smelled of fast food, my skin shone with grease, and my hair stuck to my forehead from wearing a paper hat all day. I peeled off my once-white tee-shirt and grease-stained dishwasher trousers, still feeling dirty as I put my everyday clothes back on. Walking back to the children's home was strangely relaxing after the constant noise and looped Top of the Pops tribute music all day. I was learning the value of hard work and perseverance.

The home had become a safe place for me. We all knew our pecking order, so the night-time struggles and fights were mostly history. Saturday mornings were my favourites. Most people were out early on a Saturday, visiting family or going to work. My job started at midday, so I would lie in until 9 a.m., when the baker's van came down our small street. I would run downstairs, out the massive front door and garden gate, to purchase a chilled chocolate éclair and a bottle of red cola. Then, in the common room or TV room, I would watch the Saturday morning western movie. I identified with the misunderstood, lonely, heroic main characters. Vicariously, I lived those testing moments in my fourteen-year-old imagination: confronting the baddies, saving the beautiful woman, then riding off into the distance. Although, to be honest, that last bit was a struggle, as I would have preferred to stay and receive the adoration. But it had to be done, because that's what heroes are like, apparently.

With money came new opportunities. Suddenly, I could afford nice clothes, fashionable, tasteful, and stylish. I dressed well, and as the weeks went by, I made a point of staying on trend, changing with the fashions: one week a David Bowie look, the next college jerseys, then Oxford Bags or stay-press trousers. Long gone were the days of relying on the social work department for clothes vouchers.

At one point, not long after I arrived at the home, every boy had received a voucher and we all bought new clothes, trousers, jerseys for the colder days, and polo shirts. Within a week, they had all been stolen, and although the police recovered them, it would be another year before they were returned after being kept as evidence. There was no plan B, so we all wore old clothes again for the next fourteen months.

I had settled into life at the children's home, having been there for around a year. I had a social worker. He was a nice man, patient, helpful, and never really on my case. He wasn't the smartest though. He took me to watch him play rugby when I was thirteen, and bought me my first pint of beer after the game. I remember how big the pint glass seemed, and how a passing jug filled it more than once. When he dropped me back at the home, I was drunk for the first time ever, thirteen years old, and my social worker was the enabler.

However, he was not just a poor influence; he also encouraged me to visit my parents regularly. Something I did almost against my will, although it was strange being able to say and do anything without my mum or dad being able to intervene. Still, I was mostly restrained. It was quite awkward. I would go in the evening, and they would grill me about life at the children's home. I was actually happier there than

I had ever been living at home. That's not to say the children's home was perfect, because it was not. There was a lot of bullying, some stealing, secret drinking, and occasional crazy antics.

One Friday night I went to visit my parents, and a stranger answered the door. I was confused, initially thinking I might be in the wrong tenement stairwell somehow. They asked who I was and what I wanted. I explained. They said my parents had moved away and they lived there now. I asked if they knew where my parents had moved to, and they said no. That was the start of a seventeen-year gap during which I had no contact with my mum or dad. I did not know how to find out where they were, was not really motivated to try, and my social worker never asked if I was still visiting. So it ended there, in a bizarre moment on the doorstep.

I had always felt lonely at home, unwanted, unappreciated, a mistake. Sadly, that was my prevailing memory. Nothing I did was ever enough to gain praise. Much of my young life was spent under some form of punishment, either beaten and left to whimper, or locked in a room for days. The children's home had violence at times, but it was quickly forgotten, and there was no overhanging sense of fear. Punishments were made, dressing downs were given, pocket money could be forfeited, and freedoms and privileges were always available to be reviewed. But the overriding atmosphere was acceptance and justice. The boundaries were probably not strong enough in places, but the heart was in the right place. I felt like I belonged somewhere. I felt I was learning about life. I got to contribute to the chores and the fun of the home. When friends from work or school visited, they were amazed and often envious of our safe place and the easy banter among all the resident children, like a large family. I still sometimes attended school and was ever so slightly better behaved by then.

One evening on the main landing outside the common room, some of the girls had a quarter bottle of vodka. I took a large swig of neat vodka, my first ever spirit, and everything changed in that moment.

Chapter 18

There were a couple of dogs that Iain and his wife had: a friendly Labrador and a nervous small Collie. The Collie had been raised by a cat, and was skittish at times, super friendly, but sometimes lying on its back and refusing to move. At other times, we would see it running along the top of the high garden walls, stalking the local birdlife.

It was great having the dogs around the house. They received lots of love and table scraps. I would often take both dogs for a walk up to the main part of town. It was nice walking them, and I thought I received some interested looks from girls when I was out in my "casually labelled best clothes." In my head, I was a rich young man with my own house and dogs. It was my private fantasy, a Walter Mitty moment I never told anyone about.

Part of me was living the dream in those early days at the children's home. Life was simple, fun was easy, friends were real, and money was helpful but never essential for enjoyment. I remember waking morning after morning with a light feeling. Simple pleasures such as music, reading, and walking or running were central to each day. Sometimes I would put my shorts on at night and go for a run to the local hill, through the quiet streets to the start of the park and the track to the top. I would turn quickly at the top and run back to the start as fast as I could, breathlessly checking the kitchen clock's second hand on my return for an accurate time. I wanted to improve my time each run, though I could not always remember my previous best.

The home had a cook, a busy, bustling, loud man with slicked-back hair, maybe in his forties. He and I had become good friends. I would hang out in the kitchen some days and just chat with him. He was a hard worker, did not take any cheek from the boys or girls, but was really friendly and fair. The work he did for us was a second job, as he had a full-time role cooking for a large company at their central offices. He offered to help me find a summer job there, and I agreed, as long as I could keep my Saturday job washing dishes. He was fine with that, as the offices only worked Monday to Friday.

After my social worker got me tipsy on beer at thirteen, I had, by fourteen, started occasionally going into pubs. I passed in some places as eighteen and easily obtained pints of lager and lime. Two or three of these, and I would be slurring my words and staggering home for an afternoon sleep. Night-time drinking usually involved six cans of beer from the local off-licence, shared at least two ways. These were drunk in the local park after dark, one eye open for any visiting police cars. We told each other fantastic stories about ending up in a care home or our dreams for the future. We fantasised about the girls we knew, how we would ask them out, and what the date night would be like.

Now, with my first night on vodka, I went to a whole new level. Crawling along the floor on my hands and knees, being seriously rude to everyone, and then being sick in the bath. The next morning, when I woke up, a feeling of shame and embarrassment immediately washed over me. The light feeling of happiness was tarnished, and I struggled to understand what had happened. But this was the new world open to me now, a world of crazy boundaries, bad decisions, and moments of madness. It beckoned strongly, a grown-up world. I was allowed in, even though I was anything but a grown-up. Inside me was anger, maybe at rejection, and a fear of being what my parents had told me I would be: a loser, a bad one. In their eyes, there was no hope for me. Perhaps some of their shaping had become a self-destructive vision within me that alcohol lit the touch paper of. Yet, I was free to choose my path. I know now that I was free, but back then it did not feel like freedom.

Weekends became hazy as more and more money was spent on alcohol. Soon, a night out without drinking became unthinkable. I still bought clothes, but more from necessity than from passion. I dressed well, but underneath my heart was confused. Everyone said I was on the road to life, that fun and fulfilment would be discovered on this journey, yet a faint emptiness haunted my steps, my sleep, and my awakenings. I tried to drown out the disquiet. Nightclubs became a pathway to unexpected adventures, although my intoxicated state happily curtailed the volume of dates and encounters. My happiest moments were still early morning sober ventures to watch a sunrise at a city beach.

I started to stay over at friends' houses more and more, not truly realising until too late that I had abandoned the children's home and that there would be a price to pay when I chose to return. The need to stay away became essential rather than a dalliance. When friends became bored with my constant drunkenness, or when friends' parents drew the line in the sand, I found myself sleeping rough once more. Night service buses were good for an hour's sleep before the driver would throw you off. Train stations were good for a few hours, but the police were always there looking for runaways, which I was once more. Daytime was always the best time to sleep, in a park when sunny, or in a covered shelter near one of the local ponds or city-edge parks. I kept working all through this, as money was essential to stay away.

One night, two to three weeks in, tired, wet, and probably quite smelly, I had had enough. Teary-eyed, I knocked on the door of the home after midnight. I was showered, and then a car took me away. The next morning, I awoke in the assessment centre. I was back at the start, and my future was once again in question. I learned for the first time what it really felt like to lose something that I had not fully valued when I had it. My social worker said my future was uncertain and that I might well be sent to a remand centre or an approved school for young offenders. I was shattered.

Chapter 19

So there I was, back in detention. My own choices had led me here, and I was full of regrets. I had actually been really happy at the children's home and missed it terribly. I had seen what life was like on my own and knew I was not ready for that adventure just yet. The days in detention were the same as before. I was close to fifteen now, so I was not really bullied, although a few guys tested me as "the new guy." I let them know right away that I was ready to fight. It did not really matter whether I won or lost a fight; the fact that I was prepared to fight kept most of the bullies away, as they were looking for much easier targets.

The weeks went by routinely, as did every day in the institutionalised lifestyle. My social worker came and went a couple of times; no other visitors arrived. I complied with the system, attended morning classes, worked in the vegetable gardens in the afternoons, took part in sports, kept my head down, and waited.

Then it was my day to go back to the children's panel. This time I was questioned and gave my answers of regret and learning. After a short recess, my social worker let me know that I was returning to the children's home. He warned that any repeat behaviour that brought me back to the panel would be judged differently next time.

I was so happy that night to walk back through the familiar garden gate and heavy front door, welcomed in an understated way by the staff and other children. There were a few new children since I had self-drifted away a few months earlier. I was put in a twin bedroom upstairs with one other new boy. In general, I fitted back in quickly and felt at ease. I determined in my juvenile heart that I would not make the same mistakes again.

The chef at the home told me he had a summer job for me if I wanted it. I would work at his day job in the offices helping with catering. I was so excited, as this would be an actual job with regular hours. My dishwashing job was also open for my return. I apologised to the couple who managed the restaurant for leaving them in the lurch, and they were actually glad to see me back. I had reason to thank my parents, as they had raised me to be a hard worker, just like themselves, although I would not have acknowledged that then.

My new job was amazing. I joined a group of older women at 7 a.m., cutting and buttering rolls and scones, cooking sausage patties, black pudding, and bacon to put on the rolls, filling tea and coffee urns, and loading the tea trollies ready to go around all the offices. The ladies all mothered me, joking and laughing with me, sneaking me hot filled rolls, and making lewd jokes.

Each trolley went to the lifts and was given three different levels to cover on rotation to deliver morning snacks to the office staff. There were only two trollies, so it was a massive challenge each day to reach all the offices in a reasonable time. If I remember correctly, they used some sort of token system, so no money changed hands.

I was a bona-fide tea-trolly-lady. When I set off with my trolley, the rest of the team cleaned up in the prep room before heading down to the ground floor kitchens to help make lunch for hundreds of office staff. I would finish my rounds, clean down my trolley, have my short morning break, and then start serving lunch in one of the serveries.

After lunch service, we had an hour's break before an afternoon trolley service. Another young man joined our team, we were the only two males, and he became the other trolley-dolly. We became instant friends, playing foosball and table tennis in the office rec rooms on our breaks nearly every day, and sometimes tennis at the nearby university sports grounds in the evenings.

The chef oversaw the whole operation every day, caring for hundreds of staff and looking after his team of full-time and part-time workers. He was amazing. I think now, in retrospect, that the work he did in the children's home was so poorly paid that he saw it as a way of giving something back.

Back at the home, I was adjusting as well, doing my own laundry. Out in the garage, every time we switched on the washing machine, we got an electric shock that numbed the whole hand. None of us were bright enough to report it, so we put up with it every week. My bed had to be made every morning, no duvets then, just sheets and blankets with hospital-style bed ends as the minimum expectation. If something needed ironing, I ironed it. I had chores to do in the home, cleaning the common room or vacuuming the stairs. I received pocket money from the home each week, and dishwashing money on Saturdays as a weekly wage for my full-time office job. All my work was within an hour's walk of the home, so I tended to walk to work and back.

I learned the joys of Chinese food, daytime cinema visits on days off, and buying nice clothes for myself as well as occasional gifts for others. When I think back, birthdays and Christmases were non-events, with no celebration or gifts. However, as we were all in the same boat, nothing seemed odd to any of us.

One Saturday evening, when I got back after work, I was told there was a meeting in the dining room, a room that was basically never used. We were told in muted silence that the home was being closed and the building sold. There was an outpouring of feelings and disbelief that day. In the weeks that followed, a general helplessness consumed most of us. We would be split up and moved, and it was a lot to take in. The foundations had just shifted.

Chapter 20

Freedom was the most thrilling difference at our children's home, although if we messed up we were definitely called to account, but there was a gentleness in the correction. I messed up countless times, and time after time I was treated with a firmness combined with care. Every day brought a completely new experience.

Looking back, emotional gratitude surfaces, whereas when I reflect on my family home life, mystery and disbelief are the remains uncovered, although forgiveness has since cleansed these whitened bones.

I remember one day at school, and I am embarrassed to admit it now, that I stole a Gary Glitter 45rpm single from another boy. Once back at the children's home, I rushed upstairs to play it on repeat on our old record player. The single did not have a small central hole for the spindle but a large half-crown sized gap (single inserts often came separately), so it took three or four attempts to centre the disc on the ribbed rubber playmat. Once set, and with the needle steady, I played the song at full volume on repeat. I think it was about being the leader of a gang. None of the other kids were home yet, but one of the staff was.

Surprisingly, he came into the common room, switched the record player off, and told me to go to the office immediately. I knew I was in trouble. It turned out someone from the school had phoned and asked him to check if I had the record. I was grounded, lost pocket money for two weeks, and had to return the record to the boy I had stolen it from. The remarkable thing, looking back, was that it was all handled with such kindness and care. I think this approach started to soften my hardened heart; for the first time in my life, I felt accepted and cared for.

The team at the first children's home achieved things my parents had not. I was allowed to be myself with no judgement or harsh discipline aimed at forcing change, a method that had only succeeded in driving my crushed spirit further into hiding. I loved my life there. I flourished, even if some of my branches often needed severe pruning. The encouragement to grow was enough to draw my spirit out of hiding and into the immaturity of mistakes that would eventually bring maturity. Night after night, I slept feeling safe from being dragged out of bed and beaten in the dark hours. Fear receded into the shadows of the sloped ceiling attic room, slipping quietly further from my secret thoughts each night. Perhaps I would not have recognised it then, but sleep without fear was one of the most stabilising aspects of children's home life.

Even if our escapades were more Enid Blyton than Hans Christian Andersen, there was risk and testosterone, but also a childlikeness about some pranks that allowed grace to coexist with them. Fights were usually about pecking order and were fast and furious, followed by handshakes and hugs, with sworn allegiance to each other and the home as a bonding glue we believed then was eternal. We got to know each other and what we stood for.

One other boy who lived there took me to visit his parents one day, we would both have been around fourteen, adventurous, full of tall tales, and ready for a fight.

The first time we went, his mum was in bed drunk, a sight I had never seen before, and she flung out her arm, trying to pull me under the covers. He shouted at her, and we left the room. In another room, a lone suitcase, grey with leather-riveted edges, sat under a shallow metal-framed single bed. Nothing else was there. My friend mentioned his brother being out of jail. Our visit was short, and a few weeks later, the front door was boarded and padlocked, with a large printed sign declaring "evicted" stuck to the only visible panel.

Visiting my parents had been traumatic, but it helped put into perspective the differences in parenting styles and the experiences that can shape young lives.

Another boy at the home worked in a nearby garage, and sometimes I would join him when his manager was away and help out. It was there I first saw the "cash in hand" technique for keeping customers' money out of the till.

All this richness of life, the colour and depth of knowing others, bonding over shared hardships, and experiencing adolescent chaos, was about to be erased with the stroke of an accountant's pen. No pleading would help. There was no one to plead with. Once again, the unknown came knocking at my door, though this time I was sunning myself and hardly ready to pick up and move.

Chapter 21

Portobello in Edinburgh was the place of my childhood dreams: a long sandy beach, ice cream shops, amusement arcades, and bustling with people on summer days. Even in the wind-blown winter months, it held a mystique for me, with tired bunting hinting at happier times, drawing memories forward, and suggesting a faded re-enactment.

I was living there now, transplanted to a new children's home, new to me, at least. Most of my friends had scattered; only three of the twelve musketeers had made it to this outpost. On my first night, I discovered the doors were locked at 9 pm and we were not allowed out. That was a shock. I could no longer go to my job in the city centre in the evenings, though I could still work Saturdays. School was a million miles away, and although I was supposed to attend, I never did. I became known to the police and learned how to best avoid them, playing cat-and-mouse games, showing myself briefly, then disappearing down mossy back lanes and into derelict, eyeless buildings. I was the king of Edinburgh, wandering the streets, watching the sunrise from the beach walls at 4 am with a hot pie lifted from the all-night bakery. Night after night, I climbed out of first-floor windows, walking alone along the beachfront, not another soul in sight, only a pale moon shadow for company, head down, hands in pockets, cold wind testing my resolve.

Girlfriends were part of my life now, and over the previous year I had a series of them. Heartbreak was normal; my ways were too much for most, but girls fascinated me. I fell in with a group of girls who worked at a local fish and chip shop. Full of fun, from colourful families, and full of life, I would visit at night, buy a bag of chips, and receive extra change in my hand, leaving with both chips and a handful of 50p pieces. A pint of beer was twenty pence then.

We would all head into the city centre nightclubs on Friday and Saturday nights, in our best Falmer jeans and polo T-shirts, dancing to David Bowie, the Drifters, Barry White, and Gladys Knight, to name a few. My hair was dyed green at the front, and I wore David Bowie makeup, the lightning flash across my face, forty-inch high-waisted baggy trousers, and ridiculous platform shoes. I stood out.

I was friends with the night manager from my Saturday job. Probably around 30, he had a car and connections with the night figures of Edinburgh, restaurateurs, casino owners, bookies, and all the get-rich-quick schemers you could imagine. And when I say he had a car, that's an understatement. He lived for car auctions, constantly changing vehicles, always having Jaguars, even an E-type once. He and his friends would buy, respray, and sell cars for profit, tax-free.

We were not at the Portobello children's home for long, my memory is unclear, but three to six months at most. Then three of us were moved to a desperate, sterile place called a "family group home," run by the council with underpaid, unpleasant staff, stifling rules, constant restrictions on our freedoms, and threats of expulsion at sixteen. The home was in one of the most deprived areas on the city outskirts, known for violence, gangs, and housebreaking. Clearly, local authorities thought it suitable for vulnerable adolescents. We would certainly never live in their neighbourhoods.

I missed our first home. The memories brought emotional pain; even Portobello now seemed like a haven. It held a strange fascination for me, winter days recalling threadbare overcoats, summer nights of flowery dresses and kiss-me-quick hats. So not classy, yet it had its own kind of class. I would live there again briefly a few years later, but this unique memory of my first stay clung to me like a desperate immigrant, holding on to memories as they formed. Pale grey skies, storm clouds, warm sunrises, and Siberian winds, Portobello had it all. I loved the clustered local shops, cafés, bakeries, and newsagents, all emblems of the struggle for life. I was drawn to half-empty arcades, flashing lights, and cheesy tunes repeating from early until late. Small groups of friends huddled around their favourite games, while passersby drifted past grimy windows, coats pulled tight around them.

Chapter 22

It was an alright place, that was the highest praise I could give it, clean, tidy, with idle staff. But it was so different, this was the third change in only a few years, and just two of the original twelve were still with me. We had drifted now, something had been lost in the moves. I had my own room, there was a common room with a TV, and one wall was reinforced glass. Everywhere we went we could be seen, the kitchen opened straight onto the staff area. There was nowhere other than my small box of a bedroom where I could simply be myself. I withdrew, both physically and emotionally.

I bought myself a .177 air pistol from a sports and fishing shop in the city centre, in Frederick Street I think. I fired it out the bedroom window at night, trying to spot the tiny pellets hitting the nearby school playground fence. One day, after staying in my room all day once again avoiding all things related to education I was bored. Wondering what it might feel like to shoot myself, I chewed up a bit of paper into a mushy wad, squeezed the extra saliva out, then rolled a small pellet to fit my new gun. I loaded it, pressed the barrel against my open palm and pulled the trigger. The pain was instant and sharp, but I could not make a sound. I stuffed a corner of my pillow into my mouth, rolling around on my bed, hand clamped between my legs for support, muffled cries and groans swallowed up by the pillow.

When the pain eased I stared at my hand in surprise. A large purple bruise had already formed in the centre of my left palm. Well, now I knew for certain that it really hurts to be shot, even with damp paper.

The area we lived in was wild. So much violence. Dads often turned up drunk, shouting up at windows, abuse and screams thrown back and forth, sometimes along with belongings and clothes. Gangs of twenty to fifty teenagers roamed the streets at night, carrying clubs, sticks and bottles. I stayed at a new friend's house nearby one night, they were moving and worried someone might break in while the move was half done. So he and I slept in the lounge, and sure enough that night the living room window was pushed open and a pair of legs began to slide in behind the curtains. I was not sure if my friend was awake until I heard his low rough voice say, "Hey, can yous not use the door like anyone else". I think it was probably a rhetorical question. The legs vanished, followed by a damp thump and a short curse.

I wandered the area on drizzly days when school was an option but not a preference. Rows and rows of poor quality small houses huddled together against the Scottish weather. Mattresses with bare springs lay in some gardens, next to half-burned piles of soggy rubbish. Bins overflowed and lazy, barely readable graffiti was smeared over shared doors and gable ends. Even the grass looked disinterested, sparse, patchy and wet. Neighbouring areas had high rise flats known for the worst kinds of violence, and somehow in a strange twist of planning these areas all bordered some of the most desirable housing, scenery and facilities in the whole city. There were beaches, sea views, sprawling parks, expensive cars and even cafes.

A sense of safety tugged me towards these places. I lingered along tree-lined streets, gazing upward for chestnut trees, and sat on empty autumn waterfront benches staring out to sea, writing letters in my head and wondering what was for dinner.

This children's home was not a home for me, despite being called a family group home which I am sure sounded impressive to the middle class social workers in their city centre offices. There was no sense of family in it, no protection, and it never felt like home. At best it was a stopover, at worst it magnified my loneliness and despair. At least we were allowed to stay out late, although we had to buzz to be let in after nine. It was dangerous even walking from the nearest bus stop to the home at night.

So I worked nights and weekends, and wasted my money on alcohol, fashion and those I convinced myself were my friends. Alcohol became a problem quickly as my quiet, heavy moods spilled into anger and sometimes aggression. The couple running the home, an officious, rule-waving pair who sounded as if they had swallowed a policy manual and who I had never felt cared for by, quietly told me it was time to start thinking about moving out. My sixteenth birthday was coming. I was frightened, but rebellious enough not to show it. It was probably time to move, but where would I go?

Chapter 23

I was not scared of being homeless. I knew how to manage on the streets, where to find rest, food and a bit of shelter. But that was not my aim. What should I do?

A friend at work knew about my situation. He had a one-bedroom basement flat in a run-down tenement in a lively part of the city, near the port. He was moving with his new wife to a decent council house near the football stadium. He asked if I wanted him to speak to the landlord for me. The landlord asked me to come to his house, which I nervously did, and there I was offered a lease on the flat at the princely sum of four pounds per week, cash, paid in person every Sunday. The experience of going to the landlord's house felt like entering Jabba the Hut's territory.

I was earning fifty pence an hour washing dishes in a cafe, or it might have gone up to seventy-five pence, so four pounds was manageable. I was happy and moved in, put a new lock on the door, painted part of the hallway, bought a music system and some pillows. Everything was in the one room, a bed-sofa, a small kitchenette and an easy chair to sit in, with a tiny alcove for the sink and wobbly electric cooker.

What had held such promise soon dimmed. There was a sadness over the whole flat that the occasional splash of bright new colour only emphasised. The men were fully grown, only a few days out of prison. A menace hung over even their lighter moments. I felt intimidated, weak, powerless, and I hated myself for feeling that way. I was fifteen, nearly sixteen. They broke my things, ate my food and drank my juice, laughing with each other while I stood invisible, on the edge, with tiny shivers running through me, not knowing what to do, disoriented. I was more Walter Mitty than Walter Scott. They were the older brothers of a friend from a children's home. They had nowhere to go, and that made me worry they would never leave. But I had nowhere else either.

I had been trying to paint, clean and create a decent place for myself in this one-room basement flat. It sat down a small dark lane off a quiet street, so there was no one close enough to run to for help. The whole neighbouring tenement was condemned, empty for years, wrecked. Yesterday I had felt at breaking point and went to the police station. They took a few notes and told me to come back if the men returned. I had a mocking conversation in my head about these instructions, something like, "Oh, excuse me, gentlemen, I'm just popping over to the police station to report your rather rough behaviour towards me". I felt a sort of sadness, a bit hopeless. I just had to live with it, as they came to my place day or night, kicking the door in, helping themselves to whatever I had, forcing me into the corner to stand there alone with my tiny shivers.

Another week passed, unbearable, like slow torture. I waited each night for the knock. I was so beaten down now that they no longer kicked the door in but simply knocked, and I just opened it automatically, letting them in to do whatever they did as I sat in the corner, silent, not looking. There was a weight in my stomach most nights. They took any money I had and there seemed no end to it. I think I prayed to a God I did not know to help me. If I did not go home till late and they were already there, I felt like an intruder in my own house. At work I had good friends and one day I told one of them what was happening. He was a fair bit older than me and it just so happened that he seemed concerned.

That night he and another mate from work took me to the dog races, and I discovered the thrill of drinking beer, eating hamburgers and shouting at whichever dog I was backing to run faster. I think if I went now it would feel like a rather sad circus, but back then, at fifteen, the crowd, the lights, the roar as the traps opened and the dogs tore after the electric hare was energising, fascinating and intoxicating. I placed my bets, yelled at the top of my lungs and laughed with friends, forgetting my troubles for a while, the dark clouds lifted briefly by the wash of coloured lights.

As we were leaving, my friends said they wanted to come back to my place with me. The weight in my chest returned, heavy and invasive. They said they wanted to help. I looked at them, then thought about the brothers, their size, their history, their tempers, and I had no faith that my friends would be able to do anything. They were both a bit shorter than me, one by quite a bit. They insisted, and soon we were standing outside my house. The lights were off, no one was home. I was almost relieved, preferring the comfort of known terror to the unknown.

I stopped and apologised for dragging them there for nothing, staring down at my feet as I spoke. They pushed past me, opened the gate and walked down the short flight of steps to the hidden basement door. I hurried after them, saying the place was a mess and I had nothing for them to eat or drink. They said they were just going to wait for a while. So the three of us sat in the darkness chatting for what felt like ages.

Late that night, later than they had ever come before, I saw feet and legs appear at the top of the window as one of the brothers came in the gate and down the steps. My stomach twisted. I felt sick, nervous, holding back tears.

The older of my friends went to answer the door and we crowded in behind him, almost touching. We were two steps up as we stood there. My friend held out a finger, looked straight at the brother at the door and said, "I want to tell you a story." There was a pause for a few seconds and then suddenly punches were flying and kicks were landing. The astonishing thing was they were all coming from my friend, not at him.

The brother staggered back, turning and trying to scramble up the slippery steps to the wet cobbled street above. All I could hear were sounds like a stick thudding into a cabbage. No one said a word for almost a minute, then the shouting began as the brother, now on the main street with his three attackers behind him, tried desperately to get away. There was no sign of the other brothers.

Suddenly the police were all around us and the fight was broken up. We stood there panting, bent forward, hands on our knees, steamy breath fogging the yellow street-lit scene. I looked up at the brother. Three of his front teeth were hanging from his mouth, attached to a strip of gum, blood smeared across his face, chin and hands. The police were taking all of us to the station. One officer patted my head and said, "Come on, son, walk wi me tae the polis station, eh." It was going to be a long night.

My thoughts were all over the place as I walked. Was I in trouble now? Would the brothers come back in a week or so with more friends and maybe weapons, or was it finally over?

I did see the brothers again. Weeks, maybe months later, in a local café where I was having something to eat. They spoke briefly to me, but the threat had gone. By then I had grown closer to the older boy who had helped me that night. He turned up at my house late one night, clearly a bit drunk, and asked for my help. Someone had hit his mum and she was in hospital having a wire put into her jaw to repair it. Although I had my share of fights growing up and I knew how to handle myself, I wasn't a fighter. He wanted me to go with him to see the men who had done this. I suppose I felt obligated. And here begins another tale.

Chapter 24

We were in a taxi heading to my friend's mum's place. I had gone straight away, still wearing a white novelty T-shirt printed with a hairy chest and a pair of jeans and trainers. He was slurring slightly, talking about how two men had attacked his mum and she was in hospital needing a wire inserted to help her broken jaw heal. It sounded serious and awful. I almost wished I wasn't there, but now felt obliged to help.

The taxi took about twenty minutes to bring us from my derelict city-centre basement flat to a set of notorious high-rise blocks on the outskirts of Edinburgh.

It was a cold night and the chill hit my skin the moment the taxi door opened. My friend wore a knee-length black wool coat over a black turtleneck. Once inside the cramped, sour-smelling aluminium lift, he pulled back one side of his coat to reveal a baseball bat and a large kitchen knife taped to the inside. He said something I didn't quite catch, other than the slur in his voice and the alcohol scent filling the lift before being overtaken again by its usual stale smell.

I had just turned sixteen, cold, out of my depth, and now frightened.

The lift stopped a floor short of where we were headed, so we took the stairs for the last flight. The silence was ominous, my friend leading, his coat tails flapping in front of my confused eyes. What was I doing there? Twenty minutes earlier I had been at home thinking about a mushroom and croutons cup-a-soup with toast before bed.

We reached the small landing and my friend knocked on the door. It must have been after ten. He turned to me and chose that moment to say it was his stepfather and stepbrother's flat. I was about to walk into the middle of a long-running and violent family feud.

The door opened and the man inside looked surprised, but started to welcome us in. My friend repeated his line, "Let me tell you a story", the exact same words he had used the night at my house. What followed was frantic, brutal and overwhelming. Little was said. Blows were exchanged. My friend and his stepbrother locked into a heavy, breathless wrestle, jammed in the narrow hallway. I stood back, not knowing what to do, even if I could have done anything.

Then there was blood. On hands, faces, bare stomachs and walls. A lot of blood. The wrestling turned into a heaving tangle on the floor. Another older man joined the struggle. I won't go into more detail because it adds nothing of value here.

Neighbours called the police and an ambulance. I ended up in the back of a police car, taken to the local station to be questioned and kept overnight in a cold magnolia cell with a thin blue rubber mattress on a concrete shelf and a dull stainless steel toilet. I told my story several times. The police were gentle with me and even brought me tea and toast at one point. An older officer sat with me for a while, asking how I was. I knew I was in trouble. I was anxious and worried, but it was done, and all I could do was face whatever came next.

I think now about how easily someone's whole future can change. When I hear stories on the news about violence or injury, I wonder about everyone involved and what regrets they may be carrying. I was stunned by how quickly my life could have turned. Someone could have died, and everything would have been different. I had no desire ever to go back to institutions, that's for sure. As it happened, no one died, and I learned a harsh lesson.

No one died, although one of the men spent several hours in ICU that night. I was released at five in the morning into a foggy city, street lamps hazy in the mist. I walked home with my head down, cold, just cold. I wasn't going to work that day.

After a few hours' sleep and more toast, I walked to the hospital where my friend was being kept under police guard, handcuffed to the bed frame. I chatted with him for a few minutes. The outcome was a court case several months later, many sleepless nights for me as I had no idea what my role would be. But it was a family matter and the two relatives didn't show up at court, apparently because the family differences had been sorted out. The case was dropped on the courthouse steps. My sleepless nights and whispered promises to an unknown God became just more old memories. I had taken no part in the fight except to protect my friend once. I knew then I would never accompany anyone again into violence, no matter the reason.

I was sixteen. My flat was wrecked, I was becoming an alcoholic, and I was pulling away from all my friends. I was heading into a hard season of my life.

Chapter 25

I remember my secondary school, the lonely walks down the long approach on chilly, sullen mornings, no homework done, no school uniform on, bright-coloured fashion instead. It was like some slow-motion Groundhog Day. I would go to school and usually be sent home by lunchtime at the latest.

I was used to my own company, given to exaggeration, living in my head most days to escape the dreariness of grey winter and overheated classrooms. I recall a time when many of the other boys became Christians, wearing bright-coloured fish symbol stickers on their smart blazer lapels, meeting in classrooms at lunchtimes, happy in their belief. I teased them, trying to test the only thing I knew: that they were supposed to turn the other cheek.

My memory flicked pages and suddenly I was back in the primary school playground, shorts and a parka jacket like some odd fusion of styles too far ahead of its moment. I had been in a fight and won, but it was not a popular victory. Some boys were chanting, "If you hate Allan Brown, clap your hands," over and over.

Then I was back in secondary school, recalling an evangelist, Arthur Blessitt, carrying a cross everywhere he went. I had my own encounter with God one solitary night, shut in my room, sadness wrapped around me like a blanket. I believed. I felt a joy that had been missing, like angels were singing in my head. I told my parents, and my mum poo-hooed me, saying I was hopeless, would never change, and was heading for a bad end. A few weeks later, Christianity slipped away in despair and doubt.

So there I was in Edinburgh, ready to leave my dishevelled flat, but with nowhere to go. I searched the local evening newspaper, walked past every newsagent shop window with signs in it, and found a bed and breakfast in Portobello that was taking in long-stay lodgers for the winter months. In an instant, I was gone, carrying only some clothes in a new green haversack. The other lodgers were fine, young men, just older than me, probably university students. The rooms were cold, the bedclothes damp. But it was safe, it was familiar, and I loved walking the waterfront late at night. I held my memories close, hoping they would help me keep going each day.

Weeks and months passed, winter turned to spring, the sun appeared earlier and stayed longer, but offered little warmth. I saved as hard as I could, and soon I had enough to buy my first motorbike.

My first motorbike was a Suzuki GT 250cc. It was thrilling. A few months earlier, I had gone out as a pillion passenger to the Sunday markets on the city outskirts. I was sixteen, it was my first time on a motorbike, and I loved it. Ever since that experience, I had been planning, looking, and saving until I could afford to buy one with cash.

I went to see the bike at the seller's house and he took me for a spin. It was fast, noisy, shiny, I was hooked. I went back the next day with a new crash helmet, gloves, jacket, and a friend who could ride, and we sealed the deal. We rode my new prized possession back to my lodgings and parked it on the street.

The next day it would not start. I knew nothing about motorbikes. It had a kickstart, and I kicked forty or fifty times with no result. I pushed it to the nearest motorbike garage, about a mile away, mostly uphill. Flat battery, the day before it had been charged just enough to start! I bought a new battery, installed it, and felt ready.

Except I didn't know how to ride. Embarrassingly, I pushed the bike with its new battery back home. Then I read a book on riding, went downstairs, jumped on the bike, and decided I could drive.

Amazingly, I did not kill myself in the first two minutes, despite being on a very busy main road. Off I went, thrilled, oblivious to risk. The gears were left foot: one down, half click back up to neutral, then second, and so on to fifth, or maybe sixth. Clutch left hand, throttle right, front brake hand, back brake foot.

I stopped at a set of lights. They changed and I moved off in first gear, straight into second, revving furiously. Nothing happened. Heavy traffic, slowly drifting, revving like mad.

I panicked a little. I looked down at the gear lever and couldn't work it out, one down, two back up. I'd done that.

When I looked up, I was drifting onto the kerb and pavement, nearly into a tenement doorway where a lady stood holding tightly to her grocery bags, staring at me, partly in fear, partly in disbelief.

My first proper crash. Down I went. Heel off my new cowboy boots, knees through my jeans, and a nice dent in my brand-new helmet. One day in, six minutes of riding, and I had already pushed it further than I had ridden it. Out of pocket for a new battery, lost boots and jeans, probably needed a new helmet.

Oh, by the way, in case it isn't obvious, I had been stuck in neutral.

It would have been far cheaper to take some lessons, but, of course, I thought I knew best.

Chapter 26

Spring was coming and I loved those early mornings when the beach belonged to me and the seagulls. But my time at Portobello was drawing to a close as visitors returned and guest houses reopened.

My job at the café had changed. One day the cook did not turn up and the little Italian manageress handed me, the dishwasher, the menu and said, "you are a promoted now to cook," in her Italian accent, of course. I still remember standing in the kitchen on my own with the menu and no idea what to do, waiting for the doors to open and the first customers to arrive.

There were six or seven waiting staff, mostly young women aged around 18 to 25. They began to tell me what I had to do. There were supplies to bring up from the basement, vegetables to prepare, equipment to switch on, fridges to fill. So I set to it, sweat forming in beads on my forehead as I rushed around in a frenzy of hurried movements. I had little idea where everything belonged, so I guessed. I had no idea how much of anything we would sell and some items needed to defrost, so again I guessed.

Then it happened. The first order came in, shouted by one of the front of house team. Nothing was written down. All orders were called out and the cook kept them in his head, telling his apprentice what to do as well. Only today the apprentice had not come in, so it was me and … well, me.

The rest of the day is a blur now, but we got through it. At 9pm after 12 hours of chaos, panic, fear and confusion, it was time to clean down and pack everything away. The manageress and the front of house team, some of whom were different from the morning because most changed shifts at 5pm, came into the tiny hot kitchen carrying cold drinks and telling me how well I had done.

I was officially promoted to cook that night and my pay rose from 75 pence an hour to one pound an hour, so my take home pay in 1975 became a minimum of 40 pounds a week.

I had to find somewhere else to live though, and eventually through the local newspaper adverts I found a shared room in a huge house in a smart part of the city. There were four of us in a room big enough for forty. One bed in each corner. It was a bed and breakfast costing 25 pounds a week. Breakfast was two slices of toast each served at long tables. There must have been about 50 men staying there, most if not all unemployed and having their fees paid by the local authorities. Breakfast was chaotic and sometimes there was a fight over a single piece of toast. Butter was clearly a luxury. The owners came around occasionally. They had a Great Dane that I would play with for hours while they visited.

I had 15 pounds a week to live on, so after the motorbike costs I probably had around 8 pounds left. I got meals at work, so the 8 pounds went to the local pub. Forty pints of beer each week. I was usually broke after four or five days, waiting for my next pay. I was sixteen.

One of the men I shared the room with worked at Butlins holiday camps, but he was ill and could not go that year, so he was spending his spring and summer living on benefits and toast. He talked about Butlins a lot and, to be honest, I did seriously think about applying for a job there because he made it sound a lot of fun. I never did, but I often wonder how my life might have been if I had.

We lived near the Blackford Hills and the pond there was close to my new accommodation. On my days off I would walk there and spend the day wandering around those hills until I knew every path and connection. I loved sitting in the tall ferns while small white butterflies drifted past alongside the hum of busy bees. I found old fallen trees where no one ever walked and trees I could climb and sit in for ages, thinking. I loved my own company, lost in my thoughts and dreams, wondering, forgetting where I was or even at times who I was. My dreams were not fanciful. They were about motorbikes, adventure, travel and probably girls.

There were new bosses at the café, an Italian couple. He handled the cash and she managed the staff, around ten people most days. I got on well with them and the husband took me for a beer every night after work. Sometimes he would buy me a second beer as he left if I stayed on. I worked hard, long hours at times and under frantic pressure with several hundred customers each day and one cook, me.

He told me about some better accommodation near where he lived. A friend of his, another Italian man, had rooms for rent and I could have my own room. Each room cost 6 pounds a week, which was 19 pounds cheaper. I moved that day and began a relationship with an Italian family that lasted another five or six years. Great adventures lay ahead.

Chapter 27

My new accommodation was wonderful. It felt like I was living is an episode of "Rising Damp". The house was run down, nothing matched. Carpets clashed with wallpaper and everything seemed either on its last legs or oddly revived. Yet at the same time it was a fine old townhouse with high corniced ceilings and full length bay windows facing a busy main road. My bed would tremble at night as the large trucks from the local brewery rumbled along a fairly quiet road.

The house had three large bedrooms and one small room, two bathrooms and a shared kitchen and living area with a coal fire.

It was a five-minute walk to the city centre and the area itself was probably the best part of the new location. There were so many local shops, butchers, fishmongers, bakeries, grocers, launderettes, cafés and bookshops. It felt like living in a New York film, apart from the accents. There was a large Italian community and a slightly smaller Jewish community in the area. I still remember the Jewish bakery that opened at 4am and closed at midday, always sold out, and how I would hurry to buy my bread, especially the famous eggplant loaf.

I became well known to many of the shopkeepers over the coming years. It felt good to be recognised, to feel part of something.

My landlord was an older gentleman and he and his brother shared one of the bedrooms. His brother would become cross some days and shout a lot at everyone about everything. I learned to listen politely and then drift away while he was still mid rant. The landlord himself was kind and generous but deaf. He would walk past you and release the loudest fart I had ever heard and would not acknowledge it at all. He was separated. One day he introduced me to his wife and it was a strange moment.

It turned out his wife owned a nearby Italian restaurant where all three of his sons worked. The story was remarkable. I had been in this restaurant when I was about five years old and still remembered it. This lady had been in the next bed to my mum in a long stay convalescence hospital. They had become friends and we had been invited to visit her restaurant once my mum left hospital. We did, and I remember her giving me the biggest, shiniest and most elegant Easter egg I had ever seen. And here I was eleven or so years later meeting her again. She remembered it.

At that moment I became part of this wonderful family. The drama of Italian families was real, but so was the love, the food and the fun. There is so much more to tell about the adventures over the next few years. But we will not rush ahead. We have time to let the story unfold.

This was honestly the first stable experience I had had since leaving the original children's home. There was routine, there were people around, and I was joining a family and beginning to belong to a community. I loved those days, sitting in the launderette, talking to strangers, packing my warm clean washing back into my green haversack and feeling the softness of the towels and the warmth of tumble dried clothes bringing a sense of comfort to my still lonely heart.

The local café where a cheeseburger, fries and a drink were cheap and cheerful became my favourite. I called it the "greasy spoon." The young women who worked there caught my eye and I would try to chat to them gently as they served.

I still remember a sauna opening just across the road from where I lived. I loved the idea of having a sauna on a cold winter's day. In fact, I had taken to travelling to the local swimming pool and using the sauna there on my days off. I would fall asleep on one of the lounges after about twenty minutes of heat and then the freezing splash pool. So I went to the sauna across the road and booked a sauna session and a massage. I think it cost around three or four pounds and that included a thirty minute massage. I had never had a massage before, so I was looking forward to it.

When the time came, I climbed onto the massage table, underwear on, and a towel covering most of me. A young woman came in, set the timer and began massaging my shoulders. After about ten minutes she asked me to turn onto my front, which I did. She then asked whether I wanted any extras. I replied that I had brought my own shampoo and towel and was all set. She seemed a little surprised and then started listing some extras of a more personal nature. I declined politely. I decided I would just go back to the swimming pool from then on.

Beside the sauna there was a lane, and down the lane was a busy joinery workshop. I worked out that the bin full of offcuts outside their main roller door was free for anyone to take. So we suddenly had an almost endless supply of wood for the kitchen fire and each day I made several trips back and forth gathering it.

Another young man my age moved into the house. We became fast friends and started doing things together. We went to the sauna at the pool, joined a gym, visited local cafés and spent our days off together. I had a best friend.

About two miles from where we lived was a hill called Arthur's Seat. It was surrounded by a beautiful park and a one way road went all around the hill, including up to nearly the top. We began running from our house around Arthur's Seat and back. It took about forty five minutes and we pushed each other hard. These were good days.

My friend loved to gamble and would go to the casino from time to time. I was not particularly interested, probably because I feared losing all my money, not that I had much. One night I agreed to go with him and some of my landlord's boys to the casino. It was my first visit but it would not be my last.

Chapter 28

Soft lights, deep carpets, rich red hessian wallpaper and elegantly dressed people. I kept to myself, feeling like I did not belong. Everything felt unfamiliar. People stood around various tables, some tapping their gambling chips with one hand while holding a drink in the other.

My friends were with me but had already gone off to do what they had come to do. They were focused and determined. I quite liked the atmosphere of the casino and quickly discovered that all soft drinks were free. But I had no idea what to do. So I stood there, adopting a look I thought suggested confidence, while quietly studying everyone else.

The blackjack table made the most sense. The aim was to get cards as close to twenty one as possible and to beat the dealer. The dealer had rules about when they had to take another card and when they could not. You handed the croupier, which I learned later was what the staff were called, your money between the cards being dealt. This was called a hand. He pushed the money through a slot in the table and gave you chips in return. There were five seats at each table. Every table was full and there were people two or three deep behind each seat watching and waiting for a spot.

My friend got a seat and motioned for me to stand beside him. He told me to change money and bet with him, so I did. I changed five pounds into fifty pence chips. They were a dull orange and the cheapest chips available. I bet fifty pence on his hand and won. I won fifty pence. And just like that I was in.

My memory is a little hazy, but I think I won two or three pounds that night, which for me felt amazing. I remember walking home feeling as though I had arrived. I was a member of the casino now and could go whenever I wanted. It was open every day from two in the afternoon until four in the morning, and the lights flashed three times at five minutes to four to signal closing time.

Over the next few years I became a regular at the casino. I learned how to play all the tables and specialised in roulette and Punto Banco, also known as chemise de fer.

Life was fairly good. I had great friends at work too. Although I did not realise it then, I was being prepared for my future. I learned from other people's experiences and mistakes. Work was always busy. There was no such thing as a quiet day. We were open from eight in the morning until half past ten at night and the evening manager handled the shift from six until around midnight when the cleaning was finished.

On a busy Saturday we were short staffed and I was asked to stay on, which I did. To complicate things, a new manager was starting that night and no one on the team had met him before.

When he arrived in his new suit, shirt and tie, we all thought he looked slightly overdressed. But we wanted to work well with him, so we listened and got on with our tasks. There was a new young student behind the drinks bar who had never worked there before and had received no training. She was doing her best, and I called out instructions to help while leading the kitchen section. We were under pressure.

The manager positioned himself at the payment station near the front door and stayed there even when no one was waiting. Most managers would speak with customers at the tables and move around to check how things were going.

During a particularly hectic period the Pepsi machine ran out of syrup. In those days we filled a stainless steel tank manually and the machine mixed the syrup with soda water to dispense Pepsi.

The manager heard the discussion as I tried to help and came running down through the shop. I told him I knew how to do it and that I would fetch the syrup and fill the machine once I had finished the next table's orders. He cut me off and told me to forget it, saying he would handle the problem.

Leaving a group of impatient customers waiting to pay, he rushed downstairs to the basement storeroom, grabbed two boxes of syrup containers, ran back up and poured the contents into the tank. He switched the machine on and called out loudly, "Pepsi is back on. I have filled the tank. We are all good now." With a slightly squint tie, and a swagger he moved past the kitchen to the till, charmed the customers and cleared the backlog.

The restaurant seated about one hundred people. It was full and a queue formed at the door waiting for tables.

I was flat out in the kitchen, sweat dripping into my eyes as we tried to cook and serve everything quickly while keeping seven or eight waiting staff happy. Everything was done from memory. Nothing was written down.

At one point I looked up and saw waiting staff walking back from the drinks area with full glasses of Pepsi. People were saying it tasted strange. The glasses were stacking up on the service counter and the space was being overwhelmed.

The manager was under pressure from the line at the door and from people wanting to pay. I rushed to the drinks area, poured myself a small glass of Pepsi and tasted it. I knew immediately what had happened. In his hurry, the manager had poured containers of maple syrup, used for our pancake dishes, into the Pepsi machine. All he had seen was the word syrup. The boxes were completely different colours. He lacked experience and had refused help.

It was a setback, but we had to fix it. The manager kept his distance and offered no help. I worked out a way to empty and rinse the container as best I could, got Pepsi syrup from the basement, refilled the machine and switched it back on. Other staff were pouring the returned drinks down the drain and clearing the mess. We tried to handle everything as a team and minimise the impact on the customers.

After the first two of the three glasses of Pepsi were poured, the slight taste of maple disappeared and I was back in the kitchen moving at speed to catch up with the orders.

I never saw that manager again. None of the team trusted his leadership and he remained aloof and detached the whole night, leading by position rather than relationship. I am not sure whether he left, was moved to another shop or what happened. One thing is certain, he had a harsh introduction to management that first night.

So my days continued at work, busy with the occasional crisis, and my nights were spent at the casino trying to get rich quickly. That is where I met Dominic. He was eccentric, owned a large local café, had a three storey townhouse in the city centre where he lived with his ageing mum, and spent every night at the casino. He believed he heard voices guiding his bets. He called them his pipistrelli and you would see him playing Punto Banco most nights. At sudden moments he would pull wads of notes from his socks, inner pockets and back pockets and place a huge bet on one hand. When he lost, he claimed the voices had tricked him. Always dressed in a double breasted suit, shirt and tie, he was one of the many larger than life characters who came out at night to animate the colourful nightlife of Scotland's capital. He vaguely resembled Sean Connery, an older version perhaps, with thinning hair, always well presented and walking with a swagger. It was not long before I was working in his café some evenings and it was great fun.

Chapter 29

I was still working at the city centre café as a cook and doing long shifts, sometimes six or seven days a week. On shorter days I would rush home to shower and wash the grease away before heading up the short steep cobbled road lined with expensive sandstone townhouses where the softly lit casino sat almost unnoticed. Money became the fuel that let me play the game.

We had a new night manager at work. He was full of adventure and fun and not much older than me. I liked spending time with him. There was always something happening and he was always involved in some scheme to make money. We had fun together and did things that made you feel like you were really living.

We would visit the homeless shelters at five in the morning and share breakfast with the men there and chat with them. We would go to the car auctions where he searched for bargains he could respray and sell quickly for a profit.

He had friends who owned nightclubs, restaurants and bars and he was known everywhere. The nightlife crowd in the city were a different sort of people, coming alive at one in the morning, going to bed at sunrise and sleeping until midday. Every day felt like an adventure. I loved the excitement of not knowing what would happen next. I was young and impressionable.

But there was another side to him. A temper and a violence that could appear suddenly, unpredictable and unstoppable.

One day we decided to drive to London. We travelled through the night for about ten hours and spent the day there. The next night we drove back to Scotland. We pulled off the motorway to fill the car with petrol and grab some food.

At the petrol station another driver pulled in front of us facing our car to fill their small van. They were the wrong way for rejoining the motorway and their petrol cap was on the opposite side. We finished filling our car, paid and then found ourselves blocked in by the van.

My friend called out for him to move and the man asked us to wait a couple of minutes until he had finished, although my interpretation of his gesture may have been a bit generous.

My friend jumped out of the car and the next moment was striking the man, punching him several times through the side window of the van. This was 1970s road rage, long before road rage became a recognised problem.

He got back into our car and manoeuvred out of the tight spot. As we finally cleared the van, in his anger he pulled the gearstick out of the gearbox. It was a Ford Granada manual.

For the next three hundred miles we had a pile of our clothes covering the hole in the floor to stop the wind blowing in. Every time we slowed down we had to remove the clothes and somehow fit the gearstick back in while changing gears.

It was a long night and, if I remember correctly, it was snowing as we crossed the border back into Scotland.

That moment marked a turning point for me. I had seen glimpses of his anger before but I no longer wanted to be in those situations, no matter how much fun it was to hang out. It seemed only a matter of time before something serious happened.

My home life was good during that period. I had become close with my landlord's extended family. Nearly all of them were gamblers, which gave us a shared connection and I became more of a confidant than a tenant. Their mum, the landlord's wife, would invite me to lunch on Sundays. She lived in a comfortable bungalow not far from her husband's home. On Sunday mornings, usually a little hung over, I would walk slowly along the tree lined streets, past the busy central bus garage, and through the short iron gate. Edinburgh clouds would part and the sun would shine. The back garden was full of grandchildren playing, crying and imagining. The house buzzed with sheets of pasta hanging from the kitchen table, chicken giblets simmering on the stove for the traditional chicken noodle soup, sauces spluttering on the back rings and flour dusting every surface. Pinnies and hair were tied back and quiet concentration was broken by bursts of laughter and short words of encouragement.

My new friend Dominic had a large busy café across the four lane road from where I lived. It was past the joinery lane and beside the TV studios, before the sauna and the laundrette. My friend lived in the same house and worked some nights in the café, serving food at the takeaway counter and paid cash in hand. He asked me if I wanted to work there, so I did, on some evenings.

My job was to make the chips in the basement, accessed through a trapdoor in the main servery area. Down the steep, dusty wooden steps I would go, the trapdoor closing behind me as soon as I pulled the string for the light switch. There was a small machine, similar to a mini concrete mixer, dark blue outside and lined with fine cut glass inside. It was plumbed in, so when I switched it on I emptied half a bag of potatoes, about ten kilos, into it. As it rotated slowly, the water and glass peeled the potatoes. The potatoes were then pushed individually through a hand press that formed them into chips, which fell into a bucket of brine to wait until they were needed.

When the trapdoor opened someone would call "chips". A rope with a hook would be lowered. I clipped the bucket onto it and it would be hauled up. The door slammed shut and once the dust settled I went back to work.

The cook at the café was a larger than life, smock wearing, porn reading, black shoulder length haired older woman who laughed constantly. She made the best curry I had ever tasted and served it with spicy kibbled onions and plain steamed rice. We were fed at the end of the night after cleaning and I always hoped there would be some curry left.

One night I had to serve tables, and a table of two men ordered one lamb curry and one beef curry, both with poppadums and rice. I went to serve the food onto plates but could only find one curry in the servery, so I asked the cook. She told me both curries came from the same pot. Oh, ok then. So I served the men and laughed quietly as they tasted each other's curries and commented on how good the other one was.

So life had settled into a pattern now, with friends, community and family. I made the most of each day, but gambling was draining all my income and what little I kept went either to the pub or the machines in the pub. Occasionally I went to the bookmakers to bet on horses, but I knew so little about it that I might as well have walked in, handed over my money and walked out again. Oh wait, I did. I was hungry for a change and began to think about what that might look like.

Chapter 30

I was eighteen years old and although life was going along reasonably well at work and where I lived, I recognised that alcohol and gambling had become a problem. One day while walking past a military recruitment office in Lothian Road, Edinburgh, I stopped and on a spur of the moment decision went inside and talked with the staff. When I came out thirty minutes later I had signed up for a medical for the Royal Marines. I knew nothing about them, but I thought maybe a big change would help.

I told my friends and they were both surprised and encouraging. I started to feel the momentum as if I was on a ride I wanted to get off, but the safety bar was down and we were halfway up the first incline, so there was little chance of bailing out. I think I lacked the character to admit that I might have acted too quickly and made a mistake. Now that I had shared my big plans I found it difficult to back out without feeling embarrassed. Yet part of me recognised the need for change, and understood that unless I pushed through the discomfort and the reluctance to face the cost of change, nothing would actually shift.

The medical was completed, the offer made and accepted, train ticket vouchers supplied and a date confirmed.

I had some great friends at that time, mostly from my motorbike circles. Steve worked as a miner but really wanted to work in a library. He was a deep thinker and a good mate. He had a Suzuki 1000cc bike, but also a CZ 200cc. The CZ was not really recognised as a bike by bikers. Most bikers would nod, wave or flash their lights to each other, a kind of giant club that supported one another, but the CZ 200 was more a cheap commuter than a proper bike. It rarely attracted a nod and never a flash of lights. Steve would turn up at get togethers on his CZ200 to confuse the hard core bikers, then the next time, when they thought he was a joke, he would arrive on his Suzuki 1000cc in full leathers and cut offs and blast past them. We rode together often and I loved how he kept his Suzuki down a back lane through bollards, dropped down through a gap in a garden wall, up the garden path and through a wide doorway into the basement of his rented city flat. It was an old tenement block where the back of the houses sat one layer deeper than the front. In my mind it felt like driving into a bat cave. I loved it.

Mark worked as a chef de rang at a large city hotel and he had a Yamaha 500cc twin. It was a comfortable big bike suited to longer journeys. It was slow away from the lights and not a standout among other mid range bikes, but still a nice machine. We went for long rides together late at night and swapped bikes at times. We became good friends even when he got a job selling new cash registers and bought a car. He still kept his bike but had less time to ride it.

Gary worked at Ferranti's, a major electronics firm that dominated parts of Edinburgh towards Telford. He had a Ducati 900SS, black with gold coach lines, a V twin. We became great friends. I also became close with his mates, Deeds who had a Kawasaki 750 and Eck who rode a Yamaha 1000cc. One of their friends had a classic Moto Guzzi 850 V twin.

We would go on long evening rides along the winding coast road from Musselburgh out to Gullane or North Berwick. We would hang out on the long bends, our bodies leaning hard over the edge of the bikes as we followed the rider ahead, using centrifugal force to stay grounded. Then we would sit outside pubs with a half pint of shandy that lasted an hour while we swapped stories about incidents, near misses and accidents, the sun setting over the village green and the smell of fish and chips tempting us to finish our drinks and join the line of hungry coastal visitors. We looked fierce, with long beards, dirty jeans or leather trousers, leather jackets and torn denim cut offs over them. Some wore cardboard taped to their knees so that when a knee touched the tar on a steep bend the leather trousers would be protected.

There was camaraderie, fun, learning and life with those guys. Even on cold, bleak, slush filled Edinburgh winter nights I would sit in Gary's bedroom while we built Airfix motorcycle models, told tall tales or dreamed about bikes we hoped to own one day. His mum would bring tea and biscuits, relieved I think that it was just talk for the night. I would ride home on my straight four Suzuki 550cc, shivering and sliding slowly past frustrated drivers with fogged up windows and dim headlights. Tight as a board, shoulders locked, shivering and alert, I steered myself home. It was always worth it, even with the miserable ride back, just to catch up with friends.

Chapter 31

My bikie mates were important to me. We shared the drama, the hardships, the weather, the joys, the passion, and all the thrills and spills of owning a motorbike. I had three close friends who rode motorbikes, along with Steve and Mark, whom I have already mentioned.

Gary was slim, with thick, dark, wavy hair that sometimes tried to curl. He had a moustache at about twelve years old, or so it seemed. He was as tall as I was, just over six foot. His face was angular without being harsh, the lines softened slightly, his eyes a light blue, and he had the widest smile of anyone in the group. He was incredibly laid-back. I remember countless times in the rain, waiting at the side of the road while Gary had the seat of his Ducati lifted on its hinge, handfuls of wires sticking out as he worked through the reasons his bike had suddenly stopped. He was patient and methodical, fully aware of the cost of owning an older Italian motorcycle from the 1970s.

Deeds was thin but strong, looking almost petite on his 1000 Kawa. He was around five foot eight, I would guess. Even his hair was thin, or perhaps fine is a better word. Straight as straight could be, his dark hair sat at neck length and was parted in the middle, and his intense, inquisitive soft brown eyes seemed to search for intelligence in others. He had a small, well-proportioned, expressive face. I was honestly shocked when I visited him for the first time and discovered that he lived in a very affluent part of the city with his kind and generous parents. At times he even had the beginnings of a moustache showing.

Eck was a biker's biker. He lived in the toughest part of town and was as tall as he was broad, with light brown hair that curled at the front and at the neck but was simply wavy everywhere else. He had a pale, broad face, blue eyes, fair stubble, spoke little and rode hard. He often owned upper mid-range bikes and was the strongest in the group. We would have an interesting adventure with Eck one night in the wildest pub in the city. He wore a triple-wide motorbike chain as a belt for his jeans, a thick leather jacket that would probably injure your wrist if you punched it, not that you would, and the scraggiest jeans of all of us.

With me tagging along, we were our own three musketeers, and I think I was probably D'Artagnan, trying to be the bravest and hoping to fit in and be accepted. I remember one day in the cafe where I worked. I was in the kitchen, working hard, and when I looked up I was startled to see Deeds standing there, almost exactly half of him covered in bandages. He told me his bike had had a small accident that damaged the front wheel, so he had taken a front wheel from another Kawa that a mate kept for parts and fitted it to his own. He then set off on a test ride along a section of the Edinburgh bypass dual carriageway. He opened up the bike towards 100 miles an hour when it went into a speed wobble caused by the replacement wheel. He had come off on his left side, with no leathers on. His bike was a write-off and he had narrowly avoided going under a bus. But that was not why he had come to tell me.

He turned around a little and pulled his trousers down at the back. On his left buttock was a perfectly imprinted blue-jeans back pocket, even the stitching visible in places. It would be an awesome tattoo nowadays. I stopped what I was doing and laughed and laughed. He tried not to laugh with me. I think it hurt him to laugh. He became a legend on the spot.

My favourite bike that I owned was a Yamaha 250. When I bought it in 1978 or 1979, it was fairly standard, but it was fast. It was a two stroke, so when you slid the clutch at 8000 rpm it was hard to keep the front tyre on the deck. One day, not long after I had bought it, I was riding along a busy part of Haymarket and glanced down to check my speed. When I looked up there was a Morris Allegro parked broadside, stopped about 20 yards in front of me. I hit the wing, went over the bonnet, and as I did I noticed my petrol tank travelling beside me. I hit the road hard in the middle of rush hour traffic, rolling towards an oncoming bus. My first instinct was to jump to my feet and shout "I am all right", although it would have been muffled by my helmet and sounded more like "him hall height".

People came running from a nearby corner café. It is strange how your mind captures certain images, but I can still see the scene clearly and I think the café was called Nadia's. The people were concerned diners, walking and jogging towards me, some still holding napkins or bits of cutlery. I panicked a bit and started weaving away from them but only managed about five steps before I sat down in the middle of the road. Some people helped me back towards what was left of my bike and sat me gently down on the worn sandstone doorstep of a shop that had been closed for years. The police arrived and traffic had been stopped for ages. My bike was eventually lifted to the side of the road and lay in a pitiful heap, looking as if it would be barely recognisable later in the bike mortuary. Statements were taken, witnesses spoke up, and came over to kneel beside me, reassuring me that I had not been at fault. They were so kind, their dinners interrupted or even ruined.

It became clear that I was unlikely to be charged with anything. The young woman driving had borrowed her mum's car without permission, packed a few school friends in and set off. When she reached the junction she stamped on the accelerator instead of the brake and, as a result, I was briskly allegroed into the air. When the ambulance came I insisted that I was fine and did not need it. I think the adrenaline and shock were still in control. My emotions were everywhere, and all I could think about was my ruined bike and what that meant for the next few months. That feeling only worsened when I later discovered that the young woman had no insurance and I only had third party cover. My mind was a muddle. At one point I lay back on the broad step and almost slipped into a sort of semi-conscious sleep.

I believe the police arranged for my bike to be taken to a repair shop, as I had no idea what was happening. Eventually the blue and red lights faded away and the empty ambulance left for another emergency. I was alone, sitting on the step, my helmet beside me as twilight gave way to darkness. The street lights flicked on suddenly and windows lit up like a scattered advent calendar. Traffic resumed and life carried on around me.

I got to my feet, wondering what to do next. I realised my right shoulder was extremely painful and even the slightest movement made me grimace. I had no experience to guide me and this was long before mobile phones. I had no money on me as I had only planned a short ride. So I walked, slowly and painfully, from Haymarket to Princes Street, then to the Mound and up towards the Castle, eventually passing Greyfriars Bobby. Every step was slow, with occasional stops. My shoulder was throbbing. Bright streets and moving traffic lights followed me the whole way. Very few pedestrians were around.

Eventually I walked into the Emergency Department and told my story, rejected ambulance and all. I was seen after a few hours and diagnosed with a dislocated shoulder. I was given some strapping and told to rest. I already knew I would not be able to work for a while. I walked from the hospital to my work to explain what had happened. I suppose I was so young that I did not think to take any painkillers and the hospital had not mentioned them either. I was really struggling. My boss let me rest in a storeroom where I fell asleep on top of a large chest freezer. I spent the night there, the shop closed and empty, with only the odd cockroach for company.

Chapter 32

I was out of action for a couple of weeks. But the dream of rebuilding was born then. It was still more than six months before I would walk down to Waverley Station and get on a train for Devon to start my basic training with the RMCs.

In the late 1970s and early 1980s motorbikes were fairly simple unless someone chose to customise their own. These days you can buy a bike that looks ready for the racetrack, but back then only real enthusiasts took that route.

So, I dreamed, and planned, and worked, and saved, ready for my Yamaha Phoenix project.

I found a back street mechanic in Dalkeith who loved projects and charged fair prices, so the remains were moved from the bike mortuary to their bike lab, an old lock-up in a back lane, in a back street, in a back town. Perfect.

Next I asked around my friends to find an artist who could help. I found a young man in Musselburgh who also lived down a back lane. He had never done anything like this before but he was willing to have a go.

The wreckage was checked. The frame was fine and the engine was salvageable. Game on.

I bought parts as I could afford them and took them by bus in the evenings and on days off to the mechanic and the artist. A six gallon alloy tank from a dealer in Ireland, an oblong headlamp from a specialist car shop, rear sets and clip on racing handlebars from a specialist supplier, black matt expansion exhausts from a Yamaha racing company, and a full racing fairing from a fibreglass factory in England. There was more, but those were the key pieces.

The bike would be glossy black, including the full fairing, with seventeen hand applied coats of lacquer. Gold hand painted coach lines would run along the fairing and side panels, while the tank would stay shiny alloy. This small two stroke racing bike would be impossible to catch around the city, its acceleration unlike anything else on the market then. On a straight motorway it would be vulnerable at top speed as larger engines could simply outrun it, but on twisting roads and city streets it would be impossible to catch and unstoppable. The tank was so large that I could only fit a single seat.

The square headlamp set it apart from every other bike of the time and above it I had written, in a flowing curve below the cockpit windscreen, in boxy white letters, YAMAHA.

I still remember when we rolled it out of the lock up into the weak late evening sunlight. It sat there ready, begging for a professional photoshoot, gleaming black, dangerous, thrilling and completely unique. I had taken the pain, both physical and financial. I had swallowed the anger of an unfair court decision that left the young woman with a few points and a small fine while I lost two weeks of pay and several hundred pounds. I let it go, and focused on what I could do, what I could influence, and it just so happened that was important for my future.

I started the bike. It roared into life, growling, spluttering and cracking with the odd internal backfire as the injection carbs flooded the chambers. Wearing full leathers, I straddled the bike, kicked the side stand back into place, and growled my way out of the back lanes, skittish on the damp cobbles.

I had so much fun on that machine. Yes, I had a couple of spills and was off work again, but the bike was repaired good as new each time by the same team and it drew looks of envy everywhere I parked. People stopped to take photos and ask questions. Heads turned everywhere I went and neighbours grimaced when I revved it in the street before heading out on my regular late night rides.

I decided to rent a small lock-up garage in the new town if possible, and a friend put me in touch with a lawyer who had offices and an unused garage. I would go there at nights to work on the bike or sometimes just to polish it. I knew that if I parked it on the street it would either get damaged or stolen. One morning I arrived at the lock-up to see the padlock hanging from the hasp, and my bike was gone.

The police came and took down the story. They did not sound hopeful. My insurance would not cover anything close to what I had spent on it. About a year later the police contacted me to tell me the frame had been found. They told me the name of the person who had stolen it, and it was the older brother of another young man who had a motorbike and whom I had occasionally gone for a ride with. He had a chopper motorbike and I thought of him as a sort of friend, although not a close one.

I went to his door one night, and I may tell that story later.

For now, the date for my life-changing decision was almost upon me. Friends were still somewhat doubtful that I would go. I had no idea what I was about to let myself in for, or I probably would have pulled the pin.

The day came. I packed, said a few goodbyes, and was accompanied to the station by my good friends Gary, Deeds and Eck. None of us were experienced or confident with goodbyes, so it was rushed and awkward, but it was still very kind of them to come. About fifteen minutes after they left, the train shunted forward, the carriages clanking in resistance, and then I was off on a fourteen hour journey, the first part being a sleeper to Euston in London.

Chapter 33

The train station at Lympstone was at the end of a long journey. It was bleak, wind-blown, exposed, and looked almost like a mistake, except for the high barbed wire fence and what looked like the world's longest and muddiest assault course sitting on the far side, sad and abandoned in the weak winter light. On the other side of the lone dirty concrete platform, grey uninviting clouds hung low and cold over an exposed estuary, where puddles of seawater and mud stretched out to the horizon, looking like a set from an apocalyptic film.

Then we were being marshalled up through a gate in the fence, across the assault course, through a few blocks of square concrete buildings, and into a small lecture theatre. We made our vows, received our kit, and then were marched, although marched is probably too strong a word for what we managed, so let us say we walked in a half-orderly fashion over to our dormitory. Other young men leaned out of the windows, shouting "you will be sorry", a phrase that somehow managed to be both playful and prophetic.

That night we were shown how to shower, iron our clothes, keep our kit tidy, and where everything in the camp was found. I had mistakenly thought that because I had gone to a gym and exercised a bit before coming that I was in decent shape. I discovered the truth on the morning of day two. The first gym session made it clear I was not fit at all. The phrase "and hold" became my personal nightmare. Halfway through sit-ups, pull-ups or press-ups, the instructor would call out "and hold". The long pauses continued until the room filled with louder groans, rasping breaths and muttered complaints.

The assault course itself was fine for me, except for rope climbing. I struggled with the leg technique and had to use mostly arm strength, which meant I was exhausted after one or two climbs instead of the expected six. Often we were covered in mud, either from the assault course or from being taken on a mud run out on the estuary when the tide was out. The commando crawl across freezing water was incredible. We had to drape halfway and then get back onto the rope in the crawl position in one movement. One time I failed and was told to release, which meant falling into the freezing water below. It truly did take your breath away.

We did load carries with sixty pounds of equipment over twenty five kilometres at double-time marching pace. I found those quite easy, but some of the smaller guys struggled. One or two collapsed and were moved back to the next class to repeat the training. One guy filled his haversack with bedding so it looked full but was light. That morning, as if they knew, the trainers weighed all our packs. They caught him and added bricks to the repacked load. He never made it.

We were taught to dismantle and reassemble weapons blindfolded and under time pressure. We learned map reading, did night exercises with parachute flares going off, and had to dive into thorny bushes for cover. We learned a range of weapons, how to shoot standing, kneeling and prone, and how to shoot when exhausted after a beasting on the assault course or freezing after thirty six hours without sleep out on the moors.

I was picked on for being Scottish. I was made to stand in front of the troop and say "I am a FRISB" over and over. FRISB was the acronym for Fucking Repugnant Ignorant Scottish Bastard. None of the English lads were made to do anything like that. Once I was made to hop around like a frog for twenty minutes shouting the phrase with every hop. Another time, while we were near the sea, I was told to say it again. This time I refused, which shocked the rest of the group. I could hear the sharp intake of breath around me. We were marched into the freezing winter sea, rifles held above our heads. I still refused. The guys near me started urging me to just say it, and I realised I had led us into a lose-lose situation. The trainers held all the power, and eventually I knew I would be forced to say it. So I did, and a lot of muttering followed.

One night I returned to the barracks after a few beers in Exeter. The lights were off and most guys were asleep. I was on a top bunk. I could not get under the sheets and at one point my foot tore through the sheet and I ended up hanging upside down along the side of the bunk. The lights went on and I was surrounded by laughing mates. They had made me an apple pie bed. When they finished laughing, they helped me back into the top bunk and fixed my bedding, although one sheet now had a size ten hole in it.

There were the odd scraps in the barracks. Some of the others thought that since the trainers picked on me, they could do the same. I corrected that idea for them, sometimes with a Glasgow kiss. But mostly we were a close bunch, learning to rely on each other.

We spent a few weeks training with specialised units. One exercise involved small rigid raiding craft out on the English Channel at three in the morning in January, swimming ashore to abandoned island beaches and meeting another group as part of the training. Freezing, always freezing. We lost all feeling from the waist down after standing chest deep in the sea at ridiculous hours, then had to do fireman's lifts up and down steep banks to get the feeling back. Sergeants and corporals came into the dormitory at four in the morning for surprise kit checks, and for any small mistake they would rip everything out of lockers. It must have been at least a hundred man-hours worth of washing, ironing, folding and storing, all dumped on the floor, with the order to do it again. The idea was simple. They were trying to break us. They wanted to break our will to continue.

Then we had leave, and I went back to Edinburgh for Christmas. I realised how much I missed my own people, how homesick I was for the little I still had that connected me to Scotland. I visited my friends, my head shorn of all hair, heavier and more muscular than I had been only two months earlier. I got drunk, I gambled, and I made a fool of myself at times, letting out some of the frustrations. I was taken in by the police one night, but it genuinely was a case of mistaken identity. I was released a few hours later.

And then, in what felt like a blur of coloured lights, Christmas songs, hot meals and late nights, I was on my own again, on a train with another fourteen hour journey ahead of me. I had two fewer days' leave than the rest of my platoon really, as I spent two days travelling on stuffy, slow trains, with three changes each way.

Mud, cold, no sleep, and exhaustion. I was back. I remember being at the top of a hill one night, on my own, hunkered down trying to stay hidden during an exercise. Far below me I could see the small village lights twinkling, and I imagined the people warm and snug in their beds, electric blankets set to low. I asked myself for the first time "why?" Why am I here doing this?

The next day we were told we had one more week to opt out, and after that we were committed for three years. I was eighteen, homesick, fed up with the constant abuse, and I understood my limits better now. I decided I was done. This was not the life for me. I understood that on the far side of the training there was a whole different world, but I was finished. The course had done what it was meant to do. It had sorted me out. I genuinely did not feel like I had failed. I had learned a lot, tried my best, and given it everything I had. I think I could have completed it, though I would have been near the bottom of the class.

One of the corporals who had constantly abused me for being Scottish came to see me alone. He asked why I was leaving. I told him I was constantly homesick and that it was a distraction. He said he was really surprised, as he thought I was the perfect person for the role and career. I did think about staying for the rest of the day, but in the end I left. I had an interview with the top officer who told me what he thought of me, some of which was good and some not so good. Then I was issued my discharge papers, given a train voucher, and left to walk to the station with my small bag of personal possessions, which was all I owned at that point.

Chapter 34

I arrived back in Edinburgh with nowhere to live, little money, and a skinhead haircut. I remember the train pulling into a station at 4am and a guard saying something over the tannoy that included "Edinburgh". I had been fast asleep, so, drowsy-headed, shirt untucked and stubbly, I zigzagged down the slowing train corridor. I must have fallen asleep in a first-class cabin and the guard had just left me there. When the train finally stopped and the last clank echoed, I opened the door. I did not recognise the station, and there were no signs on the platform. Hesitantly I stepped down, ready to jump back on. A man was standing behind me at the train door. He said, "Mate, is this Edinburgh?". We pooled our ignorance. Still half asleep, I replied, "Ah dinnae ken, mate. This must be Haymarket, ah dinnae recognise this as Edinburgh Waverley. I'd jump back oan if I wiz you and get aff at the next stoap. A'hm ok here, as I dinnae mind getting aff at Haymarket". It felt like too many words. He looked at me for a few seconds, then stepped back inside, shut the door and disappeared down the carriage.

I started walking toward the steps, and just as I reached them I realised I was on a satellite platform at the very back of Edinburgh Waverley. I turned to run back, but even as I did the train was already pulling away. I spoke out loud, although no one was there to hear it. "Oh no, the next stoap is Dundee, poor guy...".

I remember the feeling of joy at being back in my home city. I wanted to hug the familiar buildings, soak myself in Scottishness, and savour every moment of being home, even though paradoxically I had no home.

I do not clearly remember the rest of that morning, but I assume I went somewhere for breakfast. I definitely went to see my Italian landlord mid-morning, and joy of joys, he had a spare room for rent. I was back, and I had somewhere to stay. Next step was to find a job.

Next morning, bleary-eyed but still enjoying the freedom to come and go as I pleased, I walked to the nearest Job Centre. Looking for work that would be hard and pay reasonably well, I saw an advert for nightshift shelf packers at a supermarket on the outskirts of Edinburgh, about twenty minutes by bus from the city centre. I headed there straight away, on the bus within fifteen minutes. The store manager interviewed me that morning. I explained I had just left Marine training and was looking for physical work that paid decently. He hired me on the spot and I started that night. I was thrilled.

There was a team of six or seven men. We worked hard through the night, sweating constantly. First, we placed all the boxes at the point in each aisle where they would go on shelves. Then two guys followed with knives and small trolley tables. They lifted each box, cut it open, and used a price gun to label every item. This was long before barcodes and scanners. The main team came behind them, packing everything onto the shelves, and at first that was my job. We worked flat out, one break at 4am for half an hour, then back to fill the freezer and dairy sections before lifting all the packaging and mopping and polishing the floor for 7am when the staff arrived. We finished at 8am, having started at 11pm.

I worked hard and learned quickly. Before long I was on the cutting and pricing team. Then I was asked to handle frozen and dairy from the start of the night, which meant working on my own. I enjoyed the trust and responsibility. One night in the freezer, leaning against a cage as I searched through boxes looking for the items I needed to fill the gaps in the frozen section, I had a mad impulse and stuck my tongue out. It instantly stuck to the minus 25 degree metal. I ripped it off and it bled a little. You are the first person I think I have ever told this to.

I was doing well. I worked hard, stayed fit, slept during the day, went to the gym in the mornings after work, and ate properly. We played pranks at work too. One time we lifted a staff member's car and put fish boxes under each tyre. Another time we wrapped someone's car in industrial cling film. We even carried a small motorbike up three flights of stairs, which made the owner furious at 8am. The best part was watching people's reactions when they saw their cars.

I remember one morning on the bus, heading home. It was a single decker, warm and crowded. I fell asleep and slumped sideways, my head landing right in a lady's lap. Her scream woke me and startled half the bus. I mumbled, "oh ahm so sorry hen, ave jist cumoaf niteshift," but no one heard me. I got off the bus, embarrassed, and walked the last few miles home, muttering to myself.

The turning point came out of nowhere one Friday morning. We had all been paid and the guys were heading to the pub. They asked me to come along, and for some strange reason I said yes. The law in Scotland had just changed to let pubs open at 8am for night-shift workers.

I got drunk, stayed drunk all day, and did not go to work that night. Since coming back to Edinburgh I had been living clean, staying fit, and avoiding alcohol, so this was a big slip.

The next few weeks and months were a fight between my habits and my values. Some days I was healthy and focused. Other days I was drunk. I remember waking up at five to eleven one night, panicked. I threw on my clothes, ran down the stairs and got a taxi, terrified I was going to lose my job. Five minutes into the ride I realised it was my night off. I stopped the taxi, paid, got out and walked home.

The hardest thing about nightshift was trying to have days off. I never knew if I should stay up all day, or sleep all day, or flip my schedule. My body and mind were not coping, and I was drinking too much.

Then one week I missed two nights in a row. That was the moment I knew I was finished. Part of me felt guilty for letting down the day manager who had taken a chance on me. Another part of me felt relieved that I would not have to drag myself through that strange, heavy 4am feeling anymore.

I went back in during the day a week later to pick up my pay and apologise to the manager. It was time for the next chapter in my life.

Chapter 35

I was sitting in the Jobcentre, having an interview with an adviser. I wanted to do something different. I had worked as a cook in my early years and was good at it, but it was limited in terms of where it could lead. I had applied for a bricklaying apprenticeship.

The adviser gently steered me away from this. Even when I brought it back into the conversation a few times, they talked instead about other opportunities that they felt were a better fit for me. At moments, I felt condescended to. In the end, they gave me a choice: catering college to study full-time for a year to become a chef, with rent and income support, or back to the main Jobcentre area to look for another job I could apply for. I had already looked, and unless I wanted to work in a mortuary, a shoe shop, or as a commission-based salesperson, this was my other option: train to become a chef.

Telford College was out towards Drylaw and Granton, two of the less reputable areas of Edinburgh. I should fit right in. Our last children's home had been there.

I thought about my days in that children's home, where I was actually fairly happy, even when things went wrong. That happiness had nothing to do with money, because we had none. We could come and go as we pleased for much of the time, even if we had to buzz to be let in after 9 pm. I hardly went to school, most days heading into the city, especially in the summer months, then hanging around parks and shopping centres, where I connected with other like-minded fourteen-year-olds. We were known to the police, as they knew we should be at school, and we recognised the regular beat officers. We were skilled at melting away when they appeared in our peripheral vision.

One of the boys in the same home had an older brother I knew. He would have been in his early twenties, I think. He was always in trouble for fighting and was part of some poorly organised gang. One day I bumped into him in the city and he suggested I hang out with him. I was a little flattered, as he had status and was well known in the circles I moved in. At one point he went into a clothes shop and I went with him. While we were in the shirt section, he grabbed one and shoved it under my jersey, then moved towards another area of the shop. There, he started putting a jersey under his own shirt. A customer saw him and raised the alarm. He sprang into action, running through the shop and out of the front door. I caught a glimpse of the back of his head as he weaved away, fleeing the chasing staff. The same customer then pointed directly at me and told the remaining staff that I had been with the thief. They grabbed my arm and called the police.

The police arrived and took me to the nearest police box, where they had me sit while they questioned me and checked where I was from. The whole time, all I could hear was the crinkling of the plastic wrapping on the shirt that was stuck half down my trousers and half up my jersey. I could not believe they could not hear it. Eventually, the police warned me about my behaviour, instructed me to go to school, and let me go. I knew two things for certain. I was not keeping the shirt, and I was never hanging out with that guy again. His choices might have seemed right to him, but I had already seen the inside of a youth remand centre and had no desire to end up back there. The shirt went in the bin, and I went off to the park, not school, sorry.

My dad had been on the dole, and I remember the hushed conversations about money. Anxiety crept around the dinner table, and the slightest thing could set off a chain reaction of shouting and violence. I thought about what I could do to make this season work and bought a ten-speed racing bicycle. I cycled everywhere. It kept me fit, saved money, and gave me some freedom. For the next year, I really did cycle everywhere. It was actually fine. Even on windy and wet days, I had the right clothes and a haversack for my essentials. I started skipping too, buying a weighted skipping rope and building up to a thousand skips a day in sets of two hundred. I did double skips, backwards skips, squat skips, and even the occasional triple skip. I ate well, loved cycling, found the best back roads and lanes, and enjoyed having time to myself. For most of that year, I stayed teetotal, but I am getting ahead of myself.

Catering college was genuinely fun, even if it was hard work. We had theory most mornings: nutrition, menu costing, menu balance, hygiene, and so on. In the afternoons, we cooked. Our teacher was a Swiss chef who was firm but fair, and everyone wanted to impress him, me included. He had worked in top hotels and kitchens all over the world. We learned to make stock from roasted bones and roughly chopped vegetables. We learned to taste and season properly, and to clean and clear as we went, which I still do today. We made our own puff pastry and assembled a gâteau mille-feuille. We prepared canapés and whole roast pork loins with perfect crackling. Day after day, we cooked and cleaned.

I joined the Telford College Hill Walking Club. A minibus picked us up at 4 am in Charlotte Square, central Edinburgh, then drove through the early mist and up into the Highlands. We tumbled out of the van on some side road at first light, breath forming clouds as we geared up, and then we were off, climbing mountains. I loved it. I was always ahead of everyone, pushing myself as hard as I could with the summit in mind. Thighs burning, lungs working overtime, heart soaring.

I remember one winter climb where I delayed putting my crampons on, thinking I would be fine, until a fresh wind sprang up and blew the recent snow clear off the mountain. I was left standing on a vast sheet of rock-hard ice in my boots, with the offending crampons and ice axe still neatly strapped to my haversack. It took me ten minutes to put each crampon on as I moved like a snail to avoid sliding off the mountain. Lesson learned. On another climb, I was so far ahead that I stopped to look for the others. It had been snowing heavily, and at times I was wading through thigh-deep snow. I went to the edge and looked down. I could see the thin black strip of the road far below, but no people anywhere. I turned and kept going. Later, back at the van, I went to see where I had been standing. To my horror, I realised I had been on a cornice of ice overhanging a cliff with a drop of at least three hundred metres. Had it cracked, I would have been dead. Whoops.

College had a gym and an evening badminton club, so I exercised at lunchtime and fell in with Mr Iran, a bodybuilder who ate whole chickens, bones and all. He had a beautiful penthouse apartment and a flashy sports car and was studying something at college, although I do not think I ever saw him study. We trained together, spotting each other on heavy weights and encouraging one another to push harder. I was doing one hundred one-handed press-ups, sets of twenty chin-ups, and squatting 120 kg. We were good friends for that year, spending a lot of time together. He always had money; I always had none. He was generous and great fun, and we were forever going on late-night drives into the city centre to do something spontaneous. He had an array of girlfriends and other Iranian friends. I probably looked like an oddity in the group, but we were genuinely close.

Life at my Italian family's apartment was interesting during this period too. They had five Irish labourers staying while they worked on a large city project. They were fun but got very drunk at weekends. One guy I remember fell asleep in his own mess on a newly acquired second-hand white vinyl sofa. Yes, those were the days. When the Irish left, the Malaysians arrived, bringing strange-smelling food but immense hospitality. They would insist I join them for dinner and took real joy in being generous. They were studying marine engineering at Leith Nautical College. One of them knew kung fu, and I could never lay a hand on him when we play-fought. He taught me how to stand and balance to put maximum force into any strike. One day, when I had a sore back, he did something to it that I will never forget. It felt like I had been given a new back, the pain was gone. He said he had studied at a Shaolin temple. I believed him. It was extraordinary.

We became close friends, and I loved those guys. They were the real thing. At Christmas, they hired a car and went to the Highlands. They were involved in a bad crash, and my friend lost an eye. They went home shortly afterwards, and I never saw them again. Even now, the smell of Malaysian shrimp paste brings those memories flooding back. I had discovered the contagious joy of being around generous people.

Chapter 36

My work experience as a chef was in a city centre restaurant. It was a busy but small bistro at street level, with a three-hundred-seat restaurant on the first floor overlooking the world-famous Princes Street Gardens and, on warm summer evenings, the beautifully lit Edinburgh Castle.

The kitchen was compact, and I worked with two commis chefs. Preparation was everything, and it was very different from the work I had done as a short-order cook. I was dealing with top-end produce and expensive menus, alongside a dozen demanding, immaculate waiting staff and a management couple who lived upstairs in a small attached flat.

I started at 9 am, preparing for a midday lunch that could be ten people or two hundred. The advantage of only ten for lunch was that some of my evening prep was already done. We had two giant, eye-level gas grills, and the Barnsley chop, a double butterfly-cut lamb chop, was the favourite.

I learned a lot about catering, or hospitality as it was sometimes called. We worked six split shifts every week, starting at 9 am and prepping until midday, although I was only paid from 10 am. It was impossible to prep properly in such a short time. Service ran until 2.30 pm, followed by tidying up, with the official finish time supposedly 3 pm. In reality, we rarely left before 3.30 or 4 pm, yet we were only paid until 2.30 pm. We were back again at 5 pm, with just an hour to prepare for three hundred evening customers. Often, I worked straight through from lunch to dinner, doing all the prep in my own time and unpaid.

Conditions were shocking. Breaks were non-existent and support was hard to find. There was nowhere to do laundry, so with only two sets of work clothes issued and no time to wash them over six days of work, we were somehow expected to remain immaculate. As a result, we bought extra chef's clothes with our own money. Pay was poor, and although the waiting staff made hundreds of pounds a week in tips, none of it was shared with the kitchen team. This was my first experience of catering, and I was not impressed.

After the work experience, I worked there again during the college holidays over the summer. I saved up and bought a motorbike, a Honda 250 Super Dream. At least I had more freedom and was no longer limited to getting around by bicycle. College itself was enjoyable. The people in the class were a ragtag group, all struggling in life like me, all looking for a way forward. Of course, the government funnelled many of us into hospitality, often with employers who would chew people up, drain them, undervalue them, and eventually spit them out. Still, we had fun learning to cook. I dated a couple of the girls in the class too. I had long hair down my back, a big moustache, stubble, and I was bulking up, lifting heavy weights and training in the gym seven days a week.

Christmas came, and this was the time when I felt my loneliness most acutely. At times it felt like an inner ache, though it was something I never spoke about. In darker moments, I would sit on the thin carpet of my box bedroom, window shutters closed, and cry. I did not dwell on the pain or share my feelings with others. I cried, got up, and carried on.

That Christmas, the college class went out for drinks as the term ended and we would not see each other again. I went along and got drunk for the first time in a long while. Nothing bad happened, but I felt off the rails. The gym was no longer available now that college had finished, and everything that had kept me steady had shifted. I drank repeatedly over that Christmas until I had no money left for food or drink. I spent two days in my room sleeping, waiting until I felt able to face life again.

I got my old job back as a short-order cook. Nothing had changed, despite all my attempts to move on, joining the Marines, working night shifts in a supermarket, and studying for a new career. I was back in the same job, the same rented room, the same life, just with a different bike. I worked hard and took pride in being the best at what I did. I was paid well for the time. I believe I was the first person in my trade in Edinburgh to earn two pounds an hour. I was making more than my dad ever had.

I was excellent at my job. I could remember dozens of orders in my head, spinning around the small kitchen, pulling ingredients together in the right sequence and at the right moment, keeping the waiting staff and management happy day after day, then drinking myself to sleep night after night. I started gambling again too, on evenings and days off.

Around this time, I fell back in love with swimming. On quiet midweek afternoons, I would go to the pool on my days off. One pool had a translucent glass ceiling, and on sunny days the water was filled with light. I would swim up and down, fifty or a hundred lengths, sometimes as the only person there. I loved those moments.

I became good friends with one of the guys at work, Archie. Like me, he was a hard worker who wanted to excel, and he worked front of house. He had light brown, almost blond, spiky hair and questioning blue eyes set in a young, sharper, Rutger Hauer-like face. He was intelligent, and our curiosity sparked off each other. When we had days off together, we would jump on my bike and tour the used bookshops and second-hand stores near the university, hunting for bargains. We would then head upstairs in Jenners, Edinburgh's premium city centre store, Scotland's answer to Harrods, and sit by the café window sharing a pot of Earl Grey while talking about *Siddhartha*, Hermann Hesse, or whatever book we had recently discovered.

During the Edinburgh Festival, we would wander through fringe plays and street theatre, marvelling at the improvisation and brilliance of the performers. Archie sometimes performed fire-eating and unicycling as an act. I even helped his sister with a play she was doing, so I can say I was once involved in a play at the Edinburgh Festival, although that would probably be stretching the truth.

One of the guys who shared Archie's city centre flat was called Alan, and we became friends too. He introduced me to hash. It was a turning point, though I did not recognise it at the time. I had never smoked, so I ate some instead, laughed uncontrollably for about an hour, then slept deeply for the rest of the day. I was hooked. It was not long before I was smoking hash and becoming knowledgeable about Moroccan, Lebanese, and Nepalese varieties, able to tell the difference by texture, smell, and colour.

I discovered that after four or five pints of beer, smoking a very strong joint would give me a huge rush in my head before dropping me into a deep, heavy sleep. I became a solitary drinker and drug user. My hair grew longer. I left my job and drifted into cash-in-hand work, small cafés, helping a carpet fitter, and various other roles. My clothes went unwashed for longer and longer, and my friends saw less and less of me.

Loneliness became a fickle companion, sometimes offering comfort but more often bringing sorrow and grief. There was worse to come.

Chapter 37

I had worked a shift at a café for an old friend. It had been horrible, as the effects of constant drug use had begun to bring anxiety and panic attacks. My friend Archie introduced me to cocaine, and that was it. I remember the first night, staying awake until morning. I read Ecclesiastes in the Bible and was amazed by the wisdom in it. I felt emotionally euphoric and in love with everyone and everything. I recognised my own chasing after the wind and the meaninglessness of so much of life.

Weeks passed, and I was now using cocaine, hash, and various other substances, along with alcohol, every day. I would buy a two-litre bottle of cooking wine from an Italian deli near my rented room, take it back, and drink it slowly. The room was tiny and squalid. Once drunk, I would either sleep or go out to find more drugs. I think I was trying to recapture that first high, although I would not have been able to explain it at the time.

That afternoon, I was leaving my friend's café for the forty-minute bus journey home. It was a grey day, misty, with low cloud hanging over everything. I went to the familiar bus station and waited, grateful at least to be under shelter, even though the cold seemed to seep into my bones. The bus pulled in and a few straggling passengers stepped down the greasy, steep stairs onto the grey concrete concourse.

With a growing sense of paranoia, I made my way onto the bus and climbed the short steps to pay. I sat at the back on the lower deck and waited. The bus would probably leave in five minutes. It was a nice bus, with blue-speckled fabric seats, warm and relatively new. As I sat there, the paranoia kept rising. I felt anxious, nervous, and a strange, wobbling sensation passed through my head. I was convinced everyone on the bus knew how I felt and was staring at me.

I jumped up and got off through the exit door, flustered and hurried, as if I could not stay another second in the enclosed space. I stood near an indoor bus shelter, which made no sense to me at all, and stared at it. I simply stared, frozen inside my own bubble. After a few minutes, the feelings passed. I explained to the driver that I had already paid, showed my ticket, and got back on.

My hair was long and greasy from café work and neglect. My green military trousers were covered in stains, and my beard was straggly and wild. All my clothes came from charity shops, mismatched but worn with a kind of forced flair.

Seconds later, panic overtook reason again and I got off the bus for a second time. This time, I walked out of the bus station entirely. I felt strange and dangerous. I did not want to be in the enclosed bus, but I also could not cope with open spaces. All I wanted was the safety of my sad, lonely room, with its mattress on the floor, thin whitewashed plywood wardrobe, and my four-seasons sleeping bag.

I walked away from people until I reached a park. In the middle of it, I lay down on the grass, huddled with my recycled rain jacket pulled tightly around me, the side of my face pressed into the damp ground. I could not face people, buses, or open spaces. I was not doing well. I closed my eyes and think I slept there for around three hours in the light misty rain.

A schoolboy's voice woke me. "Hey mister, are you OK?" I stirred and saw school shoes stepping back quickly, then turning and running away. I stood up and tried to straighten my dishevelled clothes. My trousers clung to my legs, there was grass on my face, and my jacket was soaked through. Shivers came in spasms. I shoved my hands into my pockets, put my head down, and set off at a brisk pace in what I thought was the direction of home.

I walked for hours, choosing the quieter routes whenever I could. Eventually, long after dark, I was home. I closed the front door behind me but did not wait to hear it shut. I was in my room, undressed and inside the sleeping bag in seconds, knees pulled to my chest, shivering. I stayed like that for two days.

That became my pattern. I would reach a point where I could no longer cope with life, retreat to my room, and stay there for days, emerging only around the third day to make a cup of tea.

One day, Archie mentioned a scheme at a school in Wester Hailes, on the very outskirts of Edinburgh. Adults could sit in classes alongside fifth- and sixth-year pupils. At the time, Wester Hailes was a concrete sprawl of five-storey council flats, with a reputation as the heroin capital of Europe, reportedly having more addicts per head than anywhere else on the continent.

I applied, was accepted, and a whole new world opened up. I learned about Shakespeare and universal themes, the First World War, and the poetry of Wilfred Owen and Siegfried Sassoon. I learned to listen for meaning in language, to hear what lay beneath the words through context and imagery. I had one school year to complete two years of study, so I stayed up until one or two in the morning working on Maths, History, and English.

I became friends with some of the students and with all of the teachers. I soaked up knowledge like a sponge. Suddenly, I was quoting literature, solving algebra problems, and thinking more deeply about the world. My curiosity was coming alive.

I still struggled with drink and drugs and missed the occasional class, though not many. A few times, I even attended while paranoid, which must have been worrying for the teachers and students in hindsight. I was invited on class outings, to an evening at the theatre and to day trips to museums and exhibitions. I received government support for studying and also worked cash in hand at friends' cafés, which meant I always had money for drink and drugs.

One night, some work colleagues invited me to a party at a farm in the middle of nowhere. There was plenty of hashish, smoked in pipes over open flames, and I indulged without restraint. The house was a rambling old farmhouse with high ceilings, rustic furniture, and outbuildings. There was drink everywhere and many people I did not know. They all seemed able to enjoy the party without excess. I could not.

After a couple of hours, I began to hallucinate, seeing things as if through the wrong end of a telescope, or imagining the room was full of cats. Even now, I am not entirely sure whether there really were cats or whether that was purely the drugs. At the time, I believed it was the drugs.

I started having thoughts about harming others, mixed with paranoia and waves of anxiety. I became genuinely frightened for my own safety and for the safety of everyone else. That fear added a new and terrifying layer to my anxiety.

I left the house and went to a dark corner of the garden where there was a small pond. I stood in the water, and whenever anyone came near, I warned them forcefully to stay away in case I hurt them. There were probably a lot of curses shouted that night, at least from me.

Eventually, friends drove me home. I had to keep my head out of the window for the entire journey, terrified of what I might do to others in the confined space of a car. Then I was home again, back in my cocoon, relatively safe from harming anyone. This time, I stayed there for three days, not eating or drinking, apart from one or two hurried trips to the toilet.

Things were spiralling downwards.

Chapter 38

I was struggling on many levels during this period. I had just turned twenty years old and was addicted to cocaine and amphetamines, alcoholic, and living with undiagnosed mental health problems. I rarely washed, ate very little, and went for long walks alone in the local hills, searching for some kind of inner peace. It is hard to say now, after all these years, but it would not be too much to say that I did not like myself. At times, I think I even hated who I had become. Yet change felt beyond my reach.

I hated the bouts of anxiety and what I would now recognise as depression that came over me. I remember standing inside the tenement stair door to the street for twenty minutes, hand on the handle, frozen. I could not face the surge of anxiety that hit me at the thought of going outside. I stood there at the edge of what I was capable of, lost, alone, frightened, and too proud to ask for help.

School finished and I passed my exams. I had Higher qualifications now. What would have been unthinkable at sixteen had become possible at twenty. That fact alone kept me sane at times and pulled me away from drugs long enough to study, get on buses, attend classes, and live something resembling a normal life. I loved being awake at two in the morning, books from the local library strewn across my small bedroom table, the floor, and the bed, all open at different pages. The rain pattered onto my large cross framed bedroom window as Edinburgh turned in her sleep outside. The back lane lights were dim, casting shadows that felt both mysterious and comforting. Sometimes, around four in the morning, as early traffic began and the city stirred, I would slip into bed, warmed by new knowledge and a fragile sense of purpose.

I started looking for work and was eventually offered a job at a B&Q Home Store on the outskirts of Edinburgh. I had been living on next to nothing for a long time, visiting local Asian shops to buy damaged vegetables and potatoes. With a bag of flour and some oil, I could survive the week on potato fritters and vegetable soup. Food barely registered compared to my thoughts about drink and drugs. With this job, however, I swore off drugs and got myself clean again after a few difficult weeks. There were emotional swings, tears, nausea, bouts of self-induced sickness after eating, and what I assume were withdrawal symptoms, including night sweats.

I started work as a warehouse assistant. It was actually a great job. We handled all the store deliveries, shelving stock in the warehouse or moving it straight onto the shop floor. Twice a week, we loaded trucks to deliver customers' orders, and we also managed returns and damaged goods so they could be sent back to suppliers. There was a warehouse manager and one other assistant. Both were, to be honest, fairly lazy. I was even told to slow down so there would be something left to do. At one point, they sent me into the office roof space, which was crammed with old, unused stock, and told me to tidy it. I think they believed it was impossible. Four hours later, covered in dust and with sweat dripping from my beard, it was done.

I turned up ready to work every day, overalls on, sweatbands on my wrists and forehead. My happiest days were when the forklift was out of action and I had to unload everything by hand from incoming trucks. Sometimes that meant shifting a thousand grow bags for the garden centre. I was completely in my element. Working, sweating, eating, and living. I was always moving.

I did have one memorable moment on the forklift. They had sent me on a three-day training course, which I passed. While unloading a pallet of paint tins from a curtain-sided lorry, I swung round without realising that some of the pallet strapping had come loose. Around twenty tins, probably a gallon each, fell onto the concrete, bursting open and splattering several bystanders, including my boss, in magnolia gloss. We stayed late and cleaned it all up in our own time.

I laughed to myself all the way home that night, remembering the look on his face and his spluttered, "Ya f****** idiot, aye, look whit y'ev done!" Even now, writing this, I still snigger. He was barely five feet tall and paint covered one entire side of him. He looked like a half-finished garden ornament.

There was a decent social scene at the store. Staff went out together to play darts, dominoes, and sometimes five-a-side football. I went a few times, but once again I could not control my drinking and made a fool of myself, fighting and swearing. After that, I stopped going on staff nights out.

Pay was another problem. It was minimum wage with unpaid overtime, so by the middle of most weeks I had no money left. I no longer received government support, so rent, travel, electricity, and food all came out of my wages. I loved the work but could not survive on the pay. They promoted me to warehouse manager, which came with more money, but I hated it. I spent my days with a clipboard, directing staff and liaising with department heads about upcoming promotions. I missed grafting, sweating, and being in the thick of it in my overalls and sweatbands. Now I was expected to wear a shirt and tie every day, company policy. When one of the Saturday staff called me Mr Brown, I knew this was not for me. After a couple of months, I quit.

I went back to work as a short-order cook and also took on a night shift job, working five days and five nights each week. I was saving for my next motorbike. I would start at eight in the morning and work until five, sleep until eleven, then head out to work from midnight until six or seven. On my days off, I slept almost the entire time. I kept my cash on me, bound with rubber bands. I needed six hundred pounds for the bike I was dreaming of, a second-hand Suzuki 550cc, straight four, black with red and gold coach lines. I earned about fifty pounds a week from each job, and after living costs I was saving roughly fifty pounds a week. I also needed riding gear and insurance, so in total I had to save around seven hundred and fifty pounds. That meant fifteen weeks of double shifts.

One night, I went out for what was meant to be a single pint with a friend and fell asleep in the pub toilet. When I woke up, the lights were off, chairs were stacked on the tables, and the manager was behind the bar counting the takings. He said, "Oh, yer up. I was just aboot to call the polis." He let me out, and I walked home. Thankfully, I was not working that night.

Another morning, I fell asleep on the bus, stretched out across the back seat. When I woke up, the bus was packed, with people standing while I occupied four or five seats. I got off in embarrassment, only to realise I was still miles from home. I went into a nearby shop, bought a Mr Kipling Victoria sponge, tore the box and wrapping off, and ate the whole Victoria Sponge while walking to the next bus stop. Very classy.

The day finally came when I had enough money to buy the bike. Months of double shifts were behind me. That day was my last night shift, and I would not be going back. I had also been offered overtime at my daytime cooking job. A friend was due in at four to cover for me so I could leave early and collect the bike. I could barely contain myself all day.

Chapter 39

It was 4 pm and, around five or ten minutes late, my friend from work arrived, got changed, and jumped in to take on my role in the kitchen as cook. I was gone in a flurry; the motorbike shop shut at five, and I was worried the bike might have been sold already.

On the bus, I fidgeted and squirmed at every traffic light, constantly putting my hands in my pocket to check the wad of cash was still there. I had my new leather jacket and crash helmet with me, which felt a bit odd on the bus. Finally, the bus stop I was getting off at! I walked briskly on a warm Edinburgh evening towards my prize. There it was, still in the showroom window: black paint deep and lustrous, red and gold coach lines elegant, and four gleaming exhaust pipes promising balance and power on demand. I paused for a moment to take it all in, but it was already ten to five; the shop shut in ten minutes.

I went inside. A doorbell jangled as the door slowly swung shut behind me, and the salesman looked up. There was a fleeting look of disappointment across his face, but he quickly regained his composure. With a watery, smarmy smile, he asked if he could help me. Actually, he said, "Kin ah help yoo son?" as if I had wandered into the wrong shop and was perhaps looking for shoe polish.

I was not to be dissuaded from my mission. I already had a vision in my mind of riding around all my friends' houses that night, showing off my hard-won prize. "Yes, I really wanna see the Suzy 550 in the windae,".I said. He glanced at his watch. Not to be put off, I added, "I'd wanna hear it run, mister."

I knew what was happening. He looked at my shabby clothes, recycled leather jacket, and cheap open-face crash helmet and assumed I was after credit, which would mean forms, phone calls to the credit company, and delays. It was Friday, and I suspected he was hoping I would come back tomorrow. I decided to let him sweat a little. We started the bike, and I gave it a once-over; everything looked fine. Sitting on it felt right—my feet even slightly off the ground—so it was a good fit for my six-foot-two frame.

"Ah'll take it," I said, and we moved to his desk. He started pulling out a handful of forms. I waited until they were all neatly arranged, and he had mastered the fleeting look of frustration on his face. I pulled out my wad of cash, counted six hundred pounds onto his desk, and nearly wanted to lean over and push his jaw back into place. Ha ha ha, it was a glorious moment for me. It took him only five seconds to recover; I swear he rubbed his hands together. In my mind's eye, I saw Ebenezer. I almost wanted to say, "Oh, so sorry, I think I've changed my mind," just to see his reaction. But I wanted that bike badly.

We sealed the deal, and I was out the back of the shop, straddling my new gleaming possession. I think I felt truly happy for the first time in a long while.

I rode around all my bike mates' houses that sunset evening, weaving through traffic, feeling the depth of available power—so much richer than my last 250cc. This was a four-stroke engine, not a two-stroke, so the power delivery was much smoother. Yes, I lost the explosive early thrust of the mad-revved two-stroke, but there seemed to be endless smooth acceleration in my new steed. I was back. It was summer. Life was good.

That year, I was always out on my motorbike, enjoying summer nights, cruising around my favourite haunts, taking wide sweeping curves, stopping to admire the city lights, cafes for cups of tea, friends' houses for discussions about the latest motorbikes and our dreams of owning them one day. I loved simply riding around, not going anywhere in particular, impulsively changing destinations in my head—sunrise at the beach, the all-night bakery, the highest viewpoint few people knew about, the station to watch the London train arrive, the airport to see planes land, the harbour to check out the latest ships, and streets where it was fun to accelerate hard from traffic lights, leaving everyone behind to inhale the fumes until the next set.

One Friday night, with no work the next day, I was having the best night, throwing my bike around bends, hammering down short straight busy roads, weaving in and out of traffic with glee.

Then I noticed a blue tinge in the lights around me. As I tried to identify the source, I saw the unmarked police car behind me, and I knew my goose was cooked. I put my hand up immediately, admitted my mistakes, and forty pounds and three penalty points later, I was on my way.

I was nearly home, so I went back early, a bit deflated.

The next night, all was forgotten, and out I went again. Would you believe it, same policeman, same spot, same outcome. He said, "Did ah no stoap you here last nite as weel?" Sheepishly, I acknowledged the truth, and I was off for an early bath.

The lesson was learned that second time. For a season, I was still young.

The mention of an early bath reminds me of playing rugby as a young boy. One week, I could not be bothered going on Saturday, so I stayed home at the children's home, watching TV and eating. On Monday at school, the gym teacher had me stand in front of the whole year and announce that I had not turned up because "I couldnae be bothered." I was dropped from the second fourteen to the bottom team, the sixth fourteen. That Saturday, I scored six tries as a prop. Loved it. I asked the same teacher if I could stay with this team, but the following week, I was in the first team at fourteen years old, with the other boys being sixteen to eighteen. Life is funny sometimes, hey?

Chapter 40

I think that summer on the Suzuki was one of the best of my young life. I worked long hours, enjoyed my time off, stayed clear of drugs, and only got drunk a few times. I traded the Suzy for a Yamaha 750 triple, shaft driven. It did not accelerate all that fast, but its top speed was over 120 mph.

At the end of that summer, still in my early twenties and living in Edinburgh, I decided to take a short break up to the Highlands of Scotland, where my foster father from the first Children's Home lived, in Glenfinnan. It was typical of me to decide in the middle of the night to go somewhere; I often acted spontaneously. A friend was coming with me this time. We planned to leave early in the morning to avoid traffic. Around 3.30 am, we loaded the bags onto my motorbike, put on all our leathers and protective gear, and eventually set off about 4 am. The journey would take around three hours at most, with some fantastic winding roads along the way.

The first part of the journey was motorway for about 40 to 50 miles. During this stretch, my friend on the pillion struggled to stay awake, and his crash helmet kept tapping the back of mine as his head nodded forward. It was a bit annoying and worrying for the winding sections ahead, where we needed to move together to take the challenging corners at speed. At one point it just so happened that he gave a big shove with the front of his helmet as he nearly fell asleep. My head moved forward, and my eyes glanced down at the controls. At that exact second it just so happened that the red oil warning light came on.

Instinctively, I yanked in the clutch and freewheeled to the hard shoulder. We had been travelling at around 120 mph, so it probably took close to a minute to get fully off the road and stop. Once we had stopped and dismounted, I released the clutch and checked for damage. The engine had seized. Had I not pulled in the clutch, we would have locked the back wheel at 120 mph and been lucky to survive the resulting chaos.

That red light and the clunking of helmets from my tired friend had possibly saved my life, or at least prevented serious and lasting injury. What a mystery life is sometimes.

Glenfinnan quickly became a refuge for me, and I loved spending random days off there with my foster father. We would work in his garden, chop down trees, swim in the river, eat like kings, and occasionally enjoy a home-brewed or pub-supplied beer. He was working on a school play, as he was a teacher by then, planning to take the children out on the road for the summer holidays, touring various villages and towns before ending up in Edinburgh for a week's run at the Fringe Festival, in a church just around the corner from where I had been born. In fact, I had attended Sunday school there as a very young boy. He asked me to help, and I agreed.

I took a few weeks off work and drove up to his house on a newly repaired Yamaha. (It turned out that the mechanic had not put enough oil in the bike before he sold it to me, so the repairs cost nothing—other than nearly my life, of course.)

I found myself in a large town hall during rehearsals and was ushered onto the stage as an extra in a song about to be performed. I was told to pick up the lines as we went. The play was a relational musical, really about nuclear waste dumping in the Highlands. The song started, and I tried to sing along, but none of the words made any sense. I awkwardly mouthed random words that hardly made sense even to me, sweating under the stage lights, wishing I had said no to the whole caper.

The song was in Gaelic, Scotland's national language, of which I knew not a word. Apparently, everyone on the theatre floor had been in on the joke and had a good laugh at my dreadful improvising.

And just like that, I was accepted. I was one of them.

My role on the road was to leave early with the van loaded full of the scenery, and to get that offloaded at the next venue and then organise food and accommodation the party of 34 that made up our gracious travelling troupe. I was away at 4am most days, and still up at 10pm loading the scenery, after being the starring extra role - I was given a line that got a laugh most nights. In one village we put the whole show on for one couple and we received a 10-minute standing ovation. In other locations we had full halls though and appreciative audiences. I was getting to know the children and through Iain my foster father I was starting to be fascinated with some poetry, even trying my own hand at writing some.

The Highland Tour came to its conclusion on the Island of Skye, the next stop was Edinburgh Festival after a weekend of rest.

Chapter 41

Glenfinnan became a safe haven for me, and I found myself drawn there to spend weekends or even days off with Iain. Iain and Carol had been my house-parents at the very first Children's Home I lived in. I saw Iain as my foster father, and that is how I tend to describe him.

Glenfinnan is a picturesque village, set at the head of a loch and a glen, with a now world-famous railway viaduct featured in the Harry Potter movies. I will have more to say about the people of the village later, but for now, everything was new. I loved going to the local pub with Iain, playing pool, and having just the one beer. I loved the fresh air and the countryside colours, with summer wildflowers making spectacular roadside displays long before "natural gardens" were a fad. I loved the sunlight pouring through the trees on forest walks, casting green-marbled light onto clearings that made me stop and feel comforted simply by being alive.

Carol and Iain had split up some time back, before I had truly reconnected with Iain, and he had met Joy. Joy was the best thing that ever happened to Iain. She brought laughter, life, and light into the house. Iain is no longer with us, passing away recently during the Covid pandemic, and I attended his funeral online, which, as so many of us know, just is not right. I was asked to write something for the funeral, and I have included that here to help readers see who Iain was and always will be to me.

I first met Iain when I was around 13 *years old* as he was the house parent in the children's home *I was in.* He had an ability to bring the best *out of* in all the children *in the home,* myself included.

Although we lost touch initially when the home *was* closed, we reconnected when I was around *20years old.* I would often *drive* up from Edinburgh in the early *morning* hours on my motorbike to visit *with* Iain in Glenfinnan. I think he was probably unaware of how much his *highland* hospitality, *that came so naturally to him, was impacting* me. In the middle of a life full of *crisis,* Iain's Innesfree was a refuge of safety and peace *for me.*

When Iain married Joy he found his *soul-mate* and *he* was a truly happy man. I was in the middle of a tough season in Edinburgh, and *Ian* and Joy invited me to *come and* live with them, with Joy *finding* me a job on the local fish farm.

My life was never the same - and the memories of those days in Glenfinnan are *so* precious.

Iain was passionate about helping others and *having fun in* life.

Iain's life *was marked by* difficult moments *as well, and* he never let *those get to* him, making light of things that would have floored *other people. Iain would* use his sense of humour on himself as quickly as on anyone else.

Iain had a great love of music and literature, and he was a gifted writer. *He would from* time to time pick up his guitar and play *and sing* songs he had written *that* were quite beautiful. He was *also* patient, as I lived out my fantasy as a gifted tambourine player.

I remember helping *Ian mixing* and *pouring* concrete under his house when he was finishing *building* it, hungover from a night at Innesfree, *stood* behind *a* concrete mixer *for* most of the day. I remember digging ditches for drains, both of us with tights over our heads to *try and stop* the encroaching *midge insanity.* I have vague memories of *home made* beer and wine and lost days. I remember nights of music, *and* food, and friends, where Iain and Joy helped me rediscover family, love, and hope. Most of all I remember Iain. *A* friend in *days* of trouble, whose friendship went *past* words *only, to* action and embrace. *I remember* Iain *as a man who* loved his garden and had the *required ability* and *tenacity* to create a beautiful space. *I remember Iain as a man who* loved people and had the *required* ability and tenacity to help the lost *cause*.

It was *such* a blessing *to* Wendy and *I* to have Iain and Joy *at* our wedding day.

I loved Iain, he was kind *to me, he was* in my childhood a safe father-figure, *and he* and Joy *impacted* my later life in *so many* ways that resonate *even now some* decades *further* on. *I'll* always treasure the memories of his friendship, the safety of Innesfree, and how *he and Joy* in some ways "adopted me" into their family when my life was *such a mess and so* patiently *helped* me back *onto* my feet.

Iain Morrison was a good man, a good friend, and a blessing to all who knew him.

I will miss you terribly Iain

With all that said, we return to the story, heading to Edinburgh in our hired van, scenery strapped down in the back, three of us jammed in the front, singing songs and teasing each other as the green summer miles rolled by, horizon-set mountains wishing us well on our adventures.

We got the thirty-plus youngsters settled into their dormitory accommodation and headed to the hall for rehearsals. Somehow, we were all flat, the spark was missing, and rehearsals were a struggle.

That night, during our first performance, dead-tired, I fell asleep on top of a backstage upright piano. I grunted myself awake at one point, saw the stage lights low, and jumped up, walking quickly onto the stage to grab scenery for a scene change. The low lights usually signalled a scene change.

But, oh dear, there was one part of the play where the low lights merely implied the passing of time. And this was it. The lights went up on cue, and there I was, the lone extra at the back of the stage, holding a piece of mobile scenery, a Highland backdrop if I remember correctly. As unobtrusively as possible, I slipped off the stage and curled up in the wings, laughing silently, the reaction helped along by tiredness and sheer fear of the stage.

The spirits of the whole troupe lifted, and we spluttered into life. Performances took on a new edge, and we could feel the audience leaning in, cheering the songs and laughing at the right moments. On the second night, there was a standing ovation in the packed hall, and we had turned the corner. We were tight as a group now, having been together for several weeks.

The final night came. The performance was solid, the audience lapped it up, the van was packed, youngsters' bags stuffed with laundry, and the buses and van headed off north. I was left behind in Edinburgh, and the loneliness that hit me was something entirely new. It was physical, a deep sadness low in my chest, inexpressible and unmoving.

Within days, I was back on drugs, drinking, and I gave up my job. My landlord told me the house was for sale and I would have to move. My Italian family had large gambling debts. Events were changing too fast for me.

Chapter 42

My motorcycle was fully paid for, so I kept hold of it and loved getting out along the coastal roads in the late sunset evenings. Beaches flashed past on my left as I curved around half-full caravan sites and sporadic, lonely golf courses shadowing me on my right. The shimmering tar-black road snaked into the far distance, the white lines becoming just a suggestion on sharper bends.

I loved getting the bike as far over on corners as possible, adjusting my body, helmet chin almost touching the petrol tank, leading knee stuck out as far as it would go. My centre of gravity pressed the machine into the tar, praying the rubber would hold its grip until it was time to straighten up again. Occasionally, the back tyre would slide, trying to come alongside the front, but I would wrestle the bike back into line, holding on for dear life, adrenaline keeping me sharp and focused. After a hard ride on the coast road, I was drained for hours.

I had started chamfering the end of the side stand, sparks trailing behind me as I overtook on tight bends.

One day, I had a bright idea. I thought to myself, "if ah take my side-stand off and jus use the middul stand, the bikeilbe lighter and ah'll get further over oan the bends." So I did. Needless to say, on the next ride out, I had a spectacular spill on a sharp bend, smashing my thigh against a fence post hidden in the short grass at the side of the narrow road. I howled in pain for three or four minutes, writhing and rolling on the verge. When the pain eased and I looked up through my foggy visor, I saw all four of my motorbike mates standing around my bike, deep in conversation. I slumped back into the grass, the pain receding, wondering what it would take for them to check if I was all right.

The bike needed repairs I could not afford. I was about to be homeless, and all my efforts to find somewhere new had failed. All I owned was a green haversack with some clothes and my helmet. I scraped together enough money somehow, got the bike repaired, then sold it as-is with the helmet. I advertised it as "Beautiful helmet for sale for six hundred pounds, free bike with helmet."

My friend Archie said I could sleep on the floor of his flat for a few weeks while I looked for somewhere to live. His two housemates were fine with it as well. They were both studying architecture at Edinburgh University. I worked cash-in-hand jobs wherever I could. I could not get housing benefit because I had no address. At my last place, I had eventually received housing benefit after a twelve-week wait, surviving on ten pounds a week after rent. The local authority had since changed the rules. One bloke superglued his hand to the counter in the office, the police arrived, we were all cleared out, and another day was lost. Tragic, really.

I applied for council housing as a homeless person. They told me to come back in a month. So I slipped into a kind of netherworld in central Edinburgh, sleeping on floors, using my green haversack as a pillow, working random days for cash. I started using drugs again, making it a daily habit to get drunk, stoned, and high with whatever money I had. My old friend paranoia returned, along with anxiety and depression. We had a reunion party, and afterwards I stayed home for days, sleeping on the floor.

I found an abandoned house on King Street in Edinburgh, top floor. I discovered the front door could be opened. Late at night, I crept upstairs and slept there. The ceiling joists were exposed, plaster missing from the walls, everything damp. Another homeless person moved into one of the rooms, and we became a sort of friends, staying up talking, taking drugs until sunrise, then sleeping all day. I barely ate, and when I did, I made myself sick afterwards. I am not sure why, but my self-image was in ruins. I was down to 69 kilos.

Sometimes, when I was alone, the small boy in me surfaced. I would curl up and cry, deep grief shaking my body, ugly sounds suppressed as best I could. The grief came in waves lasting thirty minutes at a time. I was inconsolable. Drugs took me away from it.

I took the overnight bus to London and stayed there for two weeks, sleeping rough, begging at railway stations, barely eating. I took two weeks' worth of drugs with me, along with my green haversack. One day, I went swimming at a local pool in a London suburb I will never remember. I do remember the cool water, floating and swimming, then the hot shower. Feeling clean felt like a luxury. That day, in my head, I was on holiday. Paranoia left me alone.

I took the overnight bus back to Edinburgh, only to find the squat I had been living in had suffered a fire and was burnt out. There was no living there now, even in desperation. I went back to the council offices, walking in the rain all day. They told me to come back tomorrow. I received an emergency payment of six pounds. I bought a pie, ate it, kept it down, and went to the railway station to sleep. I told the police I was catching the first train in the morning, as others were doing. They let me stay. That was a first. Maybe my luck was turning.

I returned to the council offices first thing, clothes stained and damp, hair matted, beard wild, skinny, paranoid, and intense. They offered me a vacant flat in a high-rise block on the outskirts of Edinburgh. It just so happened that the twin tower of the very place I had once gone to with a friend to defend his mum's honour. Irony, hey. What is the point?

Chapter 43

I was fourteen floors up. The flat next door was burnt out, windows boarded up with blistered smoke marks around the shabby pressed wood. The lifts were big enough for three people and their groceries, pale aluminium, with puddles of stale urine and used needles as decoration. They rarely worked, so that was less of an issue than one might think.

Inside my flat, there was nothing. Just grey linoleum, curled in places and stained in others. The windows looked out over nearby playing fields and other high-rise blocks.

I watched as local authority tradies spent half a day rebuilding a seven-foot concrete block wall at ground level. At lunchtime, they walked around the corner to their van. Barely out of sight, three youths ran from a back lane and kicked the still-soft wall over, disappearing again within thirty seconds. Three men's days of work destroyed. It felt like a perfect illustration of the pointlessness of everything.

It was summer. I opened the windows and lay sunbathing on the grey linoleum, shifting position as the sun moved around the building. Drugs were my default. I walked for miles through fields, back roads, and long highways into the city to score, then walked all the way home again. The journey took most of the day.

Sometimes, at a dealer's place, my paranoia would spike. There would be wads of cash, people constantly coming and going, razor-sized packets of white powder everywhere, and usually a few large, intense men who carried menace without saying or doing anything at all.

I still had friends in the city, so sometimes I would visit them, sitting in their small gardens stoned or high, talking rubbish until the evening shadows sent me homewards. After about a month of living with nothing, the local authority gave me a voucher for furniture. Certain second-hand shops would honour it and deliver. I got a worn turtle-green sofa and seat, vinyl cracked in places, a mottled four-ring electric cooker, and a small cream-coloured Russian-made fridge. There was a single divan bed with a thin new spring mattress still in its cellophane. I think there may have been a red Formica kitchen table and two uneven chairs. I was set.

It was nice to have somewhere to sit. I bought a small, heavy TV but had no licence. I took my chance, reasoning that nobody in their right mind was climbing fourteen flights of stairs to check on a TV licence.

Days passed that summer, working cash-in-hand at a café in a nearby suburb, across three fields and ten minutes on a green bus. Drugs, paranoia, loneliness, sadness, and boredom were constant companions. Between government handouts and a few days' work, I could afford my own home-brewed beer (and once, cider), drugs, and some food. I often went for long walks, sometimes the entire day, along the coast, windswept beaches, and through quiet, tree-lined, expensive-looking housing estates, occasionally buying a chocolate picnic bar to keep me company. I loved how chewy and crunchy they were.

A constant melancholy settled over my life. All I needed was some Orwellian victory gin, and I could be living the dream. I read a lot those days, my mind savouring the escape of a good story well told. Books through sleepless nights offered some solace, and as the sun crept up, I would finally fall asleep. My days were gradually becoming nights, and vice versa.

A couple of times, I managed to visit Glenfinnan. I would go up on the bus or train as soon as I had signed on for benefits, giving me a whole week before the process had to be repeated. I loved my visits there; my sanity was restored, and I slept well at night, safe, tired, and happy.

One day, we took Iain's car and a trailer to a local beach about twenty miles from his house. We loaded half a ton of fresh seaweed straight from the shore into the reversed trailer. Then up to the pub for a couple of beers, a game of pool, and a venison burger with chips. Back at the house, we forked the seaweed over the arable parts of the garden. The winter frost would break it down, and in spring the rotator would work it into the soil, the world's best fertiliser.

A phone line was installed in my Edinburgh house. Nobody called, and I had no one to call anyway. I had not even paid for outgoing calls.

But you never know; maybe one day there would be a call. And there was. My phone rang, the shrill bell startling me. I jerked off the floor, I had found I slept better on the floor than on the shallow spring mattress. I answered, expecting nothing. It just so happened that it was Joy.

"Iain and I have been talking, and we wondered if you would like to come and stay with us for a while," she said. "There are some jobs going up here on a fish farm, and I think I could help you get one of them." Her voice carried a slightly polished English tone. I needed no thought. I thanked Joy instantly and accepted. We arranged the timing, and she rang off. I stood there for a while before the tears came.

I had not realised just how loneliness had eaten at my soul. Lying solitary on my grey lino bed, crying myself to sleep, I had begged an unknown God that my doorbell would ring. Even Mormons and Jehovah's Witnesses found the place unwelcoming, the grey, harsh concrete warning off both the well-meaning and the foolish. Impatience settled on me as I thought about all I would have to do: walking into the city to tell the council, handing in keys, settling rent and electricity, removing furniture, and so on.

But an adventure beckoned. I loved Glenfinnan. I loved sitting in Iain and Joy's living room, staring out the huge rain-spattered window down the glen, mist rolling through the high trees, colours shifting with the light, never the same for two seconds. I had no idea what a fish farm was or what I might do there, but it sounded like honest outdoor work, and that in itself was exciting. I determined to stop using drugs; anyway, they would not be available in a village of around twenty houses.

It was Edinburgh Festival season, so one night I went into the city to meet friends, watch the fireworks, and say my goodbyes. The night was cloud-covered. We climbed Carlton Hill, hoping for a better view, but only reached the purple haze of clouds, uninspiring as they were. I told my friends where I was going. They looked at me as if I had told them I had eaten my own excrement the night before. They did not seem happy for me, which made my own happiness feel forced and strange. There were no hugs, no promises to keep in touch. The parting, when it came, was stilted, awkward, and chilly. I walked the several hours home feeling a little betrayed. Perhaps they were not really my friends after all. It was hard to believe; after everything we had shared.

I worked through the logistics as best I could, and three weeks later, I was boarding a train to Fort William. My life would never be the same again. There were so many adventures to come, friends to make, and dramas to unfold.

Chapter 44

Reflecting on Edinburgh was, in some ways, really enjoyable. Even today, returning brings a mixture of sadness and appreciation. It still feels very much like my hometown, even though it cared little for me in my struggles.

My early morning walks around Arthur's Seat, when I was often the only person there apart from a few shivering dog walkers in the parks below, involved timing how long they might stay before returning to the warmth of last night's embers, stoked again and fresh coal eventually added. Tuesday mornings in mid-February were spent walking around the botanical gardens, owning it with no-one else around, the occasional sound of a staff buggy breaking the illusion of millionaire status. I loved the warmth of the large greenhouse displays, pausing to stare at exotic plants, puzzled by the chilly reception when opening the cacti section.

Pots of Earl Grey tea with my friend Archie at Jenners, overlooking Princes Street Gardens, felt like living the dream. Enough money in our pockets for two second-hand books and a bag of hot chips with salt and sauce later. Hermitage walks, then up through the Blackford Hills into the Braids, no golf on Sundays, so the whole place was open to explore. I found lost golf balls as a young child there. Autumn colours stuck in my head, then flashes of winter: icing-sugar scenes, sledge rides down dusted fairways, cold butter on jam sandwiches consumed with energy and glee.

Trays of warm bread and freshly baked meat pies cooling in the back lane outside the all-night bakery. Taxi drivers lining up to buy their breakfast beside me as I, on my cycle, headed to Portobello Beach at 4 am to watch the sunrise over the waves, seeking moments of peace and fulfilment.

I wandered unknown houses searching for my next hit, asking, not wanting to sound desperate, "Do you have any speed or coke, maun eh?" Gargoyles lurked in the shadows, giving nothing away, but letting me know they were there.

Broken relationships, broken promises, broken hearts. Loneliness sat inside the front porch. No-one came. Hunger was a frequent companion, sleeping on benches, avoiding the police, drama unexpected, motorcycle friends, and tumbles. Edinburgh served me a generous slice of life, not always easy, rarely showing me a way forwards, but adding depth to the person I would become.

Leaving it behind was sad. Yet I knew the season there held no promise for the future. The helter-skelter would only take me downwards now. I had given it my best shot, full points for effort. My teachers would have nothing to add, simply "could do better," what a scholar's epitaph.

The 4 am train to Fort William was only half full, so I had four seats and a table to myself. I added a book and a homemade sandwich, thick with cheddar and butter on soft white bread. I luxuriated in anonymity. My adventure lay ahead, and I had made peace with my past, allowing forgiveness to release me from any hurt caused by my friends' lukewarm goodbyes. I was determined to leave drugs behind this time. It was a fresh start, a new me, a new season. Hope was my travelling companion as the sun rose over Rannoch Moor.

At Fort William, I changed onto the Mallaig train, next stop Glenfinnan Station. I think I had three pounds to my name and a green haversack holding well-worn underwear, a few t-shirts, and a pair of jeans. Everything else I owned was on me.

The Mallaig train was busy but not full, with lots of holidaymakers and families heading out for the day or to catch a ferry to the Isle of Skye. The mood was quiet as people settled in, wondering which side would hold the best views. The train pulled away in a series of slow shunts until its momentum became smooth and rhythmic. As we passed along Loch Eil, the late-morning mist that had been obscuring the sun began to clear, and warmth spread over the loch. The sun emerged afresh, and so did smiles. Children slid from their seats, running up and down the aisles. Doors clanged open and shut as travellers wandered through the three aged carriages. I picked up my book, re-entered the story, and felt happy, settled, and content simply enjoying the small everyday moments that had eluded me for so long.

We crossed the viaduct, the views down Loch Shiel opening up as the curved track swung the train around. The Glenfinnan Monument caught the sun briefly, all its features revealed for a moment before the train swung behind an embankment. The guard announced "Next stoap Glenfinnan." I was the only person to disembark. The whistle blew, and the train was gone from the platform before I was.

I made my way down the steep tar approach to the station, over the main road, and onto a dirt track that led past a wooden a-frame holiday house, which to my knowledge was never occupied. A narrow, moss-slick pedestrian footbridge crossed a stream, and another hundred yards along the path, set well up from the track on my left, was Innesfree, Iain and Joy's house. No car in the drive; it was clear they were at work. A note on the unlocked door welcomed me in and instructed me to help myself to breakfast.

I made toast and tea, sitting on the floor in front of their still-warm glass-fronted stove, staring at the view through the huge living-room window. This was my new home.

Chapter 45

I settled into my new home quickly. I had my own bedroom at the far end of the house. For the first few nights I found it difficult to sleep, and I realised it was because of the lack of noise. The total peace at night. No traffic, no shouting or screaming, no police cars or motorbikes cutting across playing fields while chasing helmetless youths on noisy little bikes. Just silence. Even the river was too far away to be heard.

I had an interview in a nearby village where fish farming was being established in the early 1980s. A small compound at the foot of threadbare hills held a tired-looking row of bungalows, offices, laboratories, and a fairly new packing shed. Behind these was a mechanical area and another compound where the salmon cages were constructed before being trucked to the various sites for assembly and eventual stocking with fish.

I was given a tour, starting at the ponds where the eggs were kept in carefully controlled conditions until they hatched, before being moved to freshwater sites in large tankers. The fish were fed and grown at these locations before their final transfer to seawater sites, again by truck and occasionally in large tarpaulins slung beneath helicopters.

The interview was brief and straightforward. The next day I was offered a start as a "farm assistant". I remember my confusion when I phoned the local bank, remember when we could do that, to set up an account for my wages. The woman on the other end kept asking which chemist I worked for. Eventually it dawned on both of us that I was not a pharmacist but a farm assistant, and we shared a good laugh over the phone.

The pay was good, but I had debts to clear in Edinburgh, so it would be two or three months before I had any disposable income, probably not a bad thing.

I learned the seafood business from the ground up. Initially, I was put in the packing shed, filling bins with ice from the ice plant in preparation for packing the harvest when it arrived, or loading ice onto a lorry heading out to one of the fish farms. We then washed the giant bins used to store harvested fish, around 350 kilos per bin. Some days I spent hours outside with a high-pressure washer and chemicals, cleaning slime and sea lice from the white harvest bins.

When the harvest came in, we graded the salmon by weight and packed them for customers all over the UK. The fish were hand-gutted and packed into polystyrene boxes with ice flakes, then handballed onto plastic pallets, as no wood was allowed in the factory. We learned every part of the operation. At night, I often stayed back for overtime, loading the packed 30-kilo boxes by hand onto flatbed trailers, then sheeting and roping the forty-foot trailers ready to be hitched and sent out.

At weekends, I helped build the wooden and polystyrene cage sections for the farms. I also loaded harvest trucks with ice and empty bins, tarpaulined and roped them down, so all the driver had to do on Sunday night or early Monday morning was check the ropes and head off to the fish farm site for harvesting. There were around thirty sites, many of them several hours away.

The work was physical and enjoyable. The craic among the team was usually good, with plenty of practical jokes, horseplay, and wind-ups. We played cards during breaks, or sometimes football if the weather and surroundings allowed. We ate as if food might run out, and day by day we grew stronger and more resilient.

I was finding my place, working, eating, sleeping, and being part of a family with Iain and Joy. Three months into the season my Edinburgh debts were cleared and I finally had wages that were mine. You can guess what happened next. I got royally drunk, made a fool of myself, and did not make it home for two days. During those drunken days I discovered that it just so happened one of our nearest neighbour was dealing drugs, mostly hash, but sometimes speed and cocaine. They used and dealt. This was not what I had expected at all, and it was a major setback for me at that point.

Chapter 46

Loneliness seemed to live inside me, dim at times, but ready to ambush me when I least expected it. Sometimes I sought out solitude, and that was healthy. I wandered through forests, searching for small clearings where I could sit and simply be. I climbed mountains, absorbed in the effort of the ascent, with nothing else existing, sometimes alone and sometimes with a friend. I tried to find contentment in those moments, but in the background, like malicious software, loneliness persisted.

With the benefit of hindsight, I can see that loneliness travelled alongside a constant fear of rejection. My wild behaviour, drunkenness, and even drug use were attempts to fit into something I was never meant to belong to.

The local inn near the fish farm shore base was nicknamed "the Gluepot", because once you went through those doors you entered a parallel universe. There was little police presence at night unless they were called, and even then it could take over an hour for them to arrive. I once came across a serious motorbike accident, with the young rider face down on rocks, every breath a rasping struggle. The ambulance took forty minutes to arrive, and tragically, the driver was the rider's father.

Back to the Gluepot. We had lock-ins, the bar open until 4 am, front lights off, but inside and around the back it was like a fairground. The bar was often unattended, others took over the bar and the till. Sometimes prices were inflated if they felt fond of the landlord, and sometimes prices were ignored altogether, just because they could. Either way, no one complained. We just ordered and drank.

The landlord, Alex, was an ex-accountant and full of dry, cutting sayings, such as greeting the early morning with, "Close your eyes before you bleed to death."

I saw people sleeping in the strangest positions, that looked impossible to me, but there they were, fast asleep in some sort of reverse plank, heels dug into the well worn carpet, and head on the bench seat, but well off the ground, fast asleep. Drugs were common currency, grass, magic mushrooms, speed and cocaine were the usual offerings, and I went back into this world with a vengeance. I turned to Gin and Bitter Lemon as my drink after five or six pints of beer, and it felt like I could drink this mix endlessly without becoming incoherent, whereas nights spent of 120 proof Whisky "As We Get It" usually did not end well for me or others.

I was given to exaggeration, even lying at times. Although a couple of times I lied when seriously drunk, and I do not remember telling the lie, but the repercussions were real in the following weeks.

I was living two and half lives. One was work. I worked ferociously hard, physically draining fourteen-hour days, sometimes seven days a week, although weekends were more often six-hour shifts. I earned and wasted enough money to buy a house. Some days I was in the pub at lunchtime. On one occasion, I drove the forklift straight through a massive walk-in chiller door. The door ended up impaled on the forks, and when I reversed it came off the top runner, swinging wildly. I shouted at the supervisor that the forklift brakes were terrible and that we had been saying so for ages. There was a grain of truth in that, but my afternoon beers were the real cause.

I needed drugs just to feel normal. What had once been recreational was becoming essential for everyday functioning.

The second life was me alone at night, getting stoned enough to fall into a heavy sleep. Paranoia became my constant companion. Outside of work, I was a mess. I tried to hold things together, but some weekends I retreated to my bedroom on Friday afternoon and did not emerge until midnight on Sunday, surfacing only for a cup of tea. Something ordinary.

The tension between these two lives never eased. I found myself living in a land of intentions, judging others by their actions and myself by what I meant to do. I intended to stop drinking. I intended to stop using drugs. I intended to be kinder to those who tried to befriend me. Yet I had a default setting that pushed people away.

My mind was in chaos. I had thoughts of harming others that felt more like impulses than passing ideas. I wished someone could tie me to my bed at night so those urges could never be acted upon. Instead, I used more drugs and alcohol to knock myself out, which only added fuel to the fire the next night.

I was not wise enough to recognise that I needed help, and probably too proud to accept it even if it had been offered. I told myself I would be better tomorrow, and that belief carried me through.

My half life was those random weeks when I actually stopped drinking and taking drugs. When I ate with Iain and Joy, cooked for them, helped around the house and garden, and did ordinary things like swimming in the river or going out for a run. There was a beautiful road that ran around the far side of Loch Shiel. It was gated and used only by the post van or emergency vehicles. I would run there for miles on my own, not wanting to turn back, yet always aware of my limits.

The mountains were sometimes reflected in the still water, their colours changing with the seasons, from deep green to brownish yellow, as hidden rocky surfaces re-emerged for their winter frosting. I pushed myself so hard that when I finally stopped back at the front door, I would dry retch for two or three minutes. My half life was my favourite, but also the most elusive part of my existence.

I was promoted at work to team leader. The tension between my work and private life grew in widening circles around me. I became moody and at times explosive, even threatening one staff member with violence when he refused to follow my instructions. I bought a motorbike, a Yamaha 500 single-cylinder off-road bike. I had a love-hate relationship with it. It only had a kick start and on cold mornings it regularly bruised my ankle and calf with kickbacks. It was a dirty white colour, tall and rugged, and brilliant for off-road exploring. I would ride it down to the rocky shoreline at times and mess around for hours, loving the feeling of being at one with the machine over uneven ground.

Iain and Joy were incredibly good to me. They were a constant blessing, showering me with acceptance and kindness. We had nights filled with songs, joined by their friends and people from the village, each with their own caricature and larger-than-life quirks. Iain and Joy had an excellent sound system with speakers in their bedroom. One night, a friend of theirs came back from the local pub and dropped in after we were all in bed. This was not unusual, as doors were often left unlocked and cars frequently had keys in the ignition.

He put some music on, Bat Out of Hell on the turntable, and when it was too quiet for his liking, he adjusted the controls, accidentally switching the sound to Iain and Joy's bedroom. He cranked the volume and nearly gave them both a post-midnight heart attack. Another neighbour stayed up all night with a bottle of whisky and his gun, trying to catch a deer that had been eating his plants. I think the intention was to scare it off rather than shoot it. Half a bottle of whisky later, around 3 am, he shot out his own front window after mistaking his reflection for the deer.

Speaking of deer, venison was plentiful. We could swap fish farm salmon kilo for kilo for venison, and with our heavy discount on salmon, both were regular dinner staples.

My time living with Iain and Joy came to an end. I loved staying there, and if I had used some common sense I would have stayed much longer and strengthened my half life, perhaps turning it into something healthier. Instead, I was offered a room in a bothy, a run-down building adapted for shared use, close to where we worked. Two of my closest friends lived there as well, and the drug and alcohol scene was intense. So I packed my trusty green haversack, loaded my bike, and set off for the next season.

Chapter 47

My season living in Glenfinnan was full of adventure and drama, despite my own struggles and mental health issues. I remember coming home from the pub one night around 2 am. It was January, with remnants of the latest snowfall still clinging to the ground, and puddles in the rutted track freezing overnight. The full moon lit my way home, and although I was weaving slightly, I managed to stay upright and out of the ditch, steadying myself whenever I stepped on ice.

I had recently purchased a Honda CX 500 motorbike, a V-twin, water-cooled beast. I think I liked the idea of a V-twin but could not afford a Moto Guzzi at the time. It was a solid bike and looked quite striking, but performance-wise it was slow off the mark, awkward on tight bends, and lacked top-end speed. Still, it looked the part.

Drunk or not, I decided to ride out to the next village, around ten miles through uninhabited wilderness. I pushed the bike off its stand and down the path until I was far enough from Innesfree not to wake anyone when starting it. Then I set off, wearing only a T-shirt, jeans, and no helmet.

At the highest point on the road, between Loch Shiel and Loch Eilt, near the railway tunnel, I hit ice while coming around a bend and went down hard. My head struck the road and I felt the skin tear away against the tar on the left side of my scalp. The bike slid into a lay-by, headlight blazing into the darkness, engine screaming. I staggered over, worried about the bike, and flicked the off switch. Silence followed. Clouds swallowed the moon. Blood dripped onto my white T-shirt. It was minus ten degrees.

I sat down on the frozen, tundra-like ground. I was dazed, but I knew I was in trouble. I was five miles from either village, injured and poorly dressed. I sat there for five to ten minutes. There would be no traffic at that hour. The next car would likely be two or three hours away, when early commuters began their journeys.

Then, slowly and dreamlike, a light appeared at the far corner of the road. An old station wagon came around the bend, yellow headlights dipped, barely cutting through the darkness. The car stopped and Mrs Cameron Head appeared beside me. She was the local estate owner and lived at Lochailort Castle. She was about eighty years old, dressed in tweeds and always ramrod straight. She helped me into the back seat and drove me to get help.

I later discovered that it just so happened she had heard what she thought was a gunshot around ten minutes before my crash. Believing poachers were hunting her deer, she had fearlessly set out in the early hours to confront them, armed only with her walking stick and natural authority.

She took me to Lochailort, where they laid me across the bar benches and called an ambulance. Around two hours later I was lying on a white-sheeted table while a doctor picked gravel from my scalp and stitched what he could. I was put on hourly checks for the rest of the night. Iain and Joy collected a remorseful and self-pitying Allan the next morning, and I stayed home for a week or two recovering.

The CX 500 was brought back to Glenfinnan and sat on a concrete block intended one day as a shed base. It stayed there for around six months until a passing mailman offered a salvage price, hoping to restore it.

That New Year in Glenfinnan, I decided to help restock the woodpile. I went up behind the house to fell a couple of fast-growing silver birch trees. Wearing my wellies and working hard, I cut right through the trunk, yet the tree did not fall. I started a new cut and felt a strange numbness in my chest. Then I heard faint shouting. Turning around, I saw Iain and Joy waving wildly and pointing above my head.

The tree was lying across the main overhead power line. A large bright yellow ball hovered above me, rumbling and crackling ominously. Thirteen thousand volts were arcing through the lines, the tree itself burning in places. I abandoned the chainsaw in the trunk and ran across the swampy ground towards safety, not stopping to find the driest route. Both wellies came off at different points, leaving me scrambling in muddy socks as a new sun flared above the power line before it finally shorted out, cutting electricity to the entire peninsula.

An hour later I sat trembling in a hot bath. But for those faint shouts, it just so happened I might have been dead. Workers came and removed the tree, and later that day full power was restored. The story, however, was retold many times.

There were some beautiful moments as well. A good friend had built his house right on the shore of Loch Shiel, and he had a canoe he was happy for me to borrow. On cool, clear summer mornings at 5 am, I would be out in the middle of the loch, paddling hard, then stopping, leaning back, arms trailing in the deliciously cool water, drifting, entranced by reflections that seemed to go on forever. The mist would slowly lift, and the sun would begin to glance across the surface as I made my way back to the shore, returning the canoe to its resting place, satisfied with my secret time.

I played soccer in the summer for Acharacle when I was selected, and five-a-side throughout the winter was one of my favourite nights of the week. The soccer was full-on competitive, and people did get hurt. The five-a-side was mostly for fun, good-natured, and usually finished with a beer and a Chinese takeaway. We became a close-knit group, travelling into town every Thursday to play in the concrete-floored old school hall, and returning to our villages with hot food in the car, the smell making us all hungry again. One of my best friends at the time was John Thomas, and his wife Marlene used to trim my beard with scissors every month or so, after we had eaten our takeaway at their house. These are genuinely happy memories. I still treasure my times with this family, John, Marlene, and their three young girls, we had so many moments of fun and laughter.

I had also grown to love squash, even though my first ever game with my college lecturer in Edinburgh had been a disaster. There were three courts in the local town, and one of the things I was passionate about was engaging in a full-on battle on the squash court. Nothing else existed when I was playing, and that was half the appeal. I would play double sessions several times a week, as well as soccer, five-a-side, and regularly go out by myself for three- or four-mile hill runs. I loved where my mind went while running; it gave me a sense of peace, what felt like true inner calm at times. With just the rhythmic sound of my breathing in my ears, I savoured the colours of the spruce trees, the smell of bursting cedar sap, and the enchanting deep peaty hues of the small streams I sometimes ran alongside.

There was a constant struggle between my healthy routines and the weeks or months when drugs and alcohol would drag me under. Each time I pushed myself back into a healthier pattern, it would last until I felt better, and then I would fall again into Allan's merry-go-round of disaster and recovery.

Now I was moving to Lochailort, thinking I was heading towards freedom. In reality, the guard rails were being removed and the stabilisers were being benched. Not good, really not good.

Chapter 48

Living in Lochailort took me back to my college days in Edinburgh, reigniting a passion for climbing local mountains in all seasons.

It was early on a Saturday morning. I worked during the week, sometimes on weekends too, but not today. Today I had a day off. The sun was up, the sky a clear blue, and hardly a sound could be heard. As I stepped quietly out the front door, there was only the faint murmur of the river in the distance and the occasional chirp from an early bird, but even they were mostly silent this morning. The village was a slow starter on most days, but Saturdays were generally even slower. Mind you, it was 4 am.

There is a story about a couple of Spanish visitors to Scotland who were down at the shore talking with two local old men repairing their nets. The Spanish visitors said to the men, "We have a saying in our country, 'mañana, mañana!' which means tomorrow, we do it tomorrow." They asked the men if there was anything similar in the Highlands. The story goes that the two locals rubbed their beards slowly for a minute or two in deep thought before replying, "No, nothing as urgent as that." That was my village on Saturdays for sure.

I had stealthily packed a bag with some food, filled a flask with hot soup, grabbed my climbing boots, and tied a warm jersey around my waist. Out the door I went, walking briskly in the chilly morning air.

I was heading for a climb to a local hill, Sgurr an Utha. The approach began with a short walk along a forest road, then I took the straight-up-the-side route, no fussing about today finding the easiest way. It was steep in places; I can still remember gripping at rocks, looking straight down between my legs at the tiny black strip of road below. Breathing hard, loving every moment, I kept pushing until I reached the summit.

It was still early when I arrived at the top. The sky was blue, completely silent, still. The view stretched out to the Atlantic Ocean and the remote inland glens. I lay on my back in the fresh summer grass, staring up at the sky. After a few minutes I noticed a small speck in my eye and kept rubbing it, but it stubbornly remained.

Lying still, I realised the speck was actually a golden eagle, soaring high above me on the morning air currents as the sun warmed the earth. It could see much further than I ever could, and spot a mouse moving through the long grass beside me. It just so happened this image stayed with me as an image relevant to my life from that day onwards.

I continued, descending to gain height for a second climb, sliding and scrambling where the terrain allowed, boots earning their keep. I passed two small glassy lochs to find the next route. Mist drifted through the trees higher up. Grey skies with flecks of pink, like uniquely Scottish opal. My mind was slowly clearing, thoughts clinging to the thrill of climbing for the day. No one else was around; only the occasional call of a curlew or oyster catcher drifted on the breeze. The nearest house was five miles away.

I traversed the hill-loch shores, knee-deep in fresh green grass, the occasional fern fighting for its place. I paused to breathe, to just be. Looking out over the glassy water, tiny islands dotted with Caledonian pines stood at attention, burnished copper bark reflecting the pink morning light. They would glow even brighter later as the sun completed its daily mission.

Each tree was planted to honour a fallen comrade who had given all so that others might be free. My thoughts drifted to my own family and loss. With a purposeful shake of my head, I turned to the waiting mountain and started the lung-testing, thigh-burning climb.

There were days like this when I felt like a survivor. But so many more were days when I felt like a victim, an addict, or a headcase (I think it is okay to say that about myself).

I remember standing in the stores awaiting a new pair of wellies for working on the fish farm. My old ones were worn through. I was handed a pair of black Dunlop wellies with rock-hard green soles. I explained to the storeman that I wanted the white wellies with soft soles as we often stood in one spot for hours at a time. He shrugged and walked away. He had a reputation for thinking the stores were all his, so I assumed the white ones cost more.

I took the black pair and slipped them on, then rode my motorbike up and down the nearby main road for five or ten minutes, feet on the ground until the hard green soles were almost worn down. Parking in front of his window, I returned the black wellies, saying, "Not really that good." He handed me a white pair, but by then we were somewhat enemies.

I was stoned most nights and, increasingly, even some days. The tension between my work life and personal life was escalating. Anxiety, paranoia, and explosive, irrational anger were constant companions that had to be medicated regularly. Relationships suffered. I would go out with a girl and then avoid her for weeks as paranoia filled my mind. I started having thoughts of suicide. With my friends, I pretended every day to be the life of the party. We went to Amsterdam on holiday, and I hated it, while they all seemed to love it. I was deep in paranoia. Thoughts of self-harm were relentless, and the most worrying part was that no amount of drugs or alcohol brought relief, in fact, they made everything worse.

I began to hide away at night and moved to a small cottage. It had a wood-burning stove for cooking and heating, one small living/dining area, and a single and double bedroom. It was damp. For seven months of the year, the sun was behind the mountains, leaving the cottage in shade.

The World Cup (soccer) was on that year, and Scotland had qualified, but there was no TV signal in our village. My so-called enemy, the storeman, said that if someone carried a roll of cable to the top of the mountain behind the village, he would put up an aerial and run the cable back to the village to connect to the existing system. He was something of a genius with anything electrical or electronic. So my best mate Quint and I set off one Saturday afternoon with the reel of cable on its wooden roller, a stick through the middle, wearing our work overalls to climb the mountain. It would have been very early May, I think.

At around 1500–2000 feet, we hit deep snow and a fresh blizzard blowing in off the Atlantic. For every three steps forward, we slipped back one or two. The snow was waist-deep in places, the cold wind cutting straight through our fish farm overalls. With sheer grit we kept going, it was pride now more than any hope that Scotland might do well in a global competition. We made it, dumped the reel at the summit, and hurried back down to the snow line and onto grass and moss. Once out of the wind, we collapsed, hands on knees, giggling hysterically for around five minutes.

On another occasion, out in a small boat on a steel-grey water and sky day, fishing with a close friend, I tried to open up about my fears, paranoia, and anxiety. He made a funny comment to my first attempt, and I abandoned the conversation, turning instead to humour as camouflage. I believed that even my closest friends could not help me. I would keep being the life of the party, even while I was dying inside. It was not sustainable, though I probably did not fully realise that. The only option I could see was to keep going.

Chapter 49

Living in Lochailort held rich and wild memories at times. Like cutting the first steak from a local venison haunch and cooking it in my salt-and oil-seasoned cast iron frying pan, a gift from my friend Raymond, on top of my wood-burning Aga stove. The inside of the Aga fire door glowed and pinged with the heat of freshly cut local wood. The whole cottage was warm.

My neighbour Annie would drop off warm pancakes and soup every Sunday morning. Pancakes wrapped in tinfoil would sit on the kitchen counter in my entranceway when I finally stirred to life. The humanity in these gestures helped me stay sane when hangover and withdrawal clawed like stealthy wolves at my throat.

I spent low-tide days scouring the foreshore, hoping to find oysters I could sell for cash, dreaming that spring tides might reveal a hidden bed. I climbed mountains for the sheer thrill, on warm summer days and frozen winter mornings, feeling alive as I clattered back down to the pub.

There were lost days of alcohol, hazy, moments of madness with friends, all piling on top of each other, destroying sofas in our wake, believing I could live like this forever. I went to the city to watch Rangers play Celtic, driving home drunk, nose pressed to the window, with no license and no heating, while everyone else slept in a pile in the back seat, disregarding seatbelts and social order alike.

I accidentally hit Quint's nose with a mock punch, blood spattering across wallpaper and radiator, trying not to laugh the next day as his nose whistled all the way up our chosen mountain, through clean white snow.

Then came the terrors. An overwhelming desire to drive my BMW 650cc motorbike into oncoming traffic. Paranoia that lasted for weeks at a time. I tried going to a local church on a Sunday, thinking maybe there could be help there, only to find the same people from the pub on Saturday night, singing different songs, wearing different clothes. New songs and clothes could not fix what was missing inside me. Back to the cottage, stoned again until I passed out, seeking some kind of temporary relief.

Work was going well. I was promoted and eventually moved to a brand-new factory in the nearest town. I passed my driving test and bought a small car as I now had to drive eighty miles a day in all weathers. My mental health problems intensified. At times I felt compelled to drive off the road or into oncoming traffic. The cost of these mental battles was overwhelming. I felt drained, afraid to go anywhere, unwilling to face panic attacks, anxiety, and the confusion that lived inside me.

I could not maintain any relationships with the women I tried to date. I could not, or would not, explain what was happening inside me, playing the expected role while tension gnawed at my soul. My unseen life was disintegrating. I carried a heavy, growing pain in my heart each day, more clumsy and unbearable than the last. I tried confiding in a friend. He patted me on the shoulder and said, "You'll be alright," and went off with his girlfriend.

I was lost. Years of drugs and alcohol, undiagnosed mental struggles, unsupported and unconfessed, were unraveling me. On a climb, my safe "go-to" activity, I was suddenly gripped by fresh anxiety and an overwhelming urge to throw myself over a steep cliff, a thousand-foot drop below. I panicked and ran down the hill. What could I do, now that even my refuge was gone?

My thirtieth birthday had passed unnoticed that week. I was at the end of my strength to resist the constant pressure to harm myself. Some internal self-destruct sequence had been triggered, and no matter how I struggled, I could not find the off switch. In movies, there would be a red wire, a pair of clippers, a hero, a woman in distress. The wire would be clipped, the woman rescued, and they would walk into sunlight, into a perfect future, drinking coffee, smiling their flawless smiles. I had the wrong script. No red wire. A toothbrush instead of clippers. The scenery all wrong. Everything was a-kilter, unrescuable. None of my life made sense.

I knew that day I was in trouble. I felt like I might kill myself, and although I recognised the thought as crazy, I had no power left to resist it. I was deeply worried. It seemed inevitable. I had been heading to this point for a long time, and I was always going to end up here, suicidal and hopeless.

Chapter 50

So here I was, a dog-day Saturday, grey cloud low on the hills, raining on and off, wind-blown, no point going anywhere. If I was well, this would be a good day to make a tray of tea and biscuits, take them through to the bedroom and curl up with either a good book or watch a black and white Sherlock Holmes film, Basil Rathbone, by far the best Sherlock ever in my thinking.

But I was not well, although I could not explain what was wrong with me. There was a malaise, a sickness in my soul, bringing a weight I could not carry. Emotional baggage? I had the whole terminal.

I needed to sleep. I had convinced myself that if I could just sleep, then tomorrow this pain would be bearable. But the one thing that eluded me was sleep. Impossible to find in the midst of paranoia, pain, and purposelessness. I was in a fight for my life. There would be no dramatic jump into oblivion for me. I had already faced that temptation and run. Driving across the road into oncoming traffic was blocked by the thought of the poor unsuspecting others.

Most likely a handful of pills, some alcohol, and sleep into oblivion, the rest I so desperately needed for my exhausted mind, soul, and emotions, surely lay on the other side. I could not carry this one more day, of that I was certain.

But still I put up a fight. Maybe if I went running I would get so tired that I would sleep. So I changed, and in that chilling grey fine rain, I ran, and ran. Physically I was done. Mentally, no relief on the horizon, no cavalry bugle sounded, just the unbearable, internal, indescribable pain. Running had been a joy and a great escape not all that long ago. Drugs and alcohol had brought consistent oblivion up until a few weeks back. Even getting clean for a few weeks was worth the distressful sojourn from time to time. But today there was no panacea, no obvious option.

I paced up and down outside my cottage, shivering in my running shorts and vest, but the cold seemed like such a trivial inconvenience when my life was on the line.

The sound of the sea on rocks was faint in the distance when the wind dropped. Seagulls whirled up high, occasionally screaming like a tortured soul. I saw a cat slink under a dilapidated shed, grass worn a dirty yellow by winter, mud oozing at the edges. The shell of what had been a white car sat raised on old railway sleepers in the mid-distance, blurred by the rain but known to my memory. My motorbike stood silent and lonely beside the end of the ash lime roadway. The Mini Cooper I had swapped for a two and a half kilo salmon was parked by the bothy, the rear end exposed.

My friends were occupied, out of reach, somehow marked off-limits after a few fumbled attempts to be me. Churches had been visited and left me with less hope than when I entered. Where was my solace, my help, my hope? I was empty, desperate, sad, alone, tired, and scared.

The tears were a surprise when they came, rushing all at once to the surface, finding expression in ugly sounds, half-wretch and half-sob, nose running freely, swept around in the swirly wind. Hands on knees, feeling the tiny drops of rain drip from my knuckles. Rain and tears mixed with snot hung from my beard as the sobs went longer and deeper than I thought was possible. I had not cried like this for years.

I leaned against the external walls of my tiny cottage. It just so happened that they were whitewashed. Whitewashing has a purpose, but it is not good when covering over deep flaws. You can only go so long before they surface again. An echo from Ecclesiastes, "meaningless, everything is meaningless", was in my soul. I was swamped with a sense of meaninglessness, of "what's the point?".

From seemingly nowhere and with no warning, a desperate cry escaped my lips. "Jesus, please help me." The words were out without my permission. But even as they made themselves known, a warm, comforting power flowed through my whole being, body, soul, emotions, mind, every part of me touched by this ethereal embrace. Something was happening, something out of my control, unexpected, unexplained, unmerited.

Time was difficult to understand, but it felt instant. Instantly I knew I was ok. Instantly I knew that I would never need drugs or drink again.

Instantly I sensed a comfort living inside me. The power settled on me, reassuring, warm like the best feeling of love in the whole world. Accepted as I am, loved as I am, healed, given a second chance. The tears had transformed from anguish to acceptance, from fear to faith, and from despair to delight. I was crying new tears, tears of peace, tears of unexpected salvation.

It had to be God, to be Jesus. He had somehow found me, standing alone in the rain, shivering, at the end of myself, looking out over the Atlantic Ocean from the doorstep of a tiny white cottage on the rugged coast of the Scottish Highlands. There he had met with me, just me and Him, alone for a few moments while he restored what had been lost and begun a whole new chapter.

Chapter 51

I knew that something foundational, fundamental, had just happened. I was not sure how to explain it, even to myself. I had cried out for help in desperation to Jesus, and it seemed to me like he had not only heard my cry, but had answered me by doing something in me that felt amazing and brought some sort of healing.

I was still standing alone, outside my cottage, in my running shorts and vest, in the rain, still shivering, but no longer felt that crushing emotional pain inside me, and no longer felt any hunger or need for drugs or alcohol.

I walked up and down to try and keep warm as I thought about what I should do next. I sensed a strong need to tell someone about what had just happened to me, but who? Who could I speak to? None of my existing friends sprang to mind. If I could not tell them about my mental health struggles, addictions, and irrational thinking, how on earth would any of this make sense to them?

I thought about a couple that I knew from work. I did not know them all that well, but I thought that perhaps they might be Christians rather than church attenders. They seemed really happy all the time, even although they had challenges in life for sure and had little income. They were not like the people I had seen in the traditional churches where I had gone searching for help in the last few months. I am not judging those people, merely stating what I found. I found people consumed with their own affairs, who did not recognise a lost soul in their midst, who gave no invitation to meet with Jesus in their service, and who allowed me to walk back out the doors to my torment and suicidal thoughts.

But this couple, maybe they knew something about Jesus, and maybe they could help me make sense of what had just happened. I could not think of anything else, or anyone else, that I could reach out to, even if it would be a little awkward to contact a couple that I barely knew.

So I changed, warmed myself up, and just as the light of the day was fading into darkness, that time called the gloaming, I sat astride my motorbike and headed the 30 miles along the quiet country road back to the nearest town where Sammy and Chatty lived. They had used to stay not far from my village, and Sammy had in the past worked as a fisherman on the local boats, but I believed that now they lived in town and had more steady work there.

Around an hour later I was parking my motorbike at the top of the hill behind the main town, in a fairly densely populated housing estate that was bordered by bare hill and moor. The surroundings felt bleak to me in that moment, although the random lights in windows all around looked more inviting.

Walking up the path towards the door, I had two thoughts. I hoped this was the right house, and I had no idea what I would say. How would I even start the conversation? I did think about stopping, turning back, and going home, but that route seemed to hold more difficult questions than the door before me right now. How would I ever work out what to do, what had happened to me, if I turned back now?

So there in the dark, standing outside a stranger's door in my motorbike gear, I hesitated for a few seconds as I gathered my thoughts. There was no turning around now.

I knocked. It was late on a Sunday evening and the outside light was not on. I heard muffled sounds of movement within, and dulled voices exchanging words that were not clear to me. Then the door opened and Sammy stood inside. He recognised me and his Highland hospitality swung into action. "Come away in, man," he said, standing aside to let me past. I walked into the warmth of the hallway and around into the living room, where his wife Chatty was rising from her seat to see who this visitor could be.

I apologised for my intrusion. "Ah'm so sorry to cum to yer door unexpected like this," was my opening. "Ah just coodnae think of who else I cood speak to."

"Come in and hay a seat, can ah get yeh a cuppa?" came the reply. I was safe. I sat and made small talk as the tea and toast were prepared and presented. I was treated as if I was an expected guest and made to feel so welcome, even although I was sure I was intruding on rare family time for them as a couple, as they had four or five kids in this three-bedroom council house. This would be called commission housing in Australia.

As we sat to have tea, I started to tell them my story of what had happened to me at Lochailort earlier in the day. They listened and asked questions. I asked them for their thoughts as I wound up my story, and I had not gone into much detail about my past struggles, just that I had been really struggling, and then the story of what happened as I stood outside my cottage.

Sammy brought through his Bible from another part of the house and started to slowly explain to me what the Bible said about sin, forgiveness, and calling out for help from Jesus. It all tied in. What I experienced was all in the book written a long time ago. Sammy and Chatty talked to me about prayer and how prayer worked, how simple it was. I remembered some Mormons in Edinburgh that I met at the park when I was young, and how they had talked to me about prayer as well. I had been quite interested in what they said, and they seemed so outgoing, always playing sport and enjoying life, that I had for a few days considered their ways. But when they told me about a guy called Joseph Smith and some golden tablets, or something like that, I cut myself off from them, thinking that they must be crazy if they thought I would believe that.

This time there was no Joe Smith, no golden tablets, just Jesus on a cross, paying for my sins. It made sense. I knew there was a debt to pay that I could never pay for all my wrongdoing, the hurt I had caused so many people, my poor choices, my deliberate actions, not to mention the mess of my thought life, full of unhealthy fantasies and worrying thoughts of harming myself or others. I knew that I needed forgiveness from God and from so many people. I knew without a doubt that I was a sinner and needed what only Jesus had, and the experience I had of his presence, his power, and his love for me just a few hours earlier proved to me that He was alive and that He was real.

I prayed the sinner's prayer, confessing all my sin, all my need of Jesus, asking for his forgiveness and healing, and committing myself to allowing him to lead my life from that moment forwards. I thanked him for saving me. It felt natural to pray, something that a few hours earlier would have seemed bizarre perhaps.

They went to bed, telling me to sleep on the sofa and bringing fresh warm bedding. I stayed up all night in their living room praying, reading the Bible until around 5 am, when they appeared again in the kitchen making tea and toast with marmalade. We chatted in the harsher morning light, shadows thrown on tired faces, but the sound of cutlery and crockery bringing a sense of peace and domestic contentment. Kids appeared, bleary-eyed and in flannel pyjamas, reaching for toast with mechanical regularity.

Voices were kept low and conversation was broken as tea was slurped and toast buttered. I left around thirty minutes later, my motorbike sweeping down the long curve of the hill with ease, heading back to Lochailort. I would go to work that day as well. I worked at Lochailort, but Sammy and Chatty both worked in the town, for the same company as me, in the company's brand new factory.

Chapter 52

I was overwhelmed with the emotion of hope and a sense of peace and purpose, even although I did not understand it. It was an amazing feeling, like walking on air. I had gone from the darkest place I could ever imagine, lost, with no hope, facing my failure to even live and choosing suicide as the way ahead, to being alive, smiling, happy on the inside, and sensing there was hope and purpose to my life.

I remember being at work and smiling a lot. A few people asked me if I was ok, and to those I trusted I told my story. There were a range of responses, from silence, incredulity, and disbelief, through to awkwardness and a sort of dismissive response. Nonetheless, I was genuinely happy.

The company I worked for had opened a massive new factory in the town, and the small factory out at Lochailort was still operating, but many people were trying to get to the new factory as it was closer to where they lived. For a few of us that had been promoted, we were all hoping to get a move as our careers would have much greater opportunities there. However, the parent company decided to install a whole new management and leadership team and not move anyone from Lochailort. To be honest, after years of backbreaking overtime and huge effort, it was a bit of a letdown.

I looked for another job and was offered a leading role in a smaller organisation in the south-west of Scotland. I would have taken the role and moved, but it required a lot of driving, which I was not so keen on, especially as I was still so focused on motorbikes. I did have my car licence, which I passed on the second attempt, hitting the kerb and driving through a red traffic light on my first attempt.

When the company found out I was looking to move away, they moved me to the new factory and asked me to take on the production supervisor's role. This was a big step up from my team leader role, and I would have four or five direct reports and around eighty staff working in my team.

The new factory was in a mess. The staff were ruling the roost, working huge, mostly unnecessary overtime hours, and there was already a lot of damage to property through forklifts and general carelessness. The factory manager had me clean out all the recesses in the building on the first day I was there. I was too dim to realise that he did not want me there and was making a point to the rest of the team by giving me such a horrible job on my very first day as a supervisor. I was taking over from another supervisor who was being shifted sideways. He was clearly very well liked by the factory manager, even although the business results were shocking. I jumped in and did a great job in those recessed areas.

I took on the production role, leading from the front, wet gear on, in the middle of the factory, hands-on all day and all overtime, getting to know everyone and seeing how things worked.

Sammy and Chatty worked there. Sammy was in a small team working on new products in an annexe area, and Chatty worked in the main factory area, hands-on. I was their boss now. That felt a bit weird to me, but they never made me feel weird about it.

They asked me round for tea about a week later, and I was so happy to go. I was living at Lochailort and had gone back to the pub and to a party, but it was not the same. Everyone there was so happy to see me. Some had heard through the grapevine that I had become a "happy clappy Christian". They chanted my name when I walked into the pub. That was a first.

The only other time my name had been chanted was at primary school after a very vicious fight, where half the school chanted, "If yoo hate Allan Broon clap yoor hands," followed by three quick claps and repeat. Yet here I was, just inside the pub door, hearing a slurry, "Allan Brown, Allan Brown, Allan Brown," and repeat. There was in my heart a hollowness about this moment. Maybe this was something I would have loved a few weeks back, maybe even yearned for as some sort of acceptance or recognition, but now it felt counterfeit somehow.

So I was round at Sammy and Chatty's house again, having macaroni and cheese sauce for dinner. I was up to my eyes in debt when I had my encounter with Jesus, and I had decided quickly that the first thing I would do would be to clear my debt, a bank loan, an overdraft, and two maxed out credit cards, several thousand pounds with nothing to show for it. The macaroni and cheese sauce hit the spot.

They asked me how I was going and I told them I was struggling a bit at Lochailort, that there was not much out there other than the pub. I had a dog as well, a rescue dog, PB (Polo Barlienos), who was a purebred Staffordshire Terrier. I would sometimes leave him in the house, or he would come to work in my car. He would chase the car for a mile or so on the way home some nights, to give him some exercise, that was until he got wise to the fact that if he sat at the side of the road I would eventually reverse back and let him back in the car. One night he ate two litres of margarine and four frozen corn cobs from my shopping in the back of my car. I had driven without a licence for a while, having swapped a Mini Cooper for a two and a half kilo salmon at the pub one night.

It just so happened that Sammy and Chatty invited Polo and me to come and stay with them for a while, until I found somewhere in town to stay. They cleared out a small box bedroom for me. I moved a few days later and gave up my cottage at Lochailort. And so began a whole new chapter of my life that would shape a whole new future.

Chapter 53

Every morning at 5 am, Sammy and Chatty had a prayer meeting in their house. Other Christians from around the town walked, cycled, and drove to their small council house at the top of the hill and came together for an hour each morning to pray.

So I got up at 4.30 am every morning, washed, changed, and came downstairs to join the prayer meeting from 5 am to 6 am. We prayed for each other, for our town, our workplaces, our families and friends, our churches, and for others' salvation. We sang songs, quietly and reverently, neither aiming to disturb neighbours nor concerned about neighbours overhearing these moments of worship. At 6 am we stopped. When I opened my eyes there were always quite a few more people in the room than when I had closed my eyes to start praying at 5 am.

Sometimes the prayer meetings would become intense, with everyone praying at once, a noisy rabble calling out to God. Other times we would take turns praying, agreeing with each other as we did. I learned to pray, and I learned something of discipleship, without ever realising that was happening.

On Wednesday night there was a Bible study at the pastor's house. The pastor was called Donald, a youngish married man with two beautiful blond-haired, blue-eyed children, a girl and a boy. His house was up a steep path into a roomy bungalow, where we sat around the table or on the sofa, a coal fire burning bright on winter evenings. I remember the first Bible study I attended there. I had already been given a Bible and had started to read it in places, a bit of the Gospel of Matthew and some of the Old Testament. My drug-infused readings of Ecclesiastes from my Edinburgh years had raised some unanswered questions in me.

I was given a concordance and shown how to use it, and I got to practise that a few times with Sammy until I had the hang of it. Then Donald read a scripture, 2 Corinthians 7:10, "For godly grief produces a repentance that leads to salvation without regret, whereas worldly grief produces death".

Donald asked a question. "So guys and girls, what is the difference between godly sorrow and worldly sorrow? Let's use the concordances and your Bibles, and you have about forty minutes, then we will stop and you can tell me what you have found out."

I was immediately learning to go to my Bible and find out for myself what I thought, and then test that with other seasoned Christians. I learned to read the Bible and I learned something about discipleship, without ever really realising that was even happening.

Chapter 54

I made friends quickly with other like-minded young men and women. I had stopped taking drugs and alcohol, not because anyone had told me to, I just knew it was the best thing for me to do. My conscience, my inner voice and guide were more alive now. There was no struggle, no fighting the desire for drugs or drink. It just was no longer there.

I read the Bible, asking and expecting that perhaps God would somehow speak to me. I listened to other Christians talk about what God had been saying to them through the Bible, their prayers, and even their thoughts. I did not really know how this worked, but I really wanted to experience it.

I decided to go to Edinburgh one day to visit my friend Archie and tell him what had happened to me. I believed that he had been on a long search for inner peace. He had confided in me one day about something that had happened in his life that he was deeply and continually troubled by. I knew now that Jesus had the answer and great peace for Archie if he would receive it.

I loved Archie and had met his mum and his sisters. All of them were always so kind to me and made me feel at home. They were artistic, painters, actors, and artistes, houses full of creativity, colourful lives, colourful hair, and lives well lived.

I put my Bible on the dashboard and set off to Edinburgh. On the way out of town a young lady was hitchhiking and I thought I recognised her. I stopped. I knew my motives were pure and I was ok if the young lady declined the lift. She came to the window and hesitantly looked in, and after a few seconds recognised me.

"Oh!" she said at the moment of recognition. "I wasnae sure who yoo were. I didnae want to take a lift off a strange man, but ah'm glad it's yoo."

She opened the door at the same time, her small bag tumbling onto the floor as she slid in, and I was indicating and pulling away as she closed the door, traffic looking frustrated on my shoulder in the rear-view mirror.

We chatted about shared friends and history. She had been in the first school play I had helped with and we had struck up a friendship then. I wondered about talking about my newfound faith, but did not know where to start. The miles went by, some in shared silence and some in stories old and new.

We came to the fork in the road. She was going to Glasgow and I to Edinburgh. On impulse I blurted, "Oh look, a've got loads of time, so ah'll take yea to Glasgow, and it's only thirty minutes for me to drive through to Edinburgh after that." It was quickly settled.

With no further delay, I asked, "I hope yea dinnae mind the Bible on the dashboard."

She said that she had hoped I would mention it and that she wanted to talk about it. Her mum had recently started going to church and she had seen a change in her. I recounted my whole story, from lost to found, over the next thirty or forty minutes, with questions asked and answered.

There was a long silence afterwards as we staccatoed into Glasgow traffic and traffic lights. We arrived at the drop-off point and fond farewells were exchanged, if a little strained now by the long silence. I said I would pray for her and her mum, and she was gone, bag swinging over her shoulder as she disappeared into the crowded streets. We never met again, to the best of my knowledge.

The previous day had been a Sunday, and at the morning church service I had an amazing experience. For some reason I could hardly control my worship, singing loudly at each chorus and hymn. One of Sammy's boys poked me in the back at one point, as if to say, "Quieten down, please." But I could not. I was just overwhelmed and overflowing with worship and gratitude.

In a moment of silence between songs, what I can only describe as an internal wind went right through me, touching every part, even under my fingernails and toenails. It swept through me in a second or slightly more, and I felt it. I went down to the altar at the front of the church and, not caring what anyone thought or said, wept like a little child for ten or fifteen minutes, sobs shuddering through me, rising in wave after wave. Just when I thought the emotions were settling, another series of waves would come.

Driving through to Edinburgh, the sun was out and I opened my car windows and started singing. I can't remember what the song was now, but I do remember that a strange language started to pour out of my mouth, and it felt alive, like the words had a life and energy all of their own. I could not stop them, or perhaps it would be fairer to say I had no desire to stop them. It felt so alive, so amazing. I wanted to lift my hands, so I did, one at a time, as I was driving on the motorway. Anyone looking across at my car would have wondered what on earth was going on, this young man seeming to sing incoherently at the top of his lungs, one hand in the air, out the window, and a look of intense pleasure on his face. When I got back to my home town, my pastor explained to me about the "gift of tongues" and a lot of things made sense to me. I had actually thought that sometimes he prayed in Hebrew, but now I realised that this was simply his heavenly language.

In Edinburgh I looked up a few old friends, telling them what had happened to me, and received a range of responses from interest to awkward silence. I met Archie and told him. He said he could see that something had happened to me, and he acknowledged that what I said was true, but that was it. There was no interest in him to find God for himself, at least not in the way I had. I was a little disappointed, as I had thought maybe this would be a great moment for Archie. We parted in a lukewarm moment, and I knew it was time for me to move on, heading back up north to what God had in store for me there. Edinburgh was my home town, and I guess it always will be.

Chapter 55

I made friends at church with young men around my age who were on the same journey, and we shared experiences together. We shared our lives together. While I was free of drugs and alcohol, my mental health was still fragile, and when driving I would still have impulses to drive into oncoming traffic. I would have moments of paranoia or anxiety, nothing like as bad as before I had my encounter with Jesus, but still there. It was a struggle at times and I did not really know what to do about it.

One weekend I booked into an open weekend at Elim Bible College in Nantwich, England, and my friend Jeff said that he would love to come with me. I was good friends with Jeff, his wife and children, and they were a blessing to me, their kindness and hospitality giving me a home from home at times and the wonder of being allowed to be part of a loving family. So off we went late one night, driving the five or six-hour journey together. We took baby cups and a flask each so that we could drink tea and coffee in the car for the journey. I had a hunger in me to learn more about Jesus, to understand the Bible better, and was looking to see if maybe Bible college was the way forwards.

Driving down, we took turns driving while the other slept. On my driving shifts I struggled with thoughts of suicide. They were pervasive, invasive, and at times just wearing. I felt worn down by them; there was no let-up ever, but I did not know what to do.

We had the most amazing weekend at Elim Bible College. It was an open weekend, so we met others who were considering attending college. Jeff had his guitar with him, and we stayed up late at night worshipping together, before a hasty breakfast and full days experiencing college life. I was sure that Bible College was for me, but it would be another twenty-five years before that dream would be realised, and that's another story for another chapter.

Driving back up the long roads on Monday night, we were tired but happy, full of stories of moments and gladness for new friends and experiences. Yet even as Jeff slept, I was battling to stay alive, with this weird contradiction and tension in my life, held by me as a secret that only I knew. Even that tension was difficult.

Back in our home town, we visited our pastor the next night to catch up and chat about our experiences. I decided in those moments that I needed to tell someone what was going on with me and to ask for help. The sheer weight of the problem was crushing the joy out of my life. So late that night, after we had regaled each other with stories, I asked if I could share something.

"Would yoo mind if I said somethin jus noo?" That was how it started. I explained how in the lead-up to my encounter with Christ, I had struggled with anxiety, panic, and suicidal thoughts and emotions. The coal fire embers gave the room a warm, safe glow. A solitary lamp gave off its low comfort, and with the dark outside clinging to the large bay windows, I talked and they listened.

At the end of what I had to say, we all sat in silence for a minute or two, reflecting. There was a sanctity about those moments; patience is the beginning of love. Then Donald, my pastor, spoke to me, explaining that sometimes we can have an oppression sitting on our lives. He confirmed to me that I was not demon-possessed, as that had been a worry because the feelings were so strong and tenacious as to almost overpower me at times. He asked if he could pray for me, and he laid his hands on my head and prayed. During the prayer, I felt the faintest sense of something slipping off me. I could have imagined it; it was that faint. But I didn't. I knew, somehow, that something had happened. I sensed a thought that was not really mine speaking to me in my core being: "Fight for the ground you have been given." I told Donald, and he smiled and said that was good.

From that day forwards, I never experienced those thoughts and oppressions again. I was free to drive in peace. Occasionally I sensed that they wanted to find a way back into my thinking, so I would pray in the car, submit my life afresh to God, and resist those thoughts, and they would be gone. I know that if you are reading this, you may think that this is strange, even that perhaps I was being brainwashed or part of a weird cult. But this was real to me; it was my experience. And I was free. It was a delirious feeling after the years of struggle. I am so grateful to God each day for my sanity. I don't take it for granted or lightly, guarding it with all my strength.

Not long after this, it just so happened that I heard about tithing and baptisms. Both were new concepts and needed some understanding. Tithing is when someone gives the first ten percent of their income to God so that others can hear about God and be supported. I knew in my inner person that I wanted to find a way to tell God thank you, and I knew right away that tithing was a good principle for a Christian. It demonstrates that our trust is not in money, it goes to the heart of our being and our generosity, and, along with offerings, it is a solid principle to build a Christian life on. As soon as I understood it, I read all I could find about it in the Bible, and I knew that this was God's best for me. No-one had to tell me any more, convince me, or pressurise me; I knew that in my heart before God I wanted to honour His ways to the very best of my ability. I was a changed man.

Baptism is a public demonstration of a private moment. The idea is that as I go under the water, the old nature, the sin nature, is symbolically washed away, and when I rise up out of the water I am identified as a new person in Jesus. It is a ceremony that has no "magical" powers, but just an expression of faith.

So the day came. It was sunny and we gathered at the River Nevis, snow still visible on the north face of Ben Nevis in the distance. The church van was there so we could get changed into old clothes before baptism, and then dry and change into warm clothes afterwards. The people from church were gathered on the bank of the river, on the grass, bright summer clothes on show, wild flowers growing all around, and crystal clear water surging by, tumbling in places where rocks were near the surface. The sunlight caught the water's movements and turned them into an eternal dance.

I waded out towards my pastor and one of the elders. It was cold, but not freezing. I had the joy many years later of baptising a friend in Loch Etive in January. Now that was freezing, and we struggled to get the words out that day. I remember baptisms in Honduras as well, that story still to be told, but oh, the delicious feeling of warm water. Anyway, back to the story. It was chilly, fresh, and the moment the water touched my waistline is still remembered and still makes me flinch a little even today. Then we were all standing together in the middle of the river, hymns and choruses floating across towards us. We spoke about baptism, its symbolism, its relevance, and its timeless practice. John, one of the pastors, asked me, "So Allan, why are ye getting baptised today?" I made my faith statement publicly. "I trust God and His only son Jesus, and I want to publicly make this statement of repentance and being born again." And then I was under the water. Silence, stillness, the sun's rays dancing on the water above my eyes. Eternity was there. And I was up, shaking water from me, smiling the broadest smile of my life to date, rejoicing. Joy was mine.

Chapter 56

This was a season of health, of life, of growth. I played squash several times a week, went hill running, where I loved my conversations with God, flourished at work, and fully enjoyed the multitude of new friends. I lost a few kilos and started to really enjoy not eating and drinking as much, feeling sharp and alive in my headspace. It was like being given a second shot at life. I was learning to pray earnestly, to wait on God, to read the Bible, and to start to discern God's voice to me, although that was not always easy, as my own internal voice could easily drown out everything else.

In church life, I was helping the pastor's wife with Sunday School. In hindsight, I should probably have just sat in the services and learned, but there was no one willing to help the younger children, so I stepped up. It was fun mostly, and I could act a bit silly and get all the kids laughing with me, which I enjoyed. We followed Scripture Union teaching, which was actually quite helpful for me as well. The church went through some changes, with Donald stepping down as the pastor and returning to full-time work as an electrical engineer, and John, one of the associate pastors, taking on the pastor's role. It was a little tricky for me, as I felt such an allegiance to Donald.

I remember one day when Donald took me fly-fishing on Loch Hourn. He was teaching me to flyfish, how to tie the knots, and enjoy the day. I really loved time with him, as we would have great discussions about scripture, and he would always ask me searching questions. The day started clear and crisp, but soon heavy grey clouds gathered, and the darkness of a storm started to settle over us. The outboard stopped working, and we were right out in the middle of the loch. Donald stripped down the carburettor and handed me a few small pieces to clutch like the proverbial straw in my deep chilled hands while he cleaned out dirt from our fuel. We were side-on to the waves, and the shoreline appeared at the top of each wave and disappeared in the troughs. I felt like God said something to me in those moments that translated as, "If this was it, there will be no advantage to you in being with your pastor when you meet with me." Those were the feelings I had, and although there was a gentleness about the moment, there was also seriousness in my soul. The colours of the day, moody steel greys, the chill in the easterly wind that had travelled from Siberia before crossing the North Sea to Caledonia, and the barrenness of the winter-coloured hills, all lent themselves to making a mark on me that day.

But change was with us, and as time passed, I realised that John was such a good man. He modelled fatherhood and being an amazing husband superbly well. I started to love being around him and his family. We had pizza and movie nights where I was adopted into the family. He was so generous with his time and his life, and so extremely patient with those whom society had marginalised. Even now, many years later, I find myself reflecting on how I wanted to have some of his great qualities in me as I care for others. I pray that even a tiny bit of his ministry lives on in me at times.

At work, I was moved to a bigger location in the town, and now I was the Production Manager over a staff of 300 working in two different locations processing farmed salmon. I still loved to get away at weekends to the farms and help hands-on with the harvests, where we would be grafting on our hands and knees for hours out on a wooden barge at sea, harvesting the salmon into massive bins of iced water.

With great gratitude, I moved away from Sammy and Chatty's house into a shared house with a colleague from work. I was settling into my new life with Jesus, still climbing mountains at every opportunity. Even though my drug abuse had created a psychotic moment where I nearly threw myself off a cliff, I knew I was healing and did not want to give in to the fear. God had bigger mountains in mind for me, that I knew nothing about at this time.

There was a lady in church who lived in Florida but also Scotland. She would travel back and forth once or twice a year, maybe summer in Scotland and winter in Florida mostly. She had access to last-minute cheap tickets, and one day she called me and asked if I would like to go to Florida. She had a return ticket for about one hundred and thirty pounds. She could not go at this point, and I had to go the next day. Nervously I asked for two weeks off work and was given the go-ahead. So off I went to Glasgow Airport and my first transatlantic flight to

Orlando via Bangor in Maine. We went through customs in Bangor, and unbelievably, I had three seats to myself on the whole flight. I was so excited and so blessed.

Arriving at Orlando Airport for the first time is still a memory that I revisit. Walking out of the concourse into the evening heat, the smell of warm earth, seeing palm trees for the first time, and feeling the warm wind. I had lived in Scotland my whole life until then, only travelling mostly to countries that were even colder. I had an instant connection to heat, to feel warm, to live in shorts and t-shirts, and to love the sunrise every morning. I loved watching the orange sun through the mosquito netting as it rose the next morning. I walked around in the garden of the home I was staying in, praying, praising, and just being. I pulled three or four grapefruits from a tree laden with them and juiced them for breakfast. I asked John, the lady from the church's husband, why people allowed the fruit to fall on the ground and rot. I could not imagine having a citrus fruit tree and not eating or giving away all the fruit. I could see trees in neighbours' gardens with oranges laying all over the ground, just rotting away. I met Alistair and Amanda for the first time. Alistair is from Kirkcaldy and had married John's daughter. Alistair has a gift of not only asking the best questions but really listening to the answers, and I found myself really loving spending time with him and his beautiful family. I wanted to be a bit more like that, to be able to draw out of people what was in them, just as Alistair was doing with me. Even now, over thirty-five years later, Alistair and I catch up on video calls every two or three weeks.

In the worst of my drug and alcohol-fuelled days, I would try to get as out of it as I possibly could and as quickly as I could, finding escape in periods of unconsciousness. On the journey to oblivion, I would often have periods of anxiety and panic. Wild thoughts would run through my mind, thoughts of damaging others or doing crazy stuff. In my desperate condition, I would wish that someone would strap me down to the bed in restraints so that I would not act on any of these murderous thoughts. They were so real, and so strong that it was like a voice in my head telling me to do horrible things and that I had no power to resist.

I shared a bit of this as my testimony with Alistair and Amanda, not realising that, as I was staying in their house for a few nights, this might be unsettling for them. Later, on future visits, I was able to joke about it with them, as I would suddenly stop talking and incline my ear upwards, staying still for a few moments and then asking in a deep voice, "Really, ye want me tae do that right now?" It was way too early to try that on this trip, of course, and I did not yet know that I would be back as many times as I would, or of the great friendship I would enter into with this family, which, as I have mentioned, is still thriving today as I sit and write this story, some thirty-five years later.

The two weeks in Florida went by far too fast, with days at Disneyland and Busch Gardens taken with ease as if it were normal life for me. All you can eat at The Golden Corral (renamed by me The Golden Trough), going to Carpenter's Home Church in Lakeland, where thousands gathered for worship each Sunday. I think we played racquetball one day, and I was smitten, playing outside in the heat. It was the best fun. Then, suddenly, I was at the airport, dropped off and farewelled. I tried to sit in the sun out on the traffic islands for a while, but the security guys moved me on real quick. I don't think they really realised or cared that I was going back to sweet Scottish rain in freezing February. Inside the terminal, I sat in the toilet cubicle silently crying, mourning the joy I had experienced and now had to hand back. And then I was on the plane, the sun locked up safely in Florida behind me as we traversed the Atlantic Ocean at 36,000 feet.

Chapter 57

The next time I was to see John (from Florida) was at the First Aid Hall in Inverlochy, Fort William, Scotland, which we hired each Sunday for church. Sundays were busy. I would dismantle my drum kit on Saturday evening into its cases, then load my car early on Sunday morning, drive over to the church and set it all up. Then I put the chairs out, switched on the heating, turned on the urn, and so on. My next job was to jump into the church minibus, pick up several of the older people, and bring them to church. Once safely back, I would play the drums for the service, and then take the kids in the minibus over to my house for Sunday School. The First Aid Hall only had one room. After around an hour or so, we would all clamber back into the bus, the house left in disarray, and head back to the hall. There I would dismantle and pack the drums away into my car, then take the people back in the minibus, before running home for lunch. Then in the evening, I would go to church again, sometimes with the drums and sometimes without.

One week I heard that a local radio station had started up and their building was just over the road from where we had our church services. I was really into contemporary Christian music, and immediately I started to dream about a Christian radio programme. I spoke to my pastor about it and he encouraged me and prayed for me. That week I reached out to the station manager. It just so happened that two of his nephews worked with me, and he invited me over on Sunday afternoon. So we prayed after our church service and I went over.

I chatted with Raymond, the manager, and we found the connection easy. He asked me what I was interested in and I told him, "Ah'd reely luv tae haf a show wae Christian music." He looked at me, poker-faced, then slowly shook his head and said, "No, ah dinny think that would work here." I was stumped at that moment but decided in my heart to launch a captain's appeal to the umpire that I was not out. Inspired, I replied, "We would focus oan all the stuff we all agree oan as Christians only, ye ken. I woodnae want to mention anything that we dinnae aw agree oan!" A lengthy pause followed, almost awkward in time. "Ok," Raymond ventured, "when could ye start?" And I was in the following week for the first-ever local Christian radio show in my hometown.

The show ran for 21 years until we emigrated to Australia, but I'm getting ahead of myself. The show became trusted to the point where I was invited to do the breakfast show at times and was allowed to play a mix of music. I entered a national Easter radio competition one year, winning a national prize for a modern-day media report from Golgotha.

Anyway, back to John (from Florida). He was at the Red Cross Hall on Friday evening, putting on his one-man play about the life of C.T. Studd. It was brilliant. Afterwards, I chatted with him and discovered that he was a full-time missionary to Honduras (I thought Honduras was in Africa at this point), and that he had a house in Florida where he went to rest for short periods between long mission trips. He was born in Florida. After listening to a few stories about mission work I spoke up and said, "Wow, that sounds amazing." He looked at me for a moment, eye to eye, before replying, "Why don't you come?" Without missing a beat, the answer was hanging in the air between us: "Yes, ok." And that was it, I was planning a trip to Honduras.

Over the next few months, I worked on both my fitness and undertook some basic Spanish lessons via a set of CDs a friend loaned me. By the time January came, I was able to point out to Mrs Soto that her lost umbrella was under the table. All I needed now was for the stars to align in Honduras and for me to bump into a Mrs Soto who was looking for her umbrella. In fact, I was quite relaxed about the name; it could even have been a Mr Soto. I could not believe that in a few days I would be flying out on my own to Orlando, Florida, for a night, and then with John we would drive to Tampa, fly to Miami, and then change to Taca Air for a flight via Belize to San Pedro Sula, and change again for La Ceiba. I was excited and nervous.

The plan changed and when I arrived in Florida, I was to fly on my own to La Ceiba the next day, where I would be met at the airport and John would arrive two days later. And that's what happened. I loved the new freedom and the anonymity of airports, just sitting and watching people come and go. Sad departure farewells and even I teared up as I saw some family reunions at various airport gates. This was all new to me.

And then there I was, walking down the steps in the dark at La Ceiba International Airport, after a seven-hour flight. Armed soldiers stood at the bottom of the aeroplane stair ramp, ushering passengers towards a small dimly lit concrete building that had actual bullet marks on the outside wall. Part of me shrunk at that moment. Fear was gripping me in a novel way. I wanted to get back up the steps and go back to Miami. Welcome to Central America. I would come to love this country and its amazing people, but at this point all I could sense was an internal desire to flee.

I walked across the tarmac to what must be the terminal building. It was chaos, people jammed in, trestle tables set up with more armed personnel dressed in military uniforms behind the tables shouting instructions. Panic was gripping me; I had no idea what was expected. I looked around desperately for dear Mrs Soto and her beautiful umbrella, but she was not here tonight.

Bags arrived, pulled alongside the building in a trailer hauled by a farm tractor. They were flung into a holding area and then random bags were lifted onto the tables and their owners requested to step forward. Some people picked up their bags and left. At the end of the small area was a wall where dozens of people stood, also shouting out to their loved ones as they waited to finally connect. The noise was constant and unsettling; the routine had no obvious order, and I had no idea what to do.

All the bags were finally in the terminal, and it was obvious to me that one of my bags had not made it to La Ceiba. I felt a tap on my shoulder and there was Richard. John had asked him to meet me and help me, and he had managed to be allowed to enter this transit area. He spoke in Spanish to the officials, my passport had a visa stapled to it, some dollars changed hands, and I was through into the main airport area. Richard spoke to the officials at one of the desks and told me we would have to come back tomorrow or the next day to see if my bag had arrived. Then we were outside, chatting, heading for his double-cab pickup. He took me into the town for a pizza and we got to know each other a little. We were both friends with John. I was going to stay at Richard's house that night with him and his family.

Post-pizza we headed back to his car. Everywhere was so poorly lit at night, and that in itself was a bit of a culture shock. Added to that was the way people stared at me openly, not just the odd person, but everyone. It was 1990, and not many white-skinned people were in La Ceiba, so I guess I was a novelty. It felt unsettling to me. I wondered if this was a little of how people with different skin colours felt in Scotland at times, although the racial discrimination went much further than openly curious looks there.

The rain came, thunder and lightning ripped through the sky, and the noise of the rain on the car roof, windows, and body made chat impossible. So I sat and peered. We drove for a few hours, through what looked like banana plantations and possibly palm or olive plantations. The road was furiously bumpy and pot-hole ridden for long stretches. We arrived at Richard's house around 1 am. I was dog-tired. The roof of the house was corrugated iron, and the noise did not allow for much chat. I greeted and hugged Patricia, Richard's wife, who had waited up to greet us. As she pointed to a mattress on the floor, I thanked them in Scottish sign language and started to make my arrangements to sleep. And sleep I did.

Very early the next morning, actually at first light, the rain had ceased and the house was super-quiet. I got up and went out the door to see where I was. The soil underfoot was sandy in composition, and an old woven hammock was strung between two palm trees in what seemed to be a front garden. Squeezing around the pickup and gazing over the fence, I realised that the house sat on the edge of a small airplane landing strip. I could feel the heat of the sun on my neck and back, and already both the heat and the humidity were in the 80s, I thought.

Wandering around the side of the house in my bedtime shorts and t-shirt, I was stopped in my tracks. The back garden of this house was part of a half-moon white-sand beach that went for about a mile in each direction. Small waves lapped the shore about twenty paces from the back door. I walked over and stood knee-deep in the warmest seawater

I had ever experienced. Turquoise blue, clear, warm, and inviting. I lay down on the edge and allowed the small waves to wash over me and gently roll me around. Oh, I was home. This was a place I could stay for sure. I noticed a small stingray nearby, just sitting in the shallows. Parrots flitted from tree to tree overhead, and other birds made sounds like monkeys in the distance. I had stepped into the pages of *Swiss Family Robinson*, I was in the story now, not reading it, but living it.

It was a day to rest and recover from travel. After all, I had made my way the furthest away from home I had ever been. Richard and Pat's house was a few minutes' drive north of Trujillo, a fairly small town with the remnants of Spanish occupiers: a whitewashed fort, cannons, and all. Richard's sons and daughter were home-schooling, but as I was a visitor we found time to connect and play around with a ball on the beach. It was a home from home: fun, food, and family. I was made so welcome and, although I was sleeping on a thin mattress on the living room floor, I never once felt like I was in the way. Richard was (and is) a brilliant children's pastor, making every kind of balloon animal possible to the great joy of the various children we came across each day. John was on his way and would join us the next day, and we would be off on our first mission trip together the very next morning.

So I settled in for a day of rest. We had porridge for breakfast, which was so ironic. The rains came late morning and the sun disappeared for a few hours. I went to look for a book to read from Richard's bookcase and it just so happened that my eye caught the title *The Highlander's Last Song* by George MacDonald. I had never heard of this book, so I grabbed it and devoured it in a few hours of noisy corrugated-iron rain. Wow, what a great read. I knew I would be looking for more from George when I got back to the USA or UK. It turned out that I would read everything he had ever written over the next few years, and I discovered that his writing was an inspiration for C. S. Lewis. Reading George's children's book *At the Back of the North Wind*, years later, I sensed a hint of Narnia. But hey, I'm going a little off track here.

We decided in the afternoon to head back to the airport to pick up John and to see if my bag had arrived. Richard was not over-confident it would be there. I had one change of clothes in my carry-on bag and essential toiletries, etc., this was well before the days of 50ml limits, of course. On the drive, the road rose slowly, and looking over the way we had come, I could see miles of banana plantation sliding slowly downwards towards the aqua-blue skyline. Richard explained that the banana plants each gave only one crop. Everything was new, except maybe the bumps in the road, which I still remembered.

As we drew closer to La Ceiba, the road started to get crowded with people walking, all brightly coloured, carrying various parcels and packages, some on their backs and some balanced on their heads. Women walked in groups, all chattering, carrying plastic basins with cloths covering the edible contents. I was amazed that so many people liked to go out for a walk each day, and even more surprised that they would take their walk along the side of the main road. It was later in the day that I realised that they were not walking for pleasure or exercise, but from necessity. I had been seeing their world through my lens.

It was great to see John, and even though my bag had not turned up, we were all in high spirits. A visit to the local Pizza Hut salad bar was the order of the afternoon. We chatted about our plans for travel, and we met a few other missionaries who were in the city for the day and had also discovered Pizza Hut. La Ceiba was hot, too hot to walk far, hot enough to keep your head covered so your brain did not slowly cook. It was dusty, noisy, and busy, like one giant market. We went to the local supermarket, and I was enthralled with so many things I had never seen before: fruits, foods, and even household items. I bought a few small gifts to take back, including some local coffee, which I have to say was amazingly good.

We drove back to Trujjio, talking and laughing over stories retold the whole way. We ate well and fell asleep, John and I both side by side on the floor on separate thin mattresses, although his mattress did look slightly thicker to me, I guess he was the senior there. I woke up at 4 am, with what I thought was John lightly stroking my hair (which I had back then). I thought this was weird and put my hand up to move his hand away, but all that happened was that a giant cockroach slid slowly off my head and onto the pillow. I was up and highland dancing in a millisecond, much to John's confusion, and later, his amusement.

We breakfasted, loaded up Richard's fairly ancient metallic blue Land Cruiser (there was at least 300,000 on the clock), and we were off on the road, me in the back, Richard driving, and John shotgun. We were heading up into the mountains to visit a village, where I would have my first of countless meetings with Hoche.

As a young man, Hoche had a terrible upbringing. He was raised by two uncles; there was no school, only hard labour in the fields each day from a very young age, and brutal punishments for random or even imagined offences. Honduras was the wild west, with guns aplenty. Banks were robbed regularly, and shootouts happened with little warning. I was involved a few times myself, with close encounters with men and guns, but we will get to those stories in due course. Hoche became a wild man, and alcohol and violence were normal. By the time he was arrested by the local police, he had murdered three other men. Any more than three murders at that time meant execution. Three or fewer and you were in federal prison for a very long time. Two of Hoche's brothers were also murdered in reprisal killings, mistaken for him, blood feuds lasting generations in some of the villages.

In prison, a small Costa Rican nun turned up one day and preached the gospel, then left. No one came forward for salvation. I think about her often. But that night in his cell, Hoche got down on his knees on his own and received Christ as his personal saviour. Over the next few years, he managed to get a few pages of a Bible. There was such a remarkable change in his behaviour that he was eventually released after serving much less time than expected.

Hoche went back up into the mountains, to the villages where the outlaws all lived, where even the police and the army would not go, and he started a church. That was where we were heading. We would drive for a day, then walk for a day to get there. Once there, we would stay with Hoche and visit his church.

Leaving before first light, we drove on made-up roads for a few hours. The miles went past easily, every corner revealing something new to my inquisitive eyes and mind. Then we turned onto dirt roads, fording small rivers and scaling steeper inclines. By mid-morning, we were well shaken when we pulled up in a tiny village that marked the end of the available road. The road did continue, but it was not really passable by car in many sections, as storm waters had eroded large parts, and flimsy homemade wooden bridges invited only the adventurous.

So we hoisted our packs onto broad shoulders, stretching and checking that shoelaces were tied well, and we were off. It was hot, like a wall of heat. My pale Scottish skin was both enthralled and vulnerable to the experience. Sunscreen was plastered on, the hat pulled down to cover some of my neck, shoulders leaned into the weight of the pack, and all the gym work was about to be tested in the reality of this day. The ground was hard clay below my feet, uneven, reflecting heat, and hard work to cover. We climbed, and we climbed; there was no let-up. I guess I was starting to see why the police and army didn't want to travel up into this area. Some sections of the road dipped down to cross ravines or small rivers, which could be muddy, with the clay mud sticking by the kilo to my shiny new off-road walking boots. I wondered if I should have saved my pennies and just worn my trainers. Occasionally, there would be some shade, and we would all stop for a few moments to sip water from our way-too-small water bottles, before adjusting shoulder straps to at least feign some relief, then moving on again.

I guess we walked for around six hours in the heat. I was starting to feel the effects of the heat and humidity, and my energy was waning. I would push myself in spurts of effort and then slump back into a more trudging gait. John told me we were nearly there, but I soon realised that John's "nearly there" and my "nearly there" came from different dictionaries.

We came upon our first house up ahead, sat on a knoll, cleared from the surrounding jungle by the well-worn ground that a few scrawny chickens bustled over. A mud adobe house with palm frond roofing, small, tidy, and well-used looking. A wise-looking lady was framed in the lone window where a bright green basin sat, full of washed crockery. She greeted us as we drew within hailing distance.

"Keery acqua porfaffor," in a broad Scottish accent, were my only words, said so that John could hear. "Si," was the short reply. The lady came out with a few plastic glasses full of water. Holding up the container, I spied a million particles floating in the sunlit tumbler. "It's time to pray," said John. And I did. I prayed sincerely, grateful and sincerely needy to God, so thankful for this simple act, and desperate not to have an upset stomach so early in the adventure. The prayers were answered.

Soon we arrived at Hoche's village, although he lived on a rise above the river, another few miles further upriver. We stopped here and were warmly greeted. Hospitality to travellers was biblical. We were fed rice, beans, and freshly made tortillas, which I am embarrassed to say at first seemed plain to me, but would very soon become one of my favourite meals in the world. I was grateful, for sure. These people had so little compared with everyone I knew back in the UK, yet they thought nothing of sharing the little they had with strangers, me, a stranger who was already wealthy beyond any of their dreams, although not seen as wealthy in my own country.

After thanking the family for our meal, we continued on to Hoche's dwelling, where I had my first meeting with this man. We hit it off immediately, playing practical jokes on each other within the hour. He had a long mud-walled house, with mahogany roof tiles, a wrap-around verandah with hammocks, and a couple of rough-looking chairs. That night, we would sling our hammocks across the room and share this space, John, Richard, and I.

We all went down to the river and bathed. It was so nice to spend time washing together and laughing, with time to waste. I walked back up the steep hill to Hoche's house very slowly, not wanting the effort and humidity to rob me of the feeling of being clean. I sat in one of the hammocks, enjoying what there was of a breeze. Then we were off again, back down to the village where we had lunched, as that was where the church was held. My first church service in Spanish, and I was excited to experience it.

The church was brightly decorated and there were musical instruments: a balsa wood guitar, a half oil drum split lengthways and modified into a double bass, and an upside-down pail with a rope through the bottom attached to a short stick, which became a secondary bass and drum set.

The church service that evening was an unforgettable experience. The prayer time was the loudest I had ever been part of, as the whole congregation of maybe a hundred people rocked the church with heartfelt prayers that went on and on. Many people had walked in from villages further away, walking through the jungle on narrow muddy paths. The village itself was high up on the banks of a river that was easily a hundred metres across. On the other side, the jungle crowded the bank, inviting and dangerous at the same time. After about an hour or so of prayer, John eventually wandered around the crowded church, tapping people on the shoulder to let them know the service was about to start, so they could bring their prayers to a conclusion.

It was a hot and still night. The back wall of the church was painted white and alive with slow-dancing mosquitoes. People were brightly dressed, and men sat on one side of the church and women on the other, even husbands and wives. Patterned bunting was layered across the wooden beams of the ceiling, and on the stage at the front was a large amplifier speaker, big enough for a stadium. The distant noise of a generator confirmed it was in use.

So, my very first Hispanic church service, in the remote areas of Central America, within shouting distance of virgin rainforest, and surrounded by fervent worshipping villagers. I mimed the words and occasionally caught the flow of a repeating chorus line so I could sing along, even if I had no idea what I was singing. John spoke from the story of Esther, and although I did not follow the actual words, I could easily follow the drama of the story and the gasps and laughs of the congregation as Haman got what was coming to him.

In the dark, we made our way along the side of the main river back to Hoche's house, where we sat together in silence for an hour, enjoying the night sky and the sense of brotherhood. Then into the hammock and deep sleep.

We were up at 4 am the next morning, dressed and having coffee on the verandah by 4.30 am. We eased into the day. At first light, we crossed the main river in a dug-out canoe and then walked along the bank to a smaller tributary. We would follow this for the day, crossing the river countless times as the easiest pathway dictated. Chest-deep in muddy water for long parts of the day, we stopped briefly to eat a tortilla stuffed with cold refried black beans, standing together, one foot on a boulder or rock as we each tried to find a resting position.

As the light faded, the jungle thinned a little and I started to notice small areas of corn growing, and some coffee plants in groups growing in the shade of larger plants. Then we walked into a small clearing and the village became visible. Six or seven mud-walled houses close together, a few with a trail of spindly smoke weaving its way through the palm fronds. In the last of the day's light, I imagined myself to be David Livingstone and wondered at this other world I was entering.

We were warmly welcomed. John was known to the villagers, and they were excited that he was visiting and that they would have an open-air church service in their village that night. We were invited to eat: a small whole fish, head, eyes and all, rice, and super-salty soft cheese. John had impressed on me before we came to Honduras the need to be grateful for all food, as it was given sacrificially, and often a family would go without so that we could eat. I ate, my face unrevealing my thoughts. I was grateful but also adjusting. The cheese was like eating salt, and I understood that with no electricity, and therefore no fridges, salt was the preservative. I smiled and thanked the lady of the house in my rudimentary Scott-Spanish and tucked in. John pointed to something outside the small house, and as the lady turned, he scooped his cheese onto my plate. I was dumbstruck. He was trying not to laugh at my face. The fish head went under the table, where a local scavenging dog crunched it far too loudly for my comfort.

The church service was beautiful under the stars, with individuals singing songs and giving testimony to what God had done in their lives. I was getting used to Hoche, and we were always playing tricks on each other, moving our seats, tapping shoulders, and hiding each other's water or anything else we could think of to gently annoy one another.

A few days went by, each day beautifully individual but similar in location and style. Then we were travelling back to Trujjio. A few days at the beach, some fish tacos to renew us, and we were good to go again. We travelled through several remote areas, driving as far as we could before walking into the rainforest and having amazing church services. My Spanish was improving, although I had yet to see a Mrs Soto or an umbrella. I had confused a village when I mistook "Todos" for "Torros" and sincerely asked God to bless their bull.

I seemed to be back in Florida far too soon, and on my way back to Scotland against my own will. On the plane journey home, I was washed in emotions as I remembered the moments of fun, the love for the Honduran people, the joy in new friendships, and just the physical adventure of the last few weeks. Misty-eyed at times, I stared way past the small screen in front of me, seeing much greater stories than would ever be told on them.

Back in terra-Scotland, I slipped back into work, feeling like I had travelled through time. I did not know whether to be overwhelmed with gratitude for all I had or consumed with guilt over my stewardship of so much. I asked my pastor, John, if we could maybe do a Honduran-style meal at church one Sunday to raise some funds for some of the needs out there, for education and for medical situations that I was now intensely aware of, even for dentistry, something I took for granted as almost a right. I had seen such pain and sadness in such a short time. So we did. We put on a meal of rice, beans, tortillas, and a little bit of banana. I still remember my confusion when one lady brought her food back and complained that she could not eat it. I was kind and refunded her money, but mumbled something less kind under my breath, to my shame now, I realised it was not her fault that she had missed the whole point of the day.

Chapter 58

I was in a fairly plum role at work, in a senior position. Although it had some pressures, like a young man who tried to punch me when I had to let him go for constantly being absent after paydays, in general, I had it cushy. I had worked hard to get here: countless late nights in the pouring rain, watching the taillights of others heading home, last-minute overtime requests, and working under constant time pressures. Now my role was to lead others through the same seasons. Most of my time was spent in my office, working on production plans, reviewing staff attendance, preparing appraisals, and liaising with other managers for logistics, sales, marketing, and planning.

I travelled a bit for work, mostly to view potential equipment: to Stavanger, Norway, where the price of a steak dinner required a bank loan; to Copenhagen, where trucks and dozers shifted snow all through the night to be dumped in the harbour; and to Gothenburg, where I sampled seven kinds of herring lunches. Life was steady, a little predictable, but really quite enjoyable. My mental health was restored, and frequently I found myself ever so happy that I no longer endured the paranoia, anxiety, and craziness of just recent times.

I helped at Sunday School on Sundays, and at a couple of youth groups during weekday evenings, mixing it on the basketball court with the older teenagers. I loved playing squash and would play double sessions regularly, even after a Saturday morning climbing a mountain. I remember climbing Bheinn Fraoch at Glenfinnan one glorious summer morning, setting out at 5 am and selecting the steepest possible ascent route as I strode towards the early rises. A few skylarks made their presence known as the tiniest hint of promised warmth touched my skin. The smell of cut grass from the game's field added to the pleasure of just being alive.

I had a light pack on with waterproofs, an emergency bag, a whistle, a compass, and a couple of oat bars. I had learned to be prepared when, at college in Edinburgh, I joined the college climbing club and had a few close encounters, once standing on an overhanging snow cornice oblivious to the hundreds of metres directly below, and another time getting lost in the mountaintop mist, sensing the panic that comes when lost and alone. I was not expecting anything dramatic today, but it was good to be prepared.

So up I went, early thigh burns, lungs heaving, sweat starting to appear, and just sheer joy in my being. At one point I stopped, needing to breathe a little. I was hanging onto a vertical ledge, feet sliding out a little in the moss, and as I looked down between my legs, I could see the tiny black strip of road that ran part of the way up Glenfinnan to the lodge house. It was exhilarating and scary, hanging there, trusting my own strength, knowing I had what it would take to get to the top, and that even though I was exhausted, my ability to recover and keep going was a deep reserve.

Then I was clambering over the final rocky outcrops, summit in sight, and the early summer grass as green as could be. I lay down on my back, pack under my head, and stared up at the cloudless blue sky. Chest heaving, breath loud in my own ears as it settled back to a more normal rhythm. I remembered the eagle of previous years, and the ability to see the big picture without losing sight of the important details.

I loved days out on the hill. I loved the aloneness, the infinite marble greens of the sunlit forest glades, pushing into places where no one had been for hundreds of years. Branches cracking and twigs snapping, the only other sounds those of Gore-Tex and leather. The stillness. The sense of colour in the air, as if I were living inside an eternal artwork. I sensed life in solitude, so different from my previous agony of loneliness. In a flashing memory, I see myself lying on the bare floor, fourteen levels up, with the neighbouring apartment boarded up after a fire, and where I cried, no, rather I sobbed, with the pain of loneliness. Yet here I am, enjoying deep, intimate conversations with my Saviour, drinking in the colours, the smell of fresh cedar sap drifting on the cool forest breeze. Even now, living in the craziness of city life, I long for those moments. I close my eyes and relive them, keeping them fresh and alive as the days themselves in my memory. Being in the moment, loving the moments more than the memories, that is a precious place to dwell.

Chapter 59

In my mind, I found myself thinking of Honduras, the world of drama, colour, noise, and smells that was unfolding there each day as I slept at night. I would find myself lost in my thoughts of Honduras at odd moments at work, on the squash court, driving, and even in the bath. I still had a few packs of their coffee left and would treat myself on Saturday mornings, the blue tin coffee pot filled with boiling water, and the fresh coffee dunked repeatedly in its cloth bag as the water went inky black and the smells percolated the room.

I started to plan another missionary trip, reaching out to John with the new-fangled email and asking how I could co-ordinate with his plans. He was pleased for me to come. I chatted to a few people at church about my plans and gradually the dates and opportunities started to align. I could take some holiday leave from work, which was quite easy to arrange at any time, and then the idea was to go when John was on one of his trips into the jungle.

At church one Sunday, it just so happened that an acquaintance, Alistair, came up and spoke to me, asking if he could come to Honduras with me. Alistair was in a wheelchair and on crutches. My first inner response, to be honest, was a sinking feeling, one of the great joys in going for me was my alone time, time just to be, away from the manager's role and church responsibilities, where I would recharge. I'm not sure what showed on my face as I politely replied to Alistair, "Ehhhh, let's hae a catch up soon an see whit yer thinkin maun?"

…And we caught up. Alistair had been in the SAS and had been on jungle exercises in Belize. After a night in town, some locals drove over him in a Land Rover and then reversed over him again. (There was always some tension between locals and the military, seemingly, and Alistair had not done anything specifically wrong.) He had been found in the morning by sentries as the sun lit up the dips in the road to the camp. He was left in a medical room for a day, as they expected him to die, but he didn't. So they sent for a surgeon. It just so happened that the army's best surgeon for this job was on a scuba diving holiday

just off the coast of Belize. He came and did what he could, and Alistair lived, although he lost the use of his legs, his spine severed, and both knees crushed under the Land Rover. Alistair sensed that it was important to him to go back to Belize and to somehow offer forgiveness to the men who had inflicted the terrible injuries on his body. He understood that going to Honduras for two weeks first was possibly his only way there, and was ready for whatever hardships came his way. So we agreed that he could come, and John was 100% behind this as well.

So we flew from Glasgow to Orlando, stayed overnight with John, and then the next day drove to Tampa, flew to Miami, and then from Miami to La Ceiba via San Pedro Sula. Once again, I enjoyed the journey out to Trijjio, through the palm, olive, and banana plantations. Even the mountains around the airport felt like a welcome home this time. Luggage all arrived.

We spent a few days acclimatising and recovering, dining out and sleeping in shaded hammocks in the heat of the day. Then we were off to Hoche's. Alistair would be strapped to a donkey at the end of the passable road, and John, Richard, and I would walk. The heat and humidity were somehow beautiful and draining, maybe after such a long time in a cold country, I was okay with excess heat.

Steadily, we made our way up to our destination, many hours' walk along hard-baked clay tracks, much better than the clinging clay mud when it rained. Occasionally the track was in shade, and those short moments were savoured by all.

And we were there, at Hoche's house, high up on a bank above the river. The wrap-around verandah gave us all room to stretch out and rest for an hour while coffee was brewed and served con leche, as Hoche had his own small herd of cows. Rice and beans with freshly made tortillas followed soon after, as we sat around chatting, sledging each other, and laughing.

We had church at the local village that night, and Alistair gave his testimony, with the assistance of a local translator and John, who speaks the best Spanish of anyone I have ever met. The worship and prayer were loud and exuberant, some ladies gave testimonies and then sang a song, one after another. The heat built up in the small church, the mozzies danced and swayed like they were on drugs. The service would normally last a few hours, after which many of the congregation faced a several-hour walk through the jungle, often carrying children, to return to their dwellings, where they had just enough land to sustain themselves and their families through back-breaking work for nine to ten months of the year.

I loved these services. They were full of life and hope, as well as noise, colour, and drama. Even though my Spanish language skills were very elementary, that was secondary to the sense of God's presence with His people. On some Sundays there would be food after church, with the ladies of the village baking and frying all day to have enough for everyone. I loved the community and fun, as well as the spice and the flavours of these after-church food fests.

We were not able to go that far during the day, although on a couple of days I went off with John on one-day walks to other smaller dwellings, leaving Alistair with Hoche and his family. After a week or so there, it was time to head back from La Rosa to the coast and Trijjio.

Early in the morning, the faint grey mist lingering in the canopy treetops and the early morning roosters signalling the day to come, we were packing in that still, sleepy silence that often accompanies 4 am starts. Our bodies were up and slowly functioning, while our minds still tried to cling to our hammocks. Soon we were on the trail, heading down the mountain towards the small village at the start of the dirt track road where we had left Richard's 4x4. Alistair, strapped to the back of a mule, swayed back and forth almost like it was a small camel he was astride.

Slowly we made our way downwards. There had been some light rain overnight, and the hard clay we had trodden over on our ascent was turning to clinging mud on our descent. We were concerned that it might rain in the mountains, as the small rivers we had easily forded on the drive inland would be impassable as we exited.

The early morning hours passed, and we trod onwards, occasional words of encouragement exchanged, but mostly in quiet, enjoying the exercise, eyes down on the many trip hazards. Clay stuck to my boots, adding at least a kilo to every step, not to mention the long stretches of muddy path where our boots stuck to the mud underfoot, making each step an effort. Finally, I glimpsed the village through the trees, around an hour away, and we would be there by 11 am, not bad, a seven-hour walk out. Alistair was pale, sitting on his mule; he looked almost done already. I wondered how he would take the next six or seven hours of bumpy roads. He was a tough man, no doubts about that, but this was definitely taking a toll on him.

When we arrived at the village and slung our packs down with relief, we helped Alistair off the mule and back onto his feet and twin crutches. Without any preamble, it just so happened that he chipped in, "Ehh guys, ah maybi took mah pain killah's twice the day, ahm no shoor." Silence, none of us knew what to say or how serious that was. He continued, "It's ok though, ave dun that afore, and it jus meens ah'll probably fa asleep in the kah."

And he did. Before he was even fully in the back seat, he was slumping over. So we put him on a mattress in the covered back tray of the car, and off we went. Black clouds were gathering over the mountains behind us, and although the sun shone on us, there was danger ahead. The rivers flooded quickly. People crossing on foot or in cars were frequently swept away by the sudden wall of water that came down with the heavy rains, often driving large trees and branches in the scrambled mess of the initial wave.

We were suddenly in a rush, hurtling along, dust cloud behind us, racing to beat the rains at the two main rivers we had crossed on the way up. Alistair was bouncing up and down on the mattress, and I thought to myself that it just so happened he had double-dozed on his drugs today, as he would never have coped with this had he been conscious and sitting in the back seat, where I was being pinballed around, head bumping on the ceiling, window, and back of the seat in front of me.

We swept around a long bend in the road and the first river came into sight. It was hard to believe, what had been around 60 metres of shallow water a few days ago was now two hundred metres of head-high, rushing muddy water. An old yellow school bus was stuck in the middle of the river, water pouring in one side of the windows and out the other. Any passengers had long since been evacuated. The rains were here long before we arrived.

As we sat in the ute watching the scene before us a it just so happened, a large quarry lorry arrived. The driver ducked under the water to attach chains to the bus. Maybe there would be a way across after all. Once the chains were on, the tipper lorry had a go at getting the bus out. The bus body snaked and shimmered in the reflective light from the river, chains tautening and slackening as the lorry engine roared. The bus was going nowhere. Chains were removed and the lorry trundled over to us, the water barely half way up its tyres. It was massive. Chains were attached, the air intake blocked from water ingress, and we were off, dragged like a puppy hanging onto its mum's tail. We bounced along, bonnet going under the water at times, and then we were there, the other side. It had seemed impossible and impassable, but somehow God had made a way. One more river to go.

The next river was so wide that it bore no resemblance to the tiny 30-metre ford we had crossed a few days before, hardly wetting the tyres. Now it was several hundred metres across, and although it did not look very deep anywhere, it was also the last light of the day, darkness closing in fast. There was a knock at the window on the driver's side, we were truly in the middle of nowhere, miles from any village or dwelling. It just so happened that a young man in a white shirt offered to guide us across. He would walk out and, once he was a fair bit ahead, we would follow the path he had taken, and then across the whole way.

There was some debate in the car, as it was dangerous, and if we did get stuck we would be a sitting target for further flash floods. But we decided to go. Away went the man; a minute later we followed. The headlights went under the water, the wheels lost traction and spun a little, but we kept inching forwards. Eventually, all holding our breath,

I think, we made it. We stopped to thank and reward the kind man, but he was nowhere to be found, and we never saw him again.

Hours later, we pulled up outside Richard's house and carried Alistair inside onto another mattress. We all washed quickly and tumbled into our various sleeping spaces, silence reigning for the next six or seven hours until the smell of morning coffee teased us awake.

The next day we were all awake at 2 am, heading to the airport where our flight was planned for 6 am. We arrived a little bleary-eyed, with a slight cotton-wool head. We went through the process until we sat in the holding area, ready to board. Alistair was going along okay; he had rebalanced his medication and was reasonably well, considering what we had gone through. On the first day back at Richard's house, he had been in a lot of pain, doubling over regularly and sweating profusely. I had carried him to the bathroom several times through the night as he also had an upset stomach. But today, heading to Belize, he had recovered.

A family sitting next to us in the waiting area started to chat, and it turned out they were missionaries from the USA, who had been living in Honduras, starting a church for the last two years. They had also started a cocoa-butter business to support their ministry, but a week earlier they had experienced a large fire at their location when a kerosene refrigerator went up in flames. They had three young children as well as the husband and wife. The husband told me, "I stood and watched as everything we have, and everything we had worked for, went up in flames. There was no real access to enough water anywhere to try to seriously stop the fire." I sat in silence, finding it hard to even imagine going through something like this, never mind with a wife and three young children. They were heading to Belize for a week with friends there, then back to Minnesota to start rebuilding their lives while staying with his parents.

Alistair fell in with them and sat with them on the plane. He was heading to Belize and had people there to meet him and care for him, while I was heading back to Florida for a few days with John's son-in-law and daughter, Alistair and Amanda.

After a few days of R&R, one of which was at Busch Gardens, I was getting ready for the flight back to the UK, back to work and friends. Alistair (the other one) flew in from Belize and we got ready to head to Orlando early the next day. At the airport the flight was delayed, first by an hour, then by another two hours, then by another two hours, and then, after those five hours had passed, it was cancelled.

We were herded over to a desk in a long line where we waited for our hotel info, our hotel was to be in Tampa, as Orlando was already overflowing, many flights having been cancelled due to storms and freezing conditions in the north, and we had been on a flight that changed in Boston.

We were both feeling the effects of our travels, the waiting, and the inactivity. Getting off the bus in Tampa was a nice feeling. Another short time and we could stretch out on our beds and have a rest, the next flight we could get home was in two days' time, so we would have two days in Tampa, food and board paid for by the flight company, Pan-Am.

I walked ahead of Alistair and opened the hotel front door. I could see inside a short line at the reception desk, which was encouraging, we were nearly first off the bus, so that helped. We checked in and I gratefully made my way to the elevator, Alistair manfully on his crutches just half a step behind. I turned to open another door and watched, mouth open, as Alistair slowly circled round on one crutch, the other falling away like the launch mount at Cape Carnaval on the opposite shore from Tampa. Alistair fell to the floor almost in slow motion, then his whole body shook for a few seconds and some ugly green phlegm exited his nostrils as foam spluttered from his mouth. And then he was still.

I was in some sort of mild shock, I think. I stood and looked for what was a second but felt like a minute, all I could think was, "How the heck do ah tell his wife that he died in a hotel in Florida?" And as I gazed through my internal fog at the mucus on his face, I heard myself think, "Ahm no touchin' that! Kiss of life, yuk, no way." Then we went from freeze frame back to normal speed with a jolt. People in the foyer were gawping. I was shouting to the receptionist, "Hey, wilyacallanambulance!" It's all one word in Scotland. Then another guest was kneeling beside Alistair and telling me it was a grand mal seizure, that his son had just had the same thing for the first time a few days earlier. He seemed to know what he was talking about, and he looked up at me and delivered the good news: "It's all ok, buddy, ya'll see that he has expelled all the air from his body, and now in a minute he will start to breathe again." And sure enough, he did.

The paramedics arrived. Alistair was still on the floor, confused, but all okay. The paramedics asked me if Alistair had insurance, and I said he did. (Weeks later he received a bill for US$30,000, and I was less sure that he had bought himself cover, which I had told him he had to do.) They whisked him off to Tampa General while I got all our bags into the room and had a quick shower before heading over to Tampa General. I was told to go to the cafeteria and someone would come and speak to me. So I went and visited an amazing salad bar.

After a few hours, a nurse came and took me to a long hallway filled with two lines of curtained cubicles and told me Alistair was in one of them, as she swiveled and vanished around the corner. I walked down the row, softly calling out, "Alistur, are ye there?" Terrified to open the curtains in what seemed to be an overflowing part of the hospital, I glimpsed families sitting with loved ones, patients alone staring up at the ceiling, and a few sitting on the bed, legs swinging as they waited for the promised help to arrive. Eventually I discovered Alistair, sitting up in a temporary bed. He looked okay.

I slipped into his cubicle and sat on the only chair while he explained that he had run out of a significant painkiller he used and had not realised the impact of suddenly stopping after years of use. We chatted about the journeys in Honduras and what God had done in his life during the trip, our voices hushed so as not to disturb anyone. As we were chatting, I heard what sounded like a girl's voice in the next cubicle, and she was sobbing. We stopped talking and were both quiet for a minute. Then I said a little louder, "Hey, are you ok? We can hear you greetin'." There were some snuffles, then a voice said, "Can you pull the curtain back a bit?" We complied.

In the conversation that followed, it just so happened that the young lady was a Christian who had drifted away from her faith, and on overhearing our conversation, she wanted to recommit her life to Jesus. We prayed with her there and then, as she recommitted her ways to follow Jesus.

I wondered at God, what would have happened to Alistair if the flight had not been cancelled, and how it just so happened that we were next to this young lady in a hospital in Tampa, on our way to Fort William. It just so happened, hey?

Chapter 60

Around this time, it just so happened that I was head-hunted for a role within a neighbouring business. It was a smaller business run by a family who were also Christians. We met up a few times and chatted around the possibilities of my taking on a role as their first "production manager." I learned a lot over the four years I was there, primarily, I learned that I probably was not ready for such a big change, from corporate business with all the layers and supports, to a family business that worked 16-hour days just to make it through. On reflection, it was the toughest season of my management experience, with the owner of the business, who could be the sweetest person, often becoming irrational, and at times screaming right in my face in front of all the staff. The values that I held were violated, boundaries were broken, and the relationship became quickly formal and strained. In all of this, I recognised that I had a lot to learn, and that the environment was unsupportive of my learning. There was little collaboration; mostly there was hierarchy and control. In the end, having given my best physically to the job, I recognised that emotionally and mentally I had checked out some time back. We agreed it was time to go.

In reflecting at this point, it strikes me that the life of a Christian is not for the faint-hearted, we are tested and tried in so many ways, and we will only progress as much as we release the reins of our life to Jesus. I would like to give an example here, this may be difficult for some people to read, but it is a true account of what it can be like becoming and growing as a Christian.

Before I became a Christian, I wanted to be a good person, but failed, and failed spectacularly at times. On one occasion I had an affair with a married woman, and although I knew it was wrong I still did it. Now, as a young Christian, this memory came back to me, and I had an overwhelming sense that I needed to somehow do something to acknowledge my wrongdoing and, if possible, ask for forgiveness. I decided that I would approach the husband and let him know what had happened, and I knew this was risky. He was a full head taller than me, had worked on a farm all his life, and was exceptionally strong and hardy. And this was his wife. Shocking, really, what I had done.

I spoke to my pastor first to gain any wisdom. He *would not provide advice, but simply said in his experience, taking the action I was proposing did not always end in a good or better outcome.* In *effect, I felt he was leaning against me going and doing this. And part of me agreed, especially the part that was scared of being assaulted in the dark by an angry husband one night. However, I had no peace, and I sensed that God was encouraging me to make my own decision. When I reflected on this, I asked myself what I would say to this man if, in five years' time, he walked into our church. I could not answer that even to myself.*

I called him on the phone (he lived a full day's drive away from us) and, with both my hands trembling and tears running down my cheeks, I launched into a story that put the full blame on me for what had happened and made no excuses for my behaviour. *He was silent. I explained my recent encounter with Christ, how that had impacted me, and that I could not imagine how he was feeling at that moment, and that I was so sorry for my inexcusable actions.*

When he spoke, he invited me to visit him where he lived, and I agreed to go there the next week. So, in the middle of the next week, I drove to where he was living and we visited. He told me his wife (they were now divorced) had been unfaithful with several men, and that I was the only one who *had got in touch, and that he was grateful for that and for my honesty. We sat on the floor in his greenhouse on a winter's day and talked man to man for well over two hours. When we stood up and I prepared to leave, he walked me to a part of his greenhouse and showed me a "passion flower" that he was growing, and we chatted for another five minutes about Jesus and the cross. As I walked across the grey and* faint *green mossy flagstones and onto the crunching gravel, my heart was both heavy and light, and my trust in Jesus deepened.*

I was unemployed for a few months. I received housing benefit and some unemployment money and I learned to live on little, cycling the 40k round trip to town, and enjoying the back tracks through the local forest most days. Eventually, I found a role as a traffic warden and I stuck at that for a year, walking around the town and memorising scripture five days a week, for just enough money to live on and save a small amount each week. I found myself regularly praying for a new job, one that I would enjoy. I had been in a great, well-paid job and my decisions had ended that, and here, now, in this small town, maybe my options were gone.

I was walking down the High Street one afternoon, and it just so happened that a lady I vaguely recognised came right up to me and asked, "Hey, are yoo lookin' fur a job?" I stopped in my tracks. "Ehhhh, yes," was all I could say. She pressed a card into my hand and said quickly, "Come and see us then." It would be thirty years and more before I would have another meaningful job interview, but that's me running ahead again.

The role was with a training agency, helping long-term unemployed people back into the workplace. I loved it. It was outside all day, and if it rained we all went home at 11 am. I had the use of a van, picked the guys up in the morning and took them to their various workplaces, and then travelled around supporting them all day. Sometimes we all worked on the one project, like repairing a broken-down dry stane dyke. I could not stop smiling; it was the best fun job ever. Although again, it was a struggle to live on the salary. I worked in this role for around 18 months, but started to get unsettled about finances and how I could get ahead.

I went for an interview for a senior role in a seafood company around 60 miles away from where I was living. I was offered the position. There were doubts for me, as I was so involved in church life, lots of social activity, evening Bible study, helping at Sunday School, playing the drums, youth nights, etc., but I pushed on, accepted the job, and did not tell anyone.

On the Sunday before I was to leave for the new role, I went to church and still had not told a soul. Sitting up the back, I silently prayed to God: "Please God, help me with this move. I have so little peace aboot it, but a've committed noo, resigned frae my job and feel like I may be making a mistake, please help me." In the middle of the worship, it just so happened that a lady from the front row walked round to stand behind me, put her hands on my shoulders and prayed over me. I had never seen her do this before, although I had known her for a few years. She prayed over me: "Stop wrestlin wae God, stay whur he's planted yea." I felt relief. Wow. What an answer, and so quickly, how does God do that? I prayed silently: "Oh God. Please close this door now."

When I got back to my house, there was a message on the answerphone (do you remember them?): "Hi Allan, this is the company who offered you the role. We have reconsidered our offer and decided to withdraw it. Please do not come here tomorrow." Wow! I called my boss, told her the story, and it just so happened that she offered me my job back while laughing. I worked with her for another several months, until it just so happened that I was approached again to apply for a role.

I had become friends with a couple from another small local church in our town: Davy and Aileen. They were a fun-loving couple; Davy was working in the forestry and Aileen was employed in the local school. Our circle of friends grew and we often had late nights hanging out, playing games, laughing, and just generally loving life. I would often be at their house, dropping in for a catch-up, Saturday morning bacon rolls, and occasionally we went for days out together. Davy and his friend Donnie both loved fishing, as did I. One weekend we even all went away on a camping fishing trip on our way to see the Camanachd Shinty Cup Final in Inverness. But I'm getting ahead of myself.

I got a call one day from a man from another church in the town. I knew him to say hello to, but not much more than that. He asked me if I was interested in speaking to the person who ran the company he worked for, as they were looking for someone to run their "smokehouse." The business had a seafood restaurant in the town I lived in as well as in Glasgow and Edinburgh, and its own processing and smoking factory on the outskirts of the town. They also had a day cruise boat that took around 125 passengers on each trip. I dropped in one day to meet the owner, and it just so happened that we had both recently read Stephen Covey's book on Seven Habits, it was 1994. We hit it off from the word go. There was a sense of purpose and intrigue about the business he ran, which he had named "Crannog", meaning "an artificial fortified island constructed in a lake or marsh, originally in prehistoric Ireland and Scotland." But his idea was more about the integration of seafood, from boat to plate. To that end, they had a couple of fishing boats that landed their catch of fish and langoustines directly to the restaurant. I joined the business, which was literally fifty metres away from the business where I had worked for a family just a short time back.

It was hard work. Even though I was called "supervisor," it was very much a hands-on role. I would often start at six in the morning and not finish until seven or eight at night. There were deliveries to make to Edinburgh and Glasgow each week, trips to Salen to pick up prawns, and even to Mallaig at times to collect fish, as well as all the processing, cutting, filleting, packing, salting, smoking, slicing, weighing, and vacuum sealing. I constantly smelled of smoke from the old brick kiln that was on 24/7 in the unit we worked in. Some days the wind would blow the smoke back into the unit and we would all be standing outside the roller door, eyes streaming, nose running, coughing and spluttering as billows of heavy oak smoke pulsed out of every open window and door. All the smoked salmon was hand sliced, which meant standing bent over at a table for hours at a time. I became very gifted at slicing smoked salmon by hand. I was given the use of the company fish van, which was a blessing and a weight, it meant no costs from getting to and from work, and also transport in the evenings or to do my grocery shopping. It also meant I was on call for the local restaurant seven days a week, which was a massive effort at times. Rising at 4 am on a Sunday was normal. I had to make up the order for the restaurant before dropping it off, then head to the radio station to do the Sunday early morning show, six till eight am. Immediately afterwards I would be heading to church to set up, etc. Weeks rolled into months and then into a year or more. I saved up and had the opportunity to put a deposit down on an apartment five floors up, on the hill overlooking the town.

I remember moving in, not far from my 36th birthday. I had just enough money left that week for a Chinese takeaway. So I sat on the carpet in the unfurnished apartment and ate my sweet and sour pork in the fading light, lost in dreamy thoughts, staring at the evening's silhouetted hill line behind the rooftops of the closest apartments in front of my new dwelling. I slept uncovered on the floor. When I woke up early, I was staring at the only thing that just so happened to be left in the house, an empty cardboard box, and printed on the side was "bananas from Honduras."

Chapter 61

I remember my first movie visit in Honduras, it was in Trijillo, on a weekday evening. *We drove over from where Richard lived, between the small airstrip and the half-moon beach, and into the town itself, parking on the outskirts. We walked through dull, unlit streets, where the lights from the small shop windows cast the only glow there was. People stared at me, which was a wee bit unsettling, but I realised that not every day a tall white male walked down the back streets of Trijillo. I felt my skin.*

We joined the line for the movie. It was a fairly recent Harrison Ford flick, I can't remember which one now, and then we were inside a makeshift movie theatre. The seats were benches, not unlike pews, and the projector was up the back of the room, set on a dozen or so upside-down juice crates. The screen and sound were great, and to my surprise, and actually to my delight, the movie was in English with Spanish subtitles, so I got to fully understand the movie and brush up on my Spanish. I kept one eye open in case either Mrs Soto or an umbrella should make a surprise visit.

Halfway through the movie, the picture started to slip off the screen, until only about a third of the image was recognisable, the other two-thirds being wrapped around the garnished wall dressing around the screen. A tall thin young man in denim and a short-sleeved shirt, sitting near the front, stood up and hurled an empty glass Coca-Cola bottle at the back of the theatre, shouting something that to my faint Spanish ear sounded like, "Hey fatty [gordo], do your job or else." The picture immediately jerked back up to fit neatly on the screen. That moment alone was worth the paltry entrance fee.

Gradually, I furnished my apartment with the help of many kind friends, and a few trips to Inverness eventually meant I had all I needed to get by. I was still working long hours at Crannog and did not mind that too much. It was a good place to work; I was trusted and encouraged to take on more responsibilities.

We were busy in the lead-up to Christmas that year, and we did a lot of home-delivery food items, which meant early starts and late nights. I remember the soreness of the long days slicing salmon. In the morning, I would lift fifteen boxes of thirty-five kilos of salmon into the wet area, where I'd open them and cut off the heads, then fillet in one smooth motion, flipping the fish over once. Those two hundred and fifty-plus fillets would then all be laid into a mix of salt and brown sugar on the stainless steel tables and left there for another nine or ten hours to slowly cure. Then came a big clean down, getting rid of all the boxes, tape, fish heads, and bones. The bones would be brined later and hot smoked and scraped clean. Heads and stripped bones went to a pig farmer, nothing was wasted.

A change of uniform now, as the next task was in the finished product area. I would roll the trolley out of the brick kiln and decant the two hundred and fifty-plus salmon fillets from the previous day into boxes. Then myself and two staff would trim the salmon fillets, removing fat, fins, belly bones, etc., before using handheld tweezers to remove the pin bones from each salmon. The three of us (the other two staff had been hand-slicing smoked salmon all morning) would usually stop for tea about now and wolf down as many calories as our stomachs would allow at eight am.

Each salmon fillet had to be hand-sliced and small discs or clear circular paper inserted between each slice, before being boarded, bagged, vacuum sealed, weighed, and labelled. That took a fair bit of time. During the day we cooked and smoked mussels and oysters in the half shell, langoustines, and also on a smaller kiln we hot-smoked salmon fillets and added flavours such as honey and ginger, black pepper, and even garlic. We made gravadlax, my favourite fish dish in the whole world. Of course, there were piles of sea bass to fillet, as well as haddock, cod, herring, halibut, turbot, ling, saithe, and many other random species. Each day was full-on, with the finish line a herculean effort. It was the best of times and the hardest of times.

The owner, Finlay, and I became friends over this period and I got to know a little more about his business. It was going through some difficulties, as the Edinburgh restaurant was not busy and the lease was a long city-centre lease. I went with him one day to Glasgow to meet with the bank people, and it was awful. We arrived and were met, the bankers were sitting around a table and, as we awaited the legal representative, they were all laughing and joking about their previous night in a lap-dancing club. I found myself getting really angry on the inside. The legal person arrived and we got down to the discussions. Finlay was way too deep in, and there seemed no way out. They offered him a route that would basically stuff everyone that Finlay owed money to, and would allow the bank to get their cash back. He would not take that route, preferring to lose all he had rather than use the law to hide behind. That was such a right moment for me, here was someone I could work alongside. It was the start of winter and the business was about to go through its quieter period, with less cash flow than at any other time.

I talked with Finlay about going on a mission trip to Honduras over the next three winter months and he agreed that I could do that. So I started to plan, get fit, and draw together the few things I needed to take with me. About this time, Davy and Aileen invited me over for dinner, and I was to meet Aileen's sister Wendy, I had not known she had a sister, actually. I met Wendy for dinner at their house one dark winter night. She was direct, had a sense of humour, dark brown eyes, an easy smile, and wavy dark hair. She was attractive and intelligent, and I liked her right away. We played snap with Davy and Aileen, then all went over to a nearby bar where Davy was playing bass in a local band. We chatted and danced and got to know each other a little. I was leaving the very next day for Honduras for three months of mission, but I think I already knew that I would look Wendy up when I came back. I remember the walk back to Davy's house, the streetlights glistening with reflection from the chilly, damp tar, our breath releasing like mini steam engines in the freezing air, as we smiled and chatted, and a future connection seemed, at least to me, inevitable.

Chapter 62

It was such an exciting thought to go to Honduras for three months and experience what it was like to be on mission for that longer period. However, when the day came to head to the airport, I found myself racked with nerves and uncertainty. I was on the verge of quitting, of not going, as I struggled internally in my thinking. I am not sure what was happening, but the outworking was a battle between my emotions and my will. I was determined that my will would win, and so I boarded the plane for Orlando and that was it, job done, no turning back now.

I spent a few days in Lakeland, Florida, with friends, gathering a few necessary items and preparing myself for what lay ahead. I was going to live for the first four weeks in a town called Progresso, with a family that I only knew very slightly, and the aim was that I would spend my days learning Spanish and adopting the culture. John came with me to Tampa, Miami, and eventually La Ceiba. There we parted company and I was on a bus to Progresso, with my 20 Spanish words, an umbrella (I am joking), and a bag of clothes, enough to last a couple of weeks.

The father from the family I was to live with met me from the bus and we got a taxi together to the outskirts of the town, where he had a small one-bedroomed house built onto the side of his church. His name is Lauriano, and he is a beautiful man of God. I met the family, mum, two sons, daughter, and a friend who boarded with them. The boys and I would sleep on thin mattresses on the church floor, the boys both already did that, of course. They were content young men, slim, honouring, with permanent brilliant smiles.

The women's early prayer meetings were at 5 am three mornings a week, so we would rise at 4.30 am on those days and tidy up before exiting the church to allow the ladies to gather for prayer. The same ladies would be there early on Sundays, with their aprons on and a dusting of maize flour on their hands, as they laughed and prepared snacks, admitting me easily and graciously to their inner circle of fun as they taught me how to make Honduran street food.

On the days when there were no community prayers, we would sleep until 5.30 am and then everyone had work, school, etc., so we were all up and at it. I found myself trying to find a rhythm that worked for me. As a result, on the days there were no early morning prayer meetings, I would stay in the church and pray by myself, often walking up and down as I prayed, pouring my heart out to God, reading scriptures and immersing myself in them for hours at a time. These times were so rich, and I found myself in a place where it was easier, and in fact a delight, to spend hours simply in God's presence. Time went by unnoticed on those days, food untouched, tears often spilled as intimacy with God was encountered.

Most days also included a few hours in the hammock, when the younger wide-grinning, brown-eyed children would gather around me and we would have a time of unofficial Spanish lessons as I practised conjugating my verbs and putting the words in the right order, much to the hilarious enjoyment of the children. Their laughter was contagious, and their ability to find joy in the simple was a life lesson. Amazingly, between spending time with this family and the hammock hours, my Spanish was coming along, and I was now conversing and understanding most basic conversations.

During these days I would at times reflect on my own childhood. The complexity of my relationship with my dad, who had endless time for the birds in the garden and so little true time for his son. My dad, who nobody had a bad word for, and who hit me repeatedly until I bruised, who kicked me off my feet, and who slapped me to my knees. My dad who worked long, torturous hours in labour-intensive work to provide for his family, his expression of love was to provide. And at times, generous, funny, and involved, but the sudden unpredictable changes laid those times to waste. Yet I love him. I have glimpses of his pain through the Second World War, and the struggle of his own parents and their relentless discipline. He had shrapnel from a grenade in his forehead and both his legs. They did not have the resources or the time in WWII to remove it all. He was patched up and shipped back to the front. He saw his close friends, clothes blown off them by a booby-trapped watch, dead but unmarked. How did he come back to shops, and fairs, and quiet streets afterwards, unsupported, unseen, and unheard, buried alive in his memories.

I fell into the swing of life in Central America, the clusters of shotgun-wielding guards outside each bank, the crazy pumping music and decorations on the local buses, the fresh fruit bars, and the rice and beans staple diet. The dust, the heat, and the sheer difficulty of living every day made their mark. I too started to think along the lines of "why do it today if you really do not have to", and it made perfect sense to me. Contrary to the Victorian values upbringing, where the mantra is "do not put off to tomorrow what you can do today", my counter stance was much more enjoyable and, in the setting, made much more sense.

I fell in love with the family I was staying with. I became fast friends with their boys and the young man lodging with them. We often stayed awake into the small hours telling stories and laughing until we hurt. One of my great memories, that I will treasure more than any other thing, is sharing my birthday with these guys on the beach at Tela, having fish and chips (Honduran style) for dinner, and just being great mates. I love those guys.

There were a few testing moments as well. One day, against advice from the older guys, I played soccer with some of the younger men. It was fast and furious, and I was a standout for around five minutes before the heat floored me. I faded fast and finally, wilted, I left the pitch, with the sound of the fast-paced game continuing behind me. The next morning I had a fever. It was as bad as, if not worse than, anything I had experienced before. I spent the day on the mattress on the church floor, alternating between sweating and shivering. I do not remember all that much, but I do recall some people lifting me and carrying me into a house where they removed my shirt and covered me in cold, wet towels. One of the pastors and his wife came and prayed with me, and he massaged my muscles. He had hands like bricks, and the pain of his massage kept me aware while they prayed.

After they left, I could hear singing in the church and realised, to my surprise, that it was already nighttime. I was lucid, and I recalled the prayer for my wellbeing. I thought of all I had seen already, the poverty, the pain, the harshness, and the struggles, and in the midst of all of that, joy and happiness, and people living with what they had, not longing for what they did not have. They had learned to live their lives in the now, in the moment, to have their joy in the moment, their fun, their camaraderie, their love of life, in the moment. And I cried. I cried that I would expect God to heal me from a fever when so many others suffered without recourse. I found myself in a dim place in my mind as I told God I could not see why he would heal me, yet let others suffer, and in fact I tried to tell God that I was struggling to believe in him at that moment. I lay there still, feeling lost.

A soft wind blew through me. It was not a breeze or an open window or door, it was something else. I sobbed and sobbed. When the crying subsided, I was healed. I stood up and slowly made my way outside. The pastor saw me and came over. He said, "O Allan que fe tan grande tienes." "Oh Allan, what great faith you have!" My Spanish was insufficient to explain to him how wrong he was. I smiled and slowly shook my head, pointing to the sky. Nothing else needed to be added. If only he knew.

Shortly after this, I somehow got amoebas in my gut and lost kilo after kilo, suffering stomach cramps and a total lack of interest in food for around two weeks. Eventually a doctor was found, medicine was purchased, and the healing was a journey. On top of that, I had a parasite living in my skin, and strips of skin started to peel away from my body. It was painful and raw, and nothing I did seemed to help. Of course, there were the usual dozens of mosquito bites, the itches, and the mild fevers. All in all, I was not looking like such a healthy specimen as the weeks went by, although my Spanish was improving and my relationship with my God was deepening and maturing.

The time with the family was up. It was time to head back to La Ceiba to meet with John and a few others as we prepared for a massive eight-week trek into the rainforests of Central America, most notably across the Mosquito Coast, crossing over at some point from Honduras into Nicaragua.

Oh, what adventures lay ahead of us.

Chapter 63

I woke up slowly. The smell of oat and honey bread was permeating the warm bedroom air. Four am. The timer on the breadmaker must have been set for around 3.30 am, was my guess. I was back in La Ceiba, staying with Kenton, Suandi, and his family. Kenton was coming with us on the trip.

Today we would organise ourselves, clothes, haversack, first aid stuff, medical supplies, washing things, hammock, etc. We had a day to get everything together, as the following morning we would depart for the coast near Brus Lagoon, our jumping-off point for the trip. A MAF pilot was going there and was happy to drop us there, but we had a strict limit on luggage weight. We enjoyed our day, fruit and bread for brekkie, taking time to do simple things and having fun with the ongoing banter. We were all pretty much ready by early lunchtime, which would be around 10.30 or 11 am in Honduras, as we rise at 4.

John decided that, as we had time on our hands, we should all go to the local Federal Prison for a visit. There was a small group of missionaries from Norway there that day, so they came with us. There would have been around six of us, four in the back tray of the pick-up and two inside, John and Kenton. So off we bounced through the humid streets of La Ceiba, and out past the airport, turning off in the middle of a pineapple plantation, following a straight as die road that seemed to be heading through the plantation to the foot of the grand mountains that framed La Ceiba.

And there was the prison, an off-grey, high-walled compound, stained with patches of green lichen-like moss. Men without uniforms but with semi-automatic weapons wandered around. Some looked like they were in the middle of a task, others looked aimless and bored. These were the guards, poorly paid, poorly trained, and lacklustre in enthusiasm.

John and I were ushered in to meet the prison governor. John had met him before and had great favour. We were to be allowed to go into the prison and hold a service and meet with the prisoners. We had brought some cheap sunglasses to give away, and John made sure the guards all got a pair first. There would have been around 25 to 30 guards on that day. We each then had two pairs to give away to prisoners once inside. We were cautioned by John to be careful and discreet. Everything has value in the prison, and we could easily start a fight just by being naïve.

So in we went. A tall metal barred gate grudgingly opened and we went into a holding area. Once that was shut, a trustee opened the inner tall metal barred gate, and in we walked to the federal prison in Central America. I noticed immediately that no guards came in with us. John explained that trustees, with pickaxe handles, ruled the prison, and if guards came in, they came in shooting because there was a riot. All new information to me that was less than comforting.

So we were in, and I was feeling uncomfortable. The atmosphere was intense and intimidating, to me at least. Men stared at me. Some came up to me and asked me for my shoes or my shirt. Some made signs that I did not fully understand, but they did not seem to be coming from a place of pleasantries. We kept moving along slowly, John chatting to a few of the guys, myself struggling with my new Spanish to really grapple with the background noise and the voices of so many people at the same time. There were over 500 men in a prison built for 200.

Eventually we arrived at a small open hacienda-style building with whitewashing that years of telling prison grime had faded, and we entered. Chairs were rearranged for a church service, and within a few minutes John was praying and opening the service. Over the next ten minutes or so, a small trickle of men drifted into the service until all the chairs were full and more were needed. Many men hung around the doors making comments that we were meant to overhear, and others leaned smirking through the glassless window spaces.

The service proceeded with a few songs, unaccompanied, and the sense of true worship was powerful to me. These men needed God. I started to realise that there was a desperation about the prayers and the worship. There was a time for testimonies, and I listened as men acknowledged their failings, taking full responsibility for their actions. These were powerful moments of men transformed in the harshest of conditions, public declarations heard by other cynical and hardened prisoners lingering around the fringes. Men cried for their loved ones, wives, mothers, children. Not many, if any, mentioned fathers. For some there would be 20 years or more to spend here. Other older men may possibly live out the rest of their lives, never seeing the outside or their families again.

At the end of the service, I was inundated with men asking me to contact their families for them, to let them know where they were. I gathered all the details I could so I could share these with John later. I swapped my good shirt for a torn and tattered sleeveless shirt and gave away one toothbrush discreetly. I sat and chatted to some of the younger men, and my Spanish was passable for these conversations.

The time came for us to head back to the main gates and say our goodbyes. The walk back was, for me at least, quite intimidating. There were so many men here, all looking to get something from me, asking for money for food, grabbing at my arms and hands continually. I could see there truly was a need for food. I felt my body shape, well fed, large-boned, some would kindly say. I thought so little of popping into Pizza Hut in downtown La Ceiba and having a salad and a single pizza for lunch, something that for any of these men would be an unbelievably joyful experience. I know, I know they had done wrong and they were there for correction, although there was little, if any, focus on that, it seemed. Almost all energy was aimed at survival. I cannot imagine what it would be like to spend a night there.

We were through the gates and the catcalls were fading as we turned the corner to jump into the back of the pick-up for the journey back to our base. I am not ashamed to say that as we drove the bumpy, dust-driven road back through the pineapple plantation, I cried, and I cried, some for the men and some for my own shame at my fear. I whispered to myself, "If I never go back there again, it will be a day too soon."

Back at base we found our space and read, chatted, dozed, and watched a movie. The evening passed into night, and then we were to be up at 4 am and off. The big adventure awaited. John, Kenton, and I would be close buddies on this trip. The Norwegian group were going to a missionary hospital in another part of Honduras, so we would say our goodbyes in the morning. None of them had enjoyed the prison trip, and I think they were keen to move on.

The next morning at breakfast, news came that the pilot was delaying a day for weather reasons, so we would be grounded at base for another day. I was ok to hang out and loved spending time reading. I was reading *Silas Marner* and was loving the story. The Norwegians were leaving in the late afternoon. John announced another prison visit. The whole Norwegian party declined, and Kenton had a bank run to do, so he would be gone for several hours, leaving John and me.

I did not want to go. Fear gripped me. But I did not want to miss what God had for me either. I tracked down John, confessed my fears, and asked him to pray. He prayed, the shortest prayer in my history as a Christian, "God, please help Allan today." When I opened my eyes, he had left the room. Wow.

So off we went, this time just the two of us, both in the truck. I was nervous and quiet as we approached the broken-down buildings, the high guard towers giving away their purpose to any passers-by, not that there were any such things. No visit needed to the chief this time, straight to the ten-foot-high rusty iron bar double gates.

It was amazing. I felt such a peace and contentment on me. My heart had compassion for all the men. Their mannerisms and jostling caused me to stop, look, and engage today, whereas yesterday I had wanted to flee. I chatted, asked questions, laughed, prayed, and engaged with anyone and everyone. A group of men led me to another part of the prison and I went willingly. We found some chairs and we sat and chatted and laughed, and one man appeared with some brushes and cleaned my shoes.

This time I had worn good shoes that I would be happy to swap, and a decent shirt again that I would swap. I had also taken a few small denomination banknotes to slip to the odd prisoner where possible. I knew they could buy extra rice and beans for a few lempira. I went round to the cells with the men and they showed me how they lived, and to the kitchen so I could see what they got to eat. John told me later that I was not supposed to do this, and that usually the men of the prison would not allow any visitors into these personal areas, so he said I was honoured.

There was a moment in time when I was with the men on the seats chatting where I felt as if Jesus was right there with us, happy, chatting away, loving the men and loving being with them. I bought a small black coral necklace with a cross, which I still have today, from one prisoner.

So prison visits became a favourite activity for me from that day forward. I actually looked forward to the times when we were able to go and visit with the guys in the prison, and I got to know a few of them a little bit over the next twenty or so years as I travelled back and forward to Honduras. This would have been around the early 1990s, but I remember my shock and horror when there was a large prison riot in 2004 and many of the prisoners were shot dead by the guards. I guess I was glad we were not there at the time, but I had a sense of sadness and waste for the way so many lives had been lived and now ended.

As the sky lightened the next morning, we were all making our last-minute adjustments and preparations for our trip into the rainforests of Honduras and Nicaragua over the next six to eight weeks. We breakfasted after hot showers, it would be a while before we would have one of them again, voices quiet around the table, humour and nerves in equal play. Loading our light kit into the ute, we were soon off to the airport to meet our MAF pilot and board the small plane out to the edge of the Mosquito Coast. What adventures must lay ahead of us.

Chapter 64

We were taking shade under the wing of an aeroplane, remarkable to me in how small it was when I was up close. The sun was brutal this morning as we awaited the pilot with his cleared flight plan for the fringe of the Mosquito Coast. Kenton and I laughed and chatted as we enjoyed these moments that may only come along once in a lifetime, if that.

John came into sight side by side with the pilot, on the fringe of the apron, framed by the flight tower rising like an old guard behind him. The pilot, Ken from Texas of the "y'all goin git sum bienes" fame, was chatting away, waving his hands as he regaled John with some sort of story. Kenton and I fell silent until such time as we could call out a greeting. Our small pile of gear lay on the concrete near our feet. Not enough to weigh us down, not enough to meet all our desires, but our basic needs of sleep and dry clothes were there, alongside one can of hidden Coca-Cola, which was being sneaked along to celebrate Kenton's birthday in a few weeks' time.

We piled into the tiny plane and soon we were what I would describe as careering down the massive runway, like the Borrowers making a getaway in a model plane.

It was around a forty-five-minute trip out to the start of the Mosquito Coast, where we touched down, busily but safely, in a field on the edge of a village. We had buzzed the runway first, simply to chase the cattle and horses away. I was really hoping they understood it was not a game, and that they would not run back on as we finalised our approach. I would have many more of these small-plane experiences in the years to come, some more hairy than others.

We walked over to the village houses where we met David Smith, a local Garifuna man who would do the upcoming journey with us. We clicked right away, laughing and joking with each other as if we were lifelong friends. We set up camp here in this village, and we would have a church service that night before setting off into the deeper parts of the rainforest. I had my hammock, a light sheet, and a fragile mosquito net. It was the middle of the day, so we rested, as is the custom. In fact, the best sleeps are often at this time. A silence reigns, hand in hand with the humidity and heat, a trinity that even the skin-and-bone rascally dogs did not disturb. Later that evening we discovered a local woman who had baked cinnamon buns. Oh, that was a happy few minutes.

The next morning, as the mist was still draped over the nearest trees, we were already packing up and sipping hot, treacle-like coffee from tiny thick tumblers, no two the same. David would pilot the dug-out canoe we would use, and Kenton and I would sit amidships for stability, while John was stern-bound with another pearly white smiling, young man who had joined the expedition team late the previous night. Here we were, this band of unlikely brothers, a Scotsman, an Ohioan, a Floridian, a Garifuna, and a Honduran. A truer display of God's amazing grace would be hard to find.

Strangely, I find myself reflecting at this time on an incident in my life from many years ago, long before I encountered Jesus. I was living in Glenfinnan at the time and had a Honda CX500. I had driven up to Lochailort on a Friday night and had several pints of beer with some friends up there. Late in the night, when I was starting to think about heading home, I was invited to a party at Glenuig, another ten miles or so up the road. I made a decision to go, not a great decision really. Drink driving was endemic in the area, as there were no police to speak of, and late opening of pubs was normal. But that is no excuse.

When I got close to Glenuig, I realised I did not know the exact house the party was at. So I stopped at the side of the road and went to put my foot down, but I was too close to the ditch and ended up upside down in it, the motorbike pinning me in place. Luckily a car stopped. They had seen what had happened and helped me out.

The car and its merry passengers were heading to the same party, and they told me where to go, jumping back into their warm vehicle, breath cut off in clouds of steam. I watched their red tail-lights disappear into the distance.

I think I sat on my bike for a few minutes and then decided that the best thing to do was to go home. So I pushed my bike until we were both facing the right way, swung my leg over the seat, and promptly emulated my antics on this new side of the road as I once again slipped into the ditch, the motorbike following.

This may be hard to believe, but the same car came back and rescued me again. I reckon they knew I was not going well, and when I did not turn up after them at the party, they decided to come looking for me.

I clambered aboard the CX, fired it up, and off I went, blurred vision, low balance, following white lines, hoping I was adroit enough to spot and avoid any oncoming traffic. How I got home in one piece I will never really know. You would think I would have learned, but this was practised behaviour by now.

One time in Edinburgh, years earlier, I had driven home from Ratho, again after a night on the beers. Not quite as drunk this time, but possibly may have not been safe. Heading back along the unlit road, a policeman stepped out, swinging a torch and indicating that I should pull in beside him. I kept my helmet on, although he asked me to turn off the engine. He asked me my number plate, and honestly I had no idea. I thought this was it, my time had come to be caught. Anyway, I mumbled something indecipherable into my helmet that would have vaguely sounded like six digits or letters. I could not believe my luck when he spoke to me, reciting my number plate, and asked that I confirm it, which I wholeheartedly did. He waved me on. I rode carefully to within walking distance of my house, parked, and walked, picking my bike up the next day.

While there are moments of Flann O'Brien satire and black humour, overall I guess I am reflecting on how many times my life may have taken a different path, but somehow it just so happens, here I am now, by the grace of God. I certainly do not look back on these memories with any sense of bravado or pride, quite the opposite. I recognise my moral compass spinning around, connecting in comparisons to those around me. I also recognise my season of judging myself by my intentions and judging others by their actions. I treated people poorly, and for that I do sense a deep sorrow. I am so grateful to Jesus for his saving and transforming power. Without Him, I am desolate.

The mangroves started to thin out a little, the sky came back into view, and we were clear of the swamp, now into a broad, fast-running river, with steep wooded banks on both sides. The first alligator was spotted, tail in the water and body in the sun, ready to snap or slither into action when opportunity presented. I think I had a moment of realisation that this was not a theme park or a game, but life and death.

After a few hours of steady progress, we arrived at a dwelling. The ochre mud walls, with a few scattered decorations, greeted us. Wisps of hopeful smoke seemed to drift through the close-knit palm fronds that constituted both roof and ceiling. I would love to say I graciously disembarked, but it was more like a giraffe climbing a spiral stairwell. I felt sure that at any moment I would be doing the upside-down terrapin at the river's edge. Somehow I made it ashore dry, but with little dignity.

The lady of the house, a mahogany-coloured woman, tall and straight-shouldered, with a swirling mass of rich grey hair, swept out of the doorway and enveloped John in a warm greeting, children following. The only sounds were the waves lapping and the children laughing. We were introduced with great ceremony, as if we were famed travellers. I think I felt a little embarrassed at my lack of credentials to live up to the greeting. We were seated and fed with rice, beans, and lake fish. We had arrived at Brus Lagoon, and we would attempt a crossing in the morning.

We held an intimate church service for this wonderful lady and her few neighbours. We prayed a lot, sang a little, and then John shared a few words of encouragement. By the time we concluded it was dark, the only light coming from a small pine-laden fireplace, from which sap also came the sweetest of smells, filling the house as peace and joy filled the group.

The lady of the house gave up her bed and left to sleep at a friend's house. The bed was wooden-framed with mahogany timber struts. No mattress, no sheet, no pillow. This was a sacrificial offering, and I slept, or perhaps I should say I lay and turned and turned on the bed until first light. I can sleep in most places, and since that night I can sleep in more, but that night I counted the minutes as more than the stars and wondered at my durability as a pale, weak Scottish specimen.

But we were up, crossing the lagoon, the sun already warm as the bow spray soaked Kenton and me over and over, until all we could do was look at each other and laugh. Having made it across, we set course to travel up the reaches of the Rio Patuca, a river that winds its way through the depths of the Mosquito Coast and at times draws close to the border with Nicaragua. Kenton and I arranged our packs behind us and used them to lean back on. We had an unusual degree of comfort and settled in for the day.

We stopped once, drawing alongside the steep, shelved bank of the slow-moving, milk-chocolate-coloured, horseshoeing river, and scaled the mud, both for a view and a pee. After hours of slow progress against the deep water, we saw signs of life increasing on the riverbanks. Fields were planted, areas were cleared, and some basic shelters stood awaiting the families that farmed this space. I would learn that families would leave their huts and go to the fields for weeks at a time to clear, plant, or harvest. Everyone would go, grandparents, parents, and all the children, and work from dawn till dusk every day before sleeping in palm-frond and branch shelters. I felt my privilege. I felt my expanded waist, and I felt my cheap emotions.

The village was called Auas, pronounced auhos, and we were welcomed into a small house where the local pastor and his family slept. The village had a small wooden-framed church, and we would sleep there that night, across the pews or in our hammocks, but for now it was rice and beans time. The meal was amazing. Even now, rice and beans thrills me.

We held a church service which packed out the small building. Prayers went on for a long spell, then some specials, where people sang or gave their testimony. John shared a message, and he leaned towards drama when sharing, which the villagers loved. They soaked up the Bible stories in their richness, and the points made went home, as demonstrated by the packed altar and prayer time at the end of the service. There was real need, deep repentance, and the sweetness of God all around. These people worked physically hard most of the year, long days, just to survive. They were totally dependent on the weather, and early or late rains were disastrous. My appreciation of what I had sat heavy with me most days.

We followed the river day after day. We met families, made friends, and saw God at work so frequently. Enough stories were heard, told, and written to fill another book, but I will only choose a couple to tell here.

Chapter 65

The next day we travelled to Wampusirpe, a reasonably sized village that also had the added advantage of having a fairly flat field where small MAF aeroplanes could, and did from time to time, land. There we met a couple from the USA, I think it was Michigan, who told us they were agricultural missionaries. They invited us to their small house for dinner, which we accepted. Once there, they explained how their skills and experience were there to support the local people, by showing how adding certain things to the soil would enhance overall health and allow a much wider selection of fruit, veg, nuts, and seeds to be grown all year round. They confessed that they were struggling, and that no matter what they did there was so little interest or uptake from any locals. I felt sad for this older couple, so far away from home and family, with so many hopes and dreams, but living with constant frustration.

We enjoyed our dinner, and then after a celebratory church service we headed to our hammocks to recharge our strength ready for what the next day would bring. As I reflected on the couple, part of me sympathised with them, and part of me sympathised with the locals. I think after being there for only a few months my own cultural values were being challenged, and as life was hard every day for us, and much more so for those people who lived in the country, my mindset was changing, from an industrial "do not put off till tomorrow what you can do today", to more of a hammock-seeking "why on earth would you do anything today, if you could put it off till tomorrow".

The next day we set off upriver, with a request to stop at the very next village to drop off a few items for a family that lived there. A family at church had asked us to do this, and we cheerfully obliged. We had not been planning to stop at this village, as it was fairly close to the one we had just spent two days in. By fairly close, I mean a twelve-hour walk.

When we got to this village I was really surprised by a few things. There were drains cut alongside the paths around the village to allow the heavy rainwater to run away from the houses, so that the houses, which were all up on stilts as they were in every village here, did not have pools of mud under them. With no mud came a massive reduction in mosquito activity around the animals and the houses.

We found the house of the family we were looking for and they invited us in. As usual, it was a small house made from long wooden slabs cut by hand from local trees. Fifteen adults and children called this place home. There was a room with a table and two chairs, a clay oven and a small alcove where the parents and youngest children slept. Everyone else found a space on the floor each night.

As we were waiting, a couple of smiling, dark-eyed teenagers came into the room with plates of cut fruit, mandarins, pineapple, apple and some berries. All of this fruit was very unusual, and some was actually out of season. I was shocked and started to ask a few questions about how they came to have all this fruit available. It just so happened that a young local boy had been sponsored to go to agricultural college in the city, and when he came back and shared his knowledge with the village about drainage and soil adjustments, everyone in the village adopted this new knowledge as their own.

I was greatly impacted by this living example of how investing in local people was the best form of support we could provide, and that this would bring much greater returns than trying to tell locals what to do as outsiders. From that day onwards, my already existing commitment to helping with education was further steeled into purpose.

The next day we decided to walk. Villagers told us that there was a path parallel to the river that, in a few hours, would take us to the next village. Of course, when they say "a few hours" it is more a general description of time, which could mean six hours or even two days. Time is different here.

But we started walking. The village houses became further apart quickly and the encroaching jungle showed its face. Then we went through a small clearing and disappeared into the dense jungle, following a narrow, elusive path.

A couple of hours into the walk we were going along well, and we stopped for a breather at an unusually twisted, gnarly tree where there was the smallest of clear spaces. We gathered ourselves for the shortest time, hands on knees, torso at 2 pm, legs at 6 pm, and then quickly pushed on, until about forty-five minutes later we arrived at an identical tree. Hmmmmm. What were the chances there were two trees like this only about an hour apart, or alternatively, what were the chances we had gone around in a circle. We pushed on, strides becoming more purposeful, as if that alone would make all the difference. An hour later we encountered the third of the triplet trees.

It was afternoon, darkness was at most three hours away, and we were truly lost in the deepest, most remote jungle, back beside our tree of nearly three hours past. I was sort of enjoying myself, but could not imagine how we would survive a night in this place. It would be impossible to keep walking, and there was nowhere to rest, so we would probably have to stand still in the mud and mosquitoes for the ten hours of darkness. Not appealing.

We decided to cut away from the path and try to find the river. Sixty minutes of hard slog later we were as close to the riverbank as the jungle would permit, and on the other side we saw a local farmer working in his small paddocks of what looked like beans. We shouted and waved until we caught his attention. There were three of us, me, John and Kenton, and a local man who was going to head back to the original village once we were safe. To be honest, I was ready to go with him.

The farmer crossed the powerful river with ease in his hollowed log and swiftly ushered us all into his dug-out canoe, offering to pole us upriver to the next village. He told us we were still hours away, either by walking or by dug-out canoe and pole. He said we were on completely the wrong track, that it was an old track not used anymore, as the river had changed its course in a storm over a year past.

So off we went, sitting rigidly still in the most unstable vessel I had ever been in. Within a few minutes my muscles were aching, but tipping into the alligator-rich muddy river was even less appealing than the pain of this transport.

Around an hour, or maybe two, went by. It was pretty dark, and we stayed close to the edge to avoid any large debris being swept downstream from the faraway mountains. The young, barebacked farmer expertly used his pole to draw us upstream, fighting for every inch. He made it look easy to stand at the front and use his pole, but I am one hundred per cent sure it was not easy.

Suddenly, it just so happened that around the bend in the river ahead came a much bigger dug-out canoe, with a motor attached and two men shining torches. A rescue party. We somehow transferred canoes, gave the farmer a wad of notes with our thanks and prayers, and in the swirling waters we turned the canoe and gunned it towards safety.

We held a church service that night when we arrived, and I think our thanksgiving was a little deeper. The next day, as usual, we spent time with several of the local pastors and did teaching sessions with them. There was time to read, and always a siesta in the heat of the day. That night many people from several smaller local villages had travelled over, and we had a massive outdoor time of prayer and worship. Then John shared the dramatic story of Esther, and I watched these amazing people lean in, laughing at the irony and gasping at how God orchestrated the salvation of the Jewish people. Such fun.

We headed further upriver the very next day to a village called Tukrum. It was from here the next morning that we would launch our walk through the jungle to Nicaragua.

As twilight slipped away, the increasing noise took me by surprise. We were slinging our hammocks in an abandoned red-mud wood and adobe dwelling high above the gorge. We could just see the far side of the river below, where virgin rainforest clambered thick to the hazy edge. Growls, howls, screams and pulsing insects built an audio impact almost tangible in force.

Days of mud-clad walking, stooped over under the claustrophobic canopy, along with intermittent hours of poling up rivers in back-breaking dug-outs, lay behind us. Tomorrow we would walk across the Mosquito Coast border from Honduras into Nicaragua. We would be in Contra Rebel territory, small remote villages where witch doctors ruled the roost alongside the ever-present cockerels, and snake bites that could quickly end your journey, full stop.

A couple of local men travelled with us. One was on his way to visit his sick mum, the other a friend accompanying him. That night there was little to eat other than a small handful of maize porridge each, gifted to us from a nearby village. We had not eaten at all the day before. Water was in plentiful supply, although the Clorox tablets, with their pale bleach taste, made me shudder occasionally. Most times I simply grimaced.

That night we sang together, me in my gruff a-musical tone, while the locals harmonised alongside their lightweight balsa wood guitars. A tired-looking laundry pail improvised as a drum. Old hymns were our favourites. Even with my tuneless singing, there were teary moments of God-breathed intimacy under a massive sparkling Milky Way, thick-black canopy sky.

As the night darkened, pigs from the local village came and made their evening repose preparations around our hammocks. The evening scents were, well, let's say interesting. All night long I fought a losing battle against the mosquito armies, as the pigs grunted, farted and grumbled, with occasional high squeals and flurries of temper. Hunger drew some self-whispered questions from my lips, if not my heart, that night.

Four a.m. is the coolest time of the day, but not the quietest. Not much sleep was had by anyone in our small group that night. At four-fifteen we were rolling up lightweight hammocks and in the half-light attempting our packer's knots.

Bags were slung over shoulders, legs stretched, backs cracked and heads wearily rubbed or scratched. Pausing to simply breathe, we steadied ourselves, gathering our strength for the day ahead. Boots would be covered in tacky clay, hidden roots in the narrow path would destabilise our momentum, backs would ache, belts would be pulled in, and a pace would be set. Nine hours was the expectation. The nine hours was mentioned once.

The banter was light, leg-pulling the order of the day, as well as the odd half-humorous cry of "oh God"!

We had each saved one small tough dehydrated piece of bread for this day. That was our battery pack, our energy source.

After fifteen minutes in the motorised dug-out, we cut the motor and drifted slowly into a tributary, landing softly on the sloping mud bank. We were out and off with no fanfare; the earliest of morning colour was just showing our feet the way. Within seconds we were swallowed whole by the virgin rainforest, as our well-booted feet gathered clay mud with every step. And that was the next nine hours: Clorox tablets, warm water, and walking torture. I pulled my belt in a notch twice that day. At one point we stopped by a giant tree, the roots rose to at least ten feet off the ground, but had my photo taken, and even now I look at that picture and wonder if that was me.

I still remember with such clarity the moment nine hours later when we surprised ourselves and popped out of the jungle. The clear sky overhead made me smile the broadest smile of that day. I slumped down on a rock beside the Rio Coco. Done, for the moment the walking was done, and so was I.

Chapter 66

A couple of locals just so happened to be heading back down to the village from their fields in their dug-out canoes. Firstly, it was so rare that anyone went up or down the river on a Sunday, that being the universal rest day in the villages in this area. And secondly, that it just so happened they came past us a few moments after we arrived at the river was remarkable provision.

I'd love to say I jumped into the canoe like a seasoned local, but it was more like a camel standing on a crocodile in reality. Once in, the muscle memory came back with the pains. One false move and I would be floating alongside an upside-down log. We went through some rapids on the way. It was both exhilarating and shockingly scary.

Within thirty minutes we were at the village. We left the canoes and ugly-clambered up a steep muddy bank, dignity left at the river.

John had been here a few years back, and many people remembered him. This whole area had been impacted by the Contra Rebels over the previous decade. We were told, in many villages, the pastors and their families had been shot first for all to see, and their houses burned. Often whole villages had been murdered and all property and animals destroyed or stolen. The Contra, which means "against", Rebels were allegedly US-funded and opposed the Marxist government at the time. This was 1990. I listened to the stories of atrocities and violence with a shocked inner man. How could these people have lived through this and have such forgiveness in their attitudes and hearts only a year or two later? They had such a hard life. The day before we arrived, eight people in this village had died from cholera, and today an eight-year-old boy was bitten by a snake while clearing long grass in a field. He was left in a makeshift bed to see if he would live or die. There was no doctor, no medicine. Any real help was days' walk away, if you had any money, which no one here did. Wealth here was animals and crops.

We slung our hammocks in the local pastor's house. There was just enough room for three hammocks side by side. Later we would feast on rice and beans, but for now we rested, preparing for a church service in a few hours. The service was packed out and full of heartfelt prayer and worship.

The next morning we held a short service for the pastor and his wife. They had never been officially married. That would mean being away from their village for a few weeks, walking to the nearest city and back, with all sorts of costs involved, which they could not pay, and how could they leave their small subsistence farm for that time anyway?

John had brought a ring with him, which the pastor put on his wife's finger in the middle of a teary-eyed service at the front of their house. I cried, they cried, even the children cried. If this had been all that we had travelled here to do, every step would have been worthwhile.

Later that morning John and I went for a walk and chat along a path by the river, just enjoying each other's company. Two militia-style men appeared. They had semi-automatic weapons slung on their shoulders in a position that would make use fast and easy. They motioned us to walk with them over to a small barn-like rough wooden building. Years of sun had bleached and softened the hard red wood into a sullen grey. If I shut my eyes right now I can still see that sun-softened wood, oblivious to my fear, safe in its impartiality.

They questioned us and had us empty out the small bags we had with us. Neither of us had any money on us. We each had our passports in zip-lock bags, and I had a small digital camera, also in a zip-lock bag. It was the only sure way to keep anything dry, knowing that you could fall in the river on any given day. It felt like I was in a B-movie, and a bad B-movie at that. Straight to TV, no cinema or DVD for this episode. Sweat ran down my face. I honestly wondered if this was it, perhaps a small article in the papers at home saying a local man had gone missing in Central America. However, my worst fears were unfounded, and within twenty minutes we were released and back on our way, although the sweating took a little longer to stop.

That afternoon we set off on foot toward a local estuary of the main river, where we were met and ferried even further inland through a breathtakingly classic mangrove swamp. The riverbanks pressed hard with intensely green growth, fighting for space and light, so much so that for much of the trip the canoe was swallowed in their shadows. As dusk fell we arrived at a small village, and the customary river mud bank was scaled. We were welcomed warmly, and rice and beans were shared. I'd guess that at this point we were at least four weeks' travel away from any town or city. The young man who sat beside me told me we were the first missionaries ever to visit this village. That was a moment when I stopped and just thanked God that he would let me do this. The church service was full of life and joy. I was so blessed simply to be part of this.

Early the next morning, just before first light, we were on our way back to the village of the wedding ring. That night in our hammocks I talked about how I regretted not having a middle name, and how amazing Latin America was, where many of the young men I met had four or more names. The very next day I was baptised Allan David Brown. I had a new middle name.

The days went by very much the same: short canoe journeys, church services, great conversations, long walks, and the obligatory rice and beans. Around a week later we headed off downstream to start completing the circle of the journey back to Ceiba. We spent most of the day navigating the huge horseshoe bends on the jungle-plaid plains, covering three times the distance the crow took. We stopped at a large village nearly halfway to the coast, and there was a sign there on the muddy riverbank that declared this village was supported by funds from the EU as well as some USA support.

I was a little shocked by the welcome when we were greeted with "what are you going to give us", the tone of voice implying that if it was not something better than what they already had, we would not be all that welcome. People from the EU had come and spent a fair bit of time here telling everyone how poor they were, and so now their mindset was "we are poor, you are rich, so we should not have to work, you should just share your wealth with us!" Every other village I had been in was poorer than this village, but nobody had ever told them that, and they were some of the happiest people I had ever been blessed to be around. In fact, I questioned my own values and lifestyle when I was around them, and as a result made several shifts to a simpler way of life. We stayed one night, sleeping on the hard church benches and eating only a bowl of rice that was donated. We had no money with us; otherwise, we would have been robbed by now anyway.

We set off downstream in a small motorised dug-out and were dropped off at a small branch of the river. From here we would walk to a small airstrip that had been set up during the war. It was far enough away from the border to avoid shelling or land attacks, but close enough to transport wounded villagers to be airvac'd out to military hospitals that the USA had set up in Honduras. Reflecting on this caused me to pause a little. The USA were allegedly arming the militia to overthrow the Marxist government. The militia did this by attacking the poorest people in the remotest part of the country to draw the government troops into a battle they would never win. Then the USA set up this small support for those poor villagers. Was that real? Anyway, the airstrip was now utilised by MAF, and we might get a lift back to Ceiba from there, which would save us another two to three weeks of walking through the jungle; instead we would be back in just over an hour.

We walked for around seven hours. This time we were on the plains, flat, trees spaced out for miles into the distance. At one point, an off-road Ute came towards us, bouncing over the uneven terrain like a small ship in a storm. The driver pulled up and jumped out; he was clearly drunk and holding a revolver. We emptied our bags at his command, and again I wondered if we would get through the day. We had nothing of value, so disappointed and angry, he vented at us, then swivelled around and zig-zagged back to the truck, gone in a flurry of dust and tundra. John and I gathered our stuff, looked at each other and had a good five minutes laughing. I was so glad when the airstrip came into sight; the short walk had felt like almost a full day. There were showers, a kitchen, and beds.

At the airstrip, I met an older gentleman who was in the process of installing a water well in a remote village, and this airstrip was his jumping-off point. It took the whole dry season to install one water well, having to ship everything to the airstrip and then, by mule and dugout canoe, transport everything to the village. The village would be a week's round trip at least, and there would be up to ten trips to get everything on site. Then came the work of installing the well and the pump, by which time the rains were starting, and it was time to move out before he was stuck for three months or more.

He had retired from work in the USA a few years back and had been doing this every year since; he was in his seventies. He had also noticed that there was a great need for dental care in every village he visited, so in his months in the USA each year between trips, he put himself through dental school. I held a flashlight for him that day, as the power was out, and we did four extractions. The men swaggered in, but once the door shut they whimpered and whined. The ladies came in stoically and sat stoically as the extraction was undertaken, without a flicker of emotion. My respect for these ladies, which was already very high, went off the chart that day. And I saw through the false bravado of the men as well.

Two days later we were airlifted out by a kind MAF pilot, and that night we cleared the salad bar in Pizza Hut; greens had never tasted so good.

I was heading up to Florida next for a week of rest, jogging, eating and recovering before I flew back to the UK. Somehow the friends I was staying with in Ceiba had received a message. It may have been an email, as I think they were starting to be a thing about this time, the mid-1990s, when I was around 37 years old. The message said that my boss had become a Christian and would meet me at the airport when I arrived in Glasgow in a week or so. Ok, wow! I immediately thought about my old boss and how they had said they were Christian, but their behaviour was anything but. That was exciting.

Chapter 67

Florida was always fun. We would usually eat out a lot, as it was relatively cheap compared to UK prices then. Clothes were super-cheap, and of course we had to go to Busch Gardens, Disney World, and a few other places such as Wet and Wild. This was for me a place where my body and soul were restored. I loved going to Lakeland Church, where the service was on the radio on the way in if you were stuck in traffic. I loved hanging out with Alistair and Amanda and their kids, as well as with John. We would just do simple things together: go to the Post Office to pick up mail, the mall for groceries, a walk or jog around the lake to stay in shape, and wow, I found I really loved running in the heat. I wrestled with time in those days, pushing my departure as far back as I was permitted. But the time always came when I had to say a teary goodbye and head home, back to Scotland in February. The security guys at the airport were often ushering me into the building as I fought for the very last bit of sun on my face, even standing once in the grass in the middle of the main road when out of the corner of my eyes I saw them stalking me. Oh well.

I was working for a good boss in the UK. I was trusted, and there was lots of scope to take on responsibility. I had already gone from overseeing one part of his business to becoming his Operations Manager, overseeing the whole operation. I found I loved what his business did, as it was all about people, and I fell in love with the team there. They truly were an exceptional bunch, and his style of trusting people brought out the best in most people. I worked long hours but was well paid and had use of a van, which saved a some expenses for my living costs.

A friend from Oban, who had moved to Inverness, was arranging a wedding dance for one of his children. I was invited, so once back in Caledonia, I called Wendy and invited her. The dance was great fun, and we learned several new Scottish Country dances. We had our first kiss at her doorway that night, before my van and I headed home, although I think I may actually have borrowed a car for this night.

At work we had a small day-cruise boat. It took around 126 people, and I'd heard we had a new skipper, a chap called Brian. I was taken to meet him, and we fell into each other's arms. It just so happened that Brian had known me in the children's home and had actually volunteered there for a year or so – we were good friends already. How good is that?

Oh, I meant to tell you that I was met at the airport, but not by my old boss, by my current one, Finlay. He had been driving down to another bank meeting in Edinburgh when his car, a jet-black SAAB, caught fire. He was stranded in the middle of Rannoch Moor. As he awaited a rescue truck (I think he stopped another car and they promised to phone for him when they got to the next town) he told me later that he sat in his car and broke down in tears. He had worked hard for years, had been close to genuine success, but it looked like he might lose everything: his businesses, his house, his reputation, and his finances. He cried out to God for help, and in that moment he remembered the pastor of my church that I and others had spoken to him about. So, I think the bankers' meeting was rescheduled, the car was carted away, and Finlay went home and, borrowing his wife's car, went unannounced to the pastor's house, loaded with questions. That night, it just so happened that he gave his heart to the Lord.

We started a massive project, taking the wooden cruise boat up the local canal and then beginning a major refurbishment, replacing beams, planks, the whole deck, and improving electrics and plumbing, as well as replacing the two main diesel engines and shafts. We had around four months to complete this. That was a scary time – the rest of the business continued to need the care and attention it always required, the basic operations and long-term forward planning. Meanwhile, this project consumed man-hours and cash like a ravenous rottweiler. Anyway, we made it: exhausted team, depleted cash, bank still on our back, but a new season was starting and we landed a massive contract with a coach company. The renovations would be paid back in full within twelve months. Cash started to flow into all areas of the business, and we were able to buy the business back from the bank. It just so happened they were gone. It felt like a miracle story

– it was certainly exceptional. God was certainly in it, orchestrating things beyond us, as we did everything we could, so many times, it just so happened.

For instance, it just so happened that an American lady dropped into our seafood restaurant for lunch one day when passing through on her way from London to Skye. It just so happened that she loved our smoked salmon (we made our own in our seafood processing business). It just so happened that she owned The Great American Bagel Factory in London and was looking for a unique smoked salmon supplier. It just so happened that she opened another twenty or more shops, and that we ended up supplying a thousand kilos of finished smoked salmon every month. It just so happened that this business transformed our seafood processing business.

As we entered this season of blessing and opportunity, I started to regularly catch up with Wendy and get to know her and her children. We would sometimes go and watch sport on a Saturday, shinty or football, her children would be with their dad. After the game we would have some soup and toast at my apartment to warm up. I so loved those days. We would at times drive from Fort William to Kingussie to watch the shinty, whizzing along the shoreline road around Loch Laggan, with the autumnal trees draping the road in deep yellows and toasty browns, as the sun shed its fading warmth on the car windows. We chatted and listened to our favourite songs. The game would be enjoyed from the touchline, with a half-time flask of soup or coffee awaiting our chilled hands and chattering teeth. We savoured the moments like connoisseurs. We loved getting the heating on in the car after the game and setting off on the drive home, making plans for dinner, Van Morrison serenading us around the first long bend in the road as the sun set behind us.

John and Jenny lived just outside Oban and were great friends. We would often visit and stay over. Their house had a garden that flowed into Loch Melfort, and a yacht in the bay. We would go out sailing for the afternoon and once went out to the small islands, anchoring in the lee and staying the night, exploring the small uninhabited islands like new settlers. We made evening bonfires on the shoreline, eating blackened sausages like haute cuisine, laughing, telling stories, and loving our lives. Further along the bay was Ardchatten, where an ancient ruined church sat halfway up the hill, hidden in a natural fold in the land. There was a sense of peace and history that drew me back there time and again. Just to be there was to experience something of history, and something of God. Historically, whenever there was a hostile ship nearby, the monks and nuns would scamper up the hill to this sanctuary until safety was declared. I would go by myself some days and just sit there, seeking God, reimagining the history, the worship brought, the prayers offered, and the lives lived in honour of their King.

I lost count of how many times we visited John and Jenny. It was always a highlight, and I would always end up in a massive fun-wrestling match with their beautiful young family at some point. We played games, sang songs, went for walks, ate sumptuous meals, and slept deeply. The best of times.

I remember Wendy and I driving back from John and Jenny's, leaving at 6am so I could do the Sunday morning breakfast radio show, starting at 8am. We could not find anything but somber music on every station. It was about 30 minutes in when the announcer provided news about Princess Diana and her dreadful accident.

During the weeks and months that followed, Wendy and I would meet up regularly. We loved to go for walks together along the canal or up the glen, and could spend hours chatting and getting to know each other. We both loved spicy food, so Indian cuisine became a thing for us, lamb and chicken balti being a regular choice. We both had feelings for each other. I think for myself I was struggling with the thought of change and commitment. I wanted both, but part of me was unwilling to take the step.

I found myself often upset at night by myself, going to my room and slowly breaking out into deep sobs and grief and pain that seemed to have no reason and no end. At one point I got hold of some teaching tapes about how God is my father, and what a father looks like. In there, in that process, just listening, God started His healing work afresh. Tears changed from grief to sadness, to sorrow, and to release. I was crying through a process of forgiveness, forgiving my mum and dad, and forgiving myself, although I knew not what for. It was a process.

There was a trip to Honduras planned again, and I was heading out this time to Roatan to help for a couple of weeks build a house for a family of three generations who were homeless. I flew from Glasgow to Orlando and had a day or two with Alistair and his beautiful family before heading for a flight from Tampa to Miami, and then on to San Pedro Sula, and finally La Ceiba for a night. The next morning I caught up with John and we flew together in a tiny wee plane to Roatan, and made our way to the quay where we would be berthed.

We built a house over water in six days. Posts went in, floor and walls fabricated, routes planned for plumbing and electric. Part of my job was to make the holes for pipes and cables to be routed once the walls were all assembled. Day three and the skeleton could be seen, the roof was started, cabling was routed. There was the constant sound of six men sawing, drilling, hammering and bantering from dawn till after dusk. We set up lights on the evening of day two as we realised that we would not finish with daylight alone. At one point I collapsed from heat exhaustion and missed the last few hours that day, but was back on board at 5am the next day. One night there was an earthquake, and I remember waking up and wondering how many people must be dancing on the roof of the house to make it sway like this – and promptly went back to sleep.

We completed the house and had a party to celebrate. Alistair was with us for this week of the trip and I had been his labourer (he is a sparky). We had the best fun! He headed back to the USA and John and I headed for a week or two on the Mosquito Coast. There we caught up with Ron the optician and together we went around half a dozen villages doing eye tests in daylight, and holding church services in the evenings.

Before I knew it I was on a plane back to Scotland, back to work, and back to my gorgeous Wendy.

Chapter 68

Wendy and I were in an on/off sort of friendship, where we would get close, then I would balk a bit and we would have space. It was hard on her. In reflection I was quite selfish, but dressed it up to myself as caring. It seems so clear now, but when I was in the middle of it, it was quite different. I could see the damage this was causing Wendy and at one point we agreed not to see each other for a while. A few months went past and we did not visit or connect. This was not really what I wanted either. And there was the issue – what did I want? I had no idea really. What to do?

I decided to take a couple of weeks off work and head over to Florida to spend time with Alistair and his family. It was not really a holiday; the idea was to have some alone time, seek God, and resolve what was in my immediate future.

Once in Florida I settled into a routine, making time to be by myself, walking up and down in the garden as I prayed and waited on God. The second night there I went to a nearby hotel for some food and it just so happened that I bumped into Ron the optician. I explained why I was there and he invited me to use his wooden shack up in Tennessee. So the next day I hired a black Ute and set off with the shack's keys, a road map, and a bottle of water. Within 30 minutes I was stopped for speeding on the highway. When the officer saw my UK licence he lost interest, gave me a warning, and sent me on my way. It did the trick; I did not speed again for the next fourteen hours. Maybe it just so happened that he saved me from something far worse than a public telling-off at the side of the road.

I loved how the radio stations changed as I travelled up north: gospel in Florida, Motown as I drove through Atlanta, and then into a mix of country and bluegrass as the road clipped Carolina and into Tennessee. I was excited, to be honest. I daydreamed of this wooden shack, lighting a fire, going down to the river to get water, sleeping on the porch under the stars perhaps. It was going to be a great adventure.

Eventually, as the light started to fade (I had set off at 5am) I arrived. Hmmm. It was definitely made out of wood, but it was three floors high, with a verandah overlooking the Smoky Mountains and a hot tub bubbling away nicely. Jacuzzi in the ensuite, cable TV, stocked fridge and freezer. I didn't know whether to laugh or cry, so I did a bit of both to be safe.

The next few weeks were a time of rest and exploration. The Smoky Mountains in a Gulf season, tree-covered mountains resplendent in autumn finery, colours shocking in their beauty. I saw black bears with their cubs and scampered back to my car when they seemed to be heading in my direction. I drove through a living museum that felt like a scene from *Little House on the Prairie*, and saw both sides of a deeply moving Cherokee reservation: the public side in a glorious exhibition centre, and the reality for those descendants when I got lost up a back road and stumbled onto their commission housing with liquor-strewn shabby lawns.

I prayed and sought God. I sat in the hot tub every evening as the sun set over those Smoky Mountains and saw with my own eyes why they were named so in the gloaming of the day. I ate well and slept well. Then the time came to take the truck back to Ocala and consider my next steps. On my way I drove over to Charlotte, South Carolina, and stayed with a family there who I had met when building a house in Roatan. It was a time of refreshing and simplicity, as we went to church, hung out, and ate together over a long weekend. I learned to love fresh pecan nuts in those days of friendship and food.

And then I was back in Florida, still with well over a week before my return flight. So, with a friend, I decided to take on another road trip and visit a family of Messianic Jews that lived in Franklin, North Carolina. And so we were off again, this time sharing the drive overnight, arriving mid-morning to the sound of bagpipes as a fully kilted marching band made its imperial way down the main street as part of another holiday weekend event.

Oh, but I should tell you of an event on the way there. We stopped at a rest stop and I went to the bathrooms, which were at the far side of a massive car park, opposite the gas station, a good 10-minute walk away. Once there, a sign on the gent's door told me that the key could be acquired from the attendant at the gas station. The ladies' bathroom was open, and there was not another car in the car park at 3am. So, in a hastily made decision-moment, I went in, had a pee as quickly as I could, and then turned to leave. As I approached the exit, a large lady filled the doorway and stared in unexpected shock at me. She looked me up and down a few times before saying "eeeeyooooo" with a look of deep distaste. I recognised that nothing I could say, even in a Sean Connery accent, would make the situation any better, so I turned sideways, slid past her as the last "ooo's" were escaping, and jogged back to our car, where my friend was still dozing. Jumping in and driving away, I was stifling my fits of giggles and for the next few minutes was unable to tell him what was so funny.

The few days in Franklin, North Carolina, were beautiful, full of rekindled friendships with a family of twelve children and their parents. We played soccer, went for walks, sat on the verandah at sunrise and sunset, ate like kings, laughed until we were sore, and prayed together in devotions.

Before I knew it, my time was up, the car was handed back, and I was at Orlando airport, awaiting a flight home. My heart was settled and I knew that God was with me and would guide me over the next season.

Wendy and I reconnected, went for walks, and chatted about our future with a greater sense of ease, and I would say we became closer friends. From that place of friendship, so much more seemed possible. I think I had felt for a season that Wendy had her sights set on me, and that unsettled me. That was not the case, but it was how I had been feeling.

As we grew closer and closer, I found myself on the brink of asking Wendy to marry me but was struggling with how and where to do that. One day we were on the sofa at her apartment chatting, and we started to talk about marriage and the future, when I said, "How about it then?" Wendy asked, "How about what?" "How about we get married..." was my response. There were tears and questions and laughter all mixed together. We told the two children the next day, and then announced it at church, to screams of surprise and joy, as well as some spontaneous applause.

When we went with the children to let Wendy's ex know, he did not handle that well. In the passing of years he has mellowed and remarried, and we can chat to each other now at family events.

Wendy and I started to plan our wedding. Finlay offered his boat for the service, so we got married out on Loch Linnhie on a glorious sunny June day, with all our friends and family aboard. We had a ceilidh band for the reception and the food included smoked salmon, langoustines, mussels, as well as hearty Scottish soup, crusty bread, endless wine, and a muffin-based wedding cake. It was a fantastic day, my face sore from smiling, and my mum and sister talked to each other for the first time in years.

That night we stayed in a hotel on the shore of Loch Lochy. The morning breakfast at a window overlooking the mountains and the loch was memorable, partly because I took the seat that the waitress had pulled out for Wendy. Oh, there was a lot to learn for this guy. The next night we stayed in Edinburgh, up at Bruntsfield, and I gave Wendy a short tour of my childhood haunts in my home city before we flew out to Turkey for ten days of sun, pools, red cabbage and yoghurt, Turkish baths, knock-off originals, sweet fruit tea, Turkish delight, and getting to know each other a little better. When I think back now I can see how, if the church had done some pre-marriage preparation with us, we would have been so much better prepared for the struggles we stepped into: financial, relational, children, and so many big decisions in a short space of time. Yet we managed somehow to muddle through. We had massive arguments and moments of tenderness. We struggled to communicate what we both wanted and were vulnerable with each other. There were so many paradoxes.

Back in the UK we moved everything into my apartment, which was bought, and handed Wendy's keys back to the landlord, the local council. There was, for sure, a period of adjustment: physically, as we resolved what to keep and what to sell, give away, or dump;

emotionally, as we both learned to live with another person; and mentally, as we made decisions about finances and our future.

Chapter 69

Life settled into a routine at work and at home. There were times of laughter, holidays, and domestic contentment, peppered with moments of stress, business, arguments, and weariness. We both worked fairly long hours and had our taxi driver duties to consider. I started to reflect on what it meant to be a parent, and at one point I wrote these notes to myself.

Parenting is about tricycles. It is about bikes with stabilisers, then bikes without stabilisers and sometimes even motorbikes. It is about dealing with stress and showing love when you want to hide and cry. It is about being strong when on the inside you feel weak. It is about responsibility, it is about provision, and it is about not losing yourself even when you are always giving yourself. Parenting is about partnership with your spouse, it is about learning about yourself, your own failings, your own hot spots, and your own strengths. It is about learning about your partner's strengths, failings, and hot spots (while trying not to laugh). It is about the amazing transition from the world's greatest genius to the slightly embarrassing parent.

Parenting is about being a taxi driver, a cook, a cleaner, a gardener, a fixer of the unfixable, and a provider of all required funds. Parenting is about being the least popular person in the house. It is about having out-of-body experiences when you hear your own parents take over your body and speak through you the very things you vowed you would never say. Parenting is about surprising yourself and others, sometimes in a good way. Parenting is about learning the best place to hide chocolate and how to always avoid any blame.

I'm not sure about the "blame" bit, but I wrote it, so I'll leave it in.

We were not long married when Wendy grabbed my hand one night and pulled me into the hallway at home and whispered to me that she was pregnant. What a moment that was. So Rachel was on her way.

Steven and Maria were now under my care and we were getting to know each other. We had nights with pizza and *The Simpsons* on TV.

They were really good about coming to church with us most weeks, even though there was so little for them to do there. Wendy and I had my mum visit every couple of months, and when she did we would often head away for a weekend together, which was amazing. Looking back on those days now I have fond memories. We were a busy, happy, normal family who had many good friends and family close around us. We would have "board games" nights over at Davy and Aileen's, usually with some food. They would go on until the early hours, and I loved the noise and banter.

When Rachel arrived nine months later it was a special day. Wendy's mum was also in the same hospital, having been operated on for cancer. I phoned her from the maternity unit to her bed in oncology and was able to let her know she had a brand new granddaughter, Rachel. Joan cried over the phone and said later that that was the moment she knew she was healing. I sat with Rachel sleeping on my chest for nearly an hour before I called the family to come over and meet her. Steven, Maria, and my mum arrived and were all immediately besotted.

Our apartment was four floors up and too small now for this newly expanded family. Even getting the pram up the stairs was epic. So, house hunting we went. In our price range there really was nothing of the size we needed in the town, so we moved to Roy Bridge, to a four-bedroom bungalow with a garden, over behind the railway line, with only two neighbours down a private road. We needed a ten thousand pound deposit, and only had five thousand saved up, but Finlay, bless him, paid me a five thousand pound bonus from the company, tax paid, and we were able to move. We had fun there, with parties, sleepovers, bonfires, and barbecues. I had my BMW 800cc motorbike still and would escape occasionally for a blast around the local winding roads on summer nights and Saturday mornings. On Sunday nights Maria would sometimes come with me to the radio station and sit with her favourite book in the guest seat while I played my favourite Christian artists and blethered over the airways.

In one of our dinner conversations at home, Steven expressed an interest in coming with me to Honduras if I was going again, so we started to plan the trip with Wendy's blessing. Around this time I had an interesting experience. I had become friendly with a man in our church. He was retired, fairly wealthy, and had been a successful businessman. We arranged to meet for lunch one day in town, and we would have a lot to chat about, as he was involved in our church as well as a great person to chat with about business.

As I entered the café, I spotted him sitting way up the back and I made my way carefully between tables towards him. Sitting over from him on another table was a minister (he had his dog collar on) and he was fussing around with several small pieces of paper with notes on them. He looked lost in his own thoughts and world, oblivious to any other people or activity around him.

As I walked towards these two very different people, one sharply dressed, smart, attentive, and focused, the other a bit rumpled, lost in something, and unaware that I even existed, I sensed God whisper to me, "Which do you want for your future?" Without missing a beat my heart answered, "God, I'll huv the journey wae the bits o paper pleez." And the moment was gone, but the season was established. Even now, as I sit here in Sydney at 5am, clicking away on my keyboard some twenty years later, that still rings true in my heart. I want to be lost in ways of caring for others, of bringing strength, hope, and purpose to as many as I can, and to do that from a place of loving God.

But back to then. Steven and I were busy preparing for a planned trip to Honduras, and before we knew it we were on the plane to Florida and the unknown. After a day to recover in Lakeland we flew down to La Ceiba and stayed with Kenton and Saundi, who were the world's best hosts. Then we were away, up to Hoche's village, where Steven got to catch, kill, and prepare a chicken, which I then cooked for the ladies of the house, an interesting role-reversal that I was surprised they were all comfortable with.

One night we went to a local village for church, and as the service was ending the rains started, so we left hurriedly, heading back up the mountain to Hoche's house. The first river we came to was in spate. We had stepped over it in two paces on the way down, but now it was a raging torrent of white water that would carry anyone foolish enough to try to cross to their death on the rocks below. We turned back, only to discover the small streams behind us were now also raging. And the light was fading. We were all on horseback. We made our way down to the bank of the main river, which was now lapping at the path along the river bank. This river was now at least two hundred yards across, a slow-moving, unstoppable force of brown, muddy water. I had been in the river when it was low and had felt the force of the water even when I was only up to my knees. I had no desire to feel any of that force tonight. The rain was driving down, the noise made talking impossible, even shouting in each other's ears was unhearable. We were in a pickle. The river was rising, my horse was now up to its knees in swirly water, and the path was unidentifiable.

Then we saw flashlights on the river, and it just so happened that some locals had seen our flashlights and had crossed the river in their dugouts to help us. They had worked out, by seeing us going back and forth, that we were in trouble. They guided each of us along the side of the riverbank, leading our horses by hand until the path started to rise again towards the village we had left, and we were safe. In all honesty, we could have easily died that night. I am ever grateful for those selfless villagers who crossed that river to find and rescue us. Steven realised the severity of what had happened. In some ways I was perhaps a little too blasé as I was used now to getting into tricky spots and always getting out.

Our adventures continued for another couple of weeks, and I have so many great memories from that trip. On the way back to Scotland we stayed in Miami for a couple of days and took a bus into the city to do some shopping for gifts together.

Back in Scotland, our little church was going through a bit of a struggle. A group of people from another church had split away and started coming along to our church. However, within a few weeks they were demanding position and dictating terms. We had many hours of meetings and discussions, which ended with them all leaving our church and starting their own, which then fell apart a short time later.

We had friends and family in this group, and that was a tougher journey than some of the walks in Honduras.

Wendy and I were going along well, loving our days, and probably loving our gin and tonics a tiny bit too much at times as well. No harm was done. Years were drifting by, kids were growing up, grass was cut, bathrooms were refitted, cars were replaced, and jobs changed. Before we knew it, we were keen to move back into town and started looking for a house. Maria was sixteen, had a boyfriend, and told us she was moving out to live with him up in Helmsdale. I did not rate him really. What to do? Did we burn our bridges with Maria or continue to be there for her and allow her to make her own decisions?

Chapter 70

Maria left home, and it was harder on Wendy than myself, I think. I did miss Maria and was worried for her at sixteen, but Wendy had that blood connection which, whatever we may say, does go deeper, I believe. Shortly afterwards, Maria told us she was pregnant, which was an exciting and joyful time for us and for Maria.

We decided to put our house on the market and look to move back into town, and now we only needed a three-bedroomed house. House prices had shot up, but we hoped we could sell our house for more than we paid for it, so it would all be relative. Wendy did not want to sell the house until Maria had her baby, as she wanted the safety net of a room for Maria should she need it for any reason.

Our house was in a nice spot, a bit remote for us, but would probably suit others. Several couples and families came to visit and see the property, and every time I thought, "This is it." And every time, it was not. Maria was close to her time, so Wendy went up to Inverness, and I stayed home and kept house, worked, etc. I had a call from the lawyer to arrange another prospective buyer to come. So I dutifully got the place ready and texted Wendy (mobile phones were a thing now, of course). The guy came with a tape measure, only said a very gruff "hello" to me, that was it. Then he was measuring the garden, up in the attic, every room, etc. He was there for about twenty-five minutes and then gone, drove off without a word. I called Wendy and said, "I dinnae think this is the one....."

That night, Maria gave birth to a beautiful baby boy, Euan, and Wendy and I laughed and cried a little on the phone. The next day it just so happened that we got an offer for our house from "tape-man," and it was twice what we had paid for it. He had sold his house and business in England, so was cashed up, and was looking for a project house, remote but near a railway station (so his kids could visit him easily). Our property had everything he needed. The soffit was a project, and the roof needed work, it just so happened that his business had been as a roofer. Perfect fit, perfect timing.

Wendy and I sped up our house search and we found "the one" in a cul-de-sac in a village called Caol (pronounced kool). It was like a Tardis, just kept opening up. Two great living areas, three bathrooms, a massive laundry area, three bedrooms, a garden, a greenhouse, and beautiful views of the mountains framed in the front windows. As soon as we went in, I knew this was the one, nothing else we had seen had that impact. So we put in a bid, rejected, second bid, rejected. I phoned the owner and asked him what he would settle for. He told me, I bid, he accepted, and we were on.

We spent almost half a day unloading our collected and stored stuff from our attic, making several trips to the recycling area as we de-cluttered. The lawyers did their stuff and dates were agreed. The day before we moved, we got a call from the owner. He said he had changed his mind and was not selling to us now. At first, I didn't believe him, but he was serious. I felt certain he was going to cop some serious financial penalties for this decision, although our immediate concern would be where to live and where to store all our belongings.

I drove into town to get a few things done at work, praying as I drove. I saw my boss at the side of the road in town at the tyre-fitters, and I remembered he had two cottages on his property and that one was empty, so I started to look for somewhere to turn the car and go back and ask him. At that moment it just so happened that it was like God whispered to me in my inner voice, "Do you trust me?" My answer was a shaky "yes." So I never turned the car and he remained unaware.

The next day our removers arrived and started decanting our house. Our lawyer had said to us to hold fast just now and see what happens. The house was empty and we were ready to go to our new home, kids in the car and all. Wendy remembered her parcel shelf for her car was inside the front door, so she ran and got that, the very last item to be moved. Our removers had told us all their horror stories of moves going wrong, but I was holding on to my God whisper. Just as Wendy closed our front door for the last time, it just so happened that my phone rang. The seller's lawyer was apologising and telling us they had dropped their price by five thousand pounds for our inconvenience and that the sale was now concluded. There was an issue with the tiny sunroom at the new house, which we could fix for $500, so that was a great outcome. And we had cash left over, so we planned a family holiday to Disneyland, nearly three weeks in the sun, beautiful rented house with a pool, massive hired car, and spending money for the theme parks. Of course, we would miss Maria not being with us, but we were set for a great break and a time to rest for a few weeks.

Our Disney trip could have been filmed for a Disney sitcom at times, we laughed, cried, fell out, and hugged. Rachel, at the age of three, headbutted the pavement (or should I say sidewalk) the first time she stepped out of the car. Finding our rental home without satnav was tricky; I still don't know how we found it, to be honest. But once we were there, we played in the pool, we ate out, we arranged our visits to theme parks, we ate out, we visited Walmart for a car seat for Rachel (which we brought back in our luggage with us), we ate out, and oh, did I mention we ate out?

I have to tell just one story from Disneyland. On our first day at the park, we had discovered freshly made giant cheese-stuffed pretzels. So, on our return visit a week later, we decided we had to try those again. When we got to the stall, there were none in the display cabinet. We had passed another seller about five minutes earlier, so I said I would walk back and see if they had any there. Wendy suggested joining the line here and asking, in case they had them but just not on display. I declined and set off on my rescue mission. (Oh, you are way ahead of me already, I think.) About forty minutes later, I returned empty-handed to be informed this stall had them, so I joined the line, bought them, and we sat in stony silence (Wendy and I) and ate, they tasted different that day. Still not talking, Wendy and I (with Steven and Rachel) set off for the Peter Pan ride and joined the line. Wendy and I looked in different directions, no words exchanged, a stony silence had settled in. Rachel skipped up to us, took Wendy's hand and then took my hand, then put my hand into Wendy's hand and glided away. Oh, how hard is it to be mad at each other and still be holding hands? Eventually the ice cracked, and we laughed at ourselves, the day only getting better from then on, and yes, I did apologise.

We visited friends in Florida, Alistair and Amanda. Alistair took Steven and me up in a plane and we flew from a small airfield outside Orlando to over the main Tampa airport, chatting with the tower control there. Wendy and Amanda went for a drive in Amanda's convertible, discovering bang-bang shrimp, and then an evening at home with gin and tonic.

Leaving Florida is always hard, and after a fantastic family holiday it's even harder. But we did leave and headed home to nursing for Wendy, and back to work as a manager for myself, as the kids returned to school to tell their friends of their American adventure.

Life went by, weeks, months and years. My role transformed at work, where I found myself managing a Commercial Diving Centre, a boat repair yard, as well as a few other smaller businesses spread out over a fairly wide geographical area. My role was to move the businesses towards being commercially viable. I worked hard at the challenges, which at times seemed overwhelming. The businesses took shape, with others involved helping, steering, challenging and growing.

A time came when I was coasting really. I was finding things for myself to do, and I recognised that in some ways I was doing things that either were not mission critical or were things that people within each business should be learning to do, so I was in some ways actually becoming a blockage. I chatted to Wendy, saying that maybe a change was coming and that it needed to be challenged, but I did not really want the organisation to make any more acquisitions of lame-duck businesses.

One day I was walking between buildings at the main offices when I bumped into the chairperson of the board. He asked me to come with him as he was keen to chat. So I went into the boardroom, where to my surprise the whole board was assembled, waiting. I sat down, wondering what was about to happen. A moment of silence, then the chairperson spoke, "So, Allan, if you could have any job, what would it be?" So I guessed he meant "any job in the company," but that's not what he said. I paused to breathe and responded from a place of butterflies, "Ehhh, a'd like tae go tae Bible college." Silence, just the faint sound of breathing. A minute passed; I think I could hear a grandfather clock ticking in my mind.

"Oh, well, I don't think any of us were expecting that response," the chairperson offered. Heads nodded slowly, chins were rubbed. "Let's adjourn and we can reschedule." And I was out in the corridor on my own, like I'd just awoken from a dream sequence.

I left early, driving home, wondering if I had somehow just sacked myself. I told Wendy that evening, and I thought she would be concerned, but she laughed and cheered and said we should go to Australia and Hillsong Bible College. Over the coming days we chatted a lot. I was keen to find a way to do Bible college in Scotland and we visited a few locations where there were Bible colleges, but nothing really clicked. But the dream was being spoken into reality. Wendy was convinced that we would go to Australia and started watching *Homes Down Under* and *Bondi Rescue*. Sometimes I would power-doze off watching Bear Grylls and when I opened my eyes fifteen minutes later, someone was being pulled from the surf half-drowned. I tried to explain to Wendy that as we had never been to Australia, it was not an option to just suddenly up and go. I don't think I really listened to her points as well as I might have.

Wendy and I talked a lot each day about the changes that were possible and how we felt. She was excited; I was nervous. Wendy is a risk-taker; I am logical in my thinking. Logic was working against me. My big sticking point was that we had never even visited Australia, so how could we just suddenly go and live there?

I got a call one day to visit the owner, and I thought to myself, "This is it, I'm getting the bullet today." So I stopped by and sat with him and his wife and we had a lovely lunch at their beautiful house. That morning Wendy had heard from Maria that Maria was going to visit Australia and her flights were being paid, and my heart was happy for Maria, but hurting for Wendy who wanted so badly to go there.

As lunch was winding up and we were reflecting on what a tough year it had been, Finlay and Lorna (the owners) suddenly said that it just so happened they would like to send Wendy, Rachel and me on a trip to

Australia, and that the company would pay for flights and accommodation. All I could think of was that this was my big argument getting blown out of the water.

I met Wendy and told her the story. At first, she was in disbelief, but then the excitement took hold. In the days to follow we spent time planning and preparing, eventually deciding that we would go to Hillsong Conference in London with Rachel, and then fly from there to Australia.

Meanwhile, another thread started to form. Months before, on a trip to London for a network leadership event for Hillsong, it had just so happened that we had connected with a Hillsong pastor, and it just so happened that his grandfather lived in the same part of Scotland that we lived in. Then he had connected us to a family who were walking the West Highland Way (which ends at our town). There had been really bad weather, so we had driven down, collected the family, and taken them back to our village, where over the next few days we became great friends. While in London at the conference, we connected with them again. They were so excited to hear we were going to Australia and gave us a few phone numbers for contacts when we were out there.

And so the adventure began. We loved the conference in London, and then boarded our flights to Australia, so excited, wondering how many movies we could watch in a day. The Australian trip turned out to be the start of another amazing series of adventures, and really they deserve their own story.

Epilogue

It Just So Happened

Looking back over these pages, I can see something I never saw clearly while living it: none of it was wasted. Not the childhood I tried to outrun, not the years in care homes, not the mistakes, not the moments of courage I didn't recognise as courage at the time. Not even the parts I would have edited out if I'd had the pen in my own hand.

Scotland shaped my bones. It taught me resilience the hard way; through cold mornings, harder knocks, and the quiet determination to keep going when nothing seemed certain. It gave me humour, grit, a sense of justice, and a way of seeing people that cuts through appearances. It gave me a hunger to understand why people do what they do, and why some rise while others fold. I didn't know it then, but those years were building the raw material for a future I couldn't have imagined.

And then came the next story, the one that unfolds in Australia, on the other side of the world, with a different sky and a different pace of life. That story deserves its own book, because it wasn't simply another chapter; it was a rebirth. A quiet rebuilding. A long obedience in the same direction. It was where the scattered pieces began to form something coherent. Where calling stopped being an idea and became a lived reality. Where I learned that God doesn't discard anything. He repurposes it.

Coaching didn't arrive as a career choice; it emerged as a lifeline. A natural extension of everything I had lived through. When you've walked through your own chaos, you learn to recognise the chaos in others. When you've found clarity the long way, you want to shorten the path for someone else. Coaching became the place where faith, skill, and experience could finally sit at the same table.

And so *The Allan Key* was born. Not out of ambition, but out of recognition, that the very things that once threatened to undo me had become the tools I now use to unlock others. Purpose, clarity, identity, courage… these weren't theories for me. They were survival skills that became gifts.

This book tells the story of what happened before I knew who I would become.

The next book tells what God can do when a broken life is placed, hesitantly, unevenly, but sincerely, into His hands. It shows that trust isn't a dramatic moment; it's a series of small surrenders stitched together over years. It shows that redemption rarely arrives with fanfare, but through steady transformation, one decision at a time.

If this story has offered anything, I hope it is this:

Your past is not the end of the story.

Your pain is not the whole story.

And when you entrust the pieces of your life to God, even the jagged ones, He has a way of turning them into something that can help others find their way home.

That is what happened to me.

It just so happened… and yet, looking back, it could not have happened any other way.

www.theallankey.com